A *hopeful* PROPOSAL

OTHER COVENANT BOOKS AND AUDIOBOOKS BY SAMANTHA HASTINGS

Secret of the Sonnets

By Any Other Name

a regency romance

A *hopeful* PROPOSAL

SAMANTHA HASTINGS

Covenant Communications, Inc.

Cover image: *Woman in White Dress Drinking Tea* © Ilina Simeonova / Trevillion Images

Cover design by Christina Marcano © 2025 by Covenant Communications, Inc.

Published by Covenant Communications, Inc.
American Fork, Utah

Library of Congress Cataloging-in-Publication Data

Name: Samantha Hastings
Title: A Hopeful Proposal / Samantha Hastings
Description: American Fork, UT : Covenant Communications, Inc. [2025]
Identifiers: Library of Congress Control Number 2024945040 | ISBN 978-1-52442-831-0
LC record available at https://lccn.loc.gov/2024945040

Printed in the United States of America
First Printing: July 2025

32 31 30 29 28 27 26 25   10 9 8 7 6 5 4 3 2 1

PRAISE FOR SAMANTHA HASTINGS

A Hopeful Proposal

"With the irresistible charm of a marriage of convenience, *A Hopeful Proposal* is a heartfelt Regency romance that will sweep readers off their feet. Sarah and Christopher's journey from reluctant partners to undeniable soulmates is brimming with wit, longing, and the kind of slow-burning love that lingers long after the final page. A delightful must-read for fans of the genre!"

—Tiffany Odekirk, author of *Summerhaven*

"In *A Hopeful Proposal*, Hastings touched all of my emotions. Both Christopher and Sarah demonstrate the power of hope, respect, and love while navigating family trials and a blooming relationship. For anyone looking for a heartwarming romance, *A Hopeful Proposal* won't disappoint.

—Chalon Linton, author of the Flying in Love series

By Any Other Name

"A tender and romantic story of grief, growth, and enduring love."

—Rosalyn Eves, author of *An Improbable Season*

"*By Any Other Name* is exactly the type of novel I've come to expect from Samantha Hastings. Witty dialogue, compulsory storytelling, brilliant characterizations, and a happily ever after that is completely satisfying. Readers will love curling up with this sweet romance as Jenny finds herself again in life and love."

—Jenni L. Walsh, *USA Today* bestselling author of *Unsinkable*

Secret of the Sonnets

"This Shakespeare-connected mystery takes on the challenge of living up to the many excellent Regency romances available. Challenge met and exceeded!"

—Historical Novel Society

"For readers who love Regency romance yet are looking for something different than the prerequisite balls and affairs of the *ton*, *Secrets of the Sonnets* is just the thing. The story will appeal to lovers of Shakespeare as well since the Bard's work is sprinkled liberally throughout the story."

—*InD'Tale Magazine*

to Ivy and Emery Larsen

ACKNOWLEDGMENTS

I am so grateful to everyone who helped with this new story: my wonderfully supportive family, the incredible team at Covenant, and my street team who help promote my books. A special shout-out to Lisa Olsen, Katie Watkins, Mindy Holt, Korbie Harrison, Holly Bleggi, Julie Carpenter, Sydney Anderson, LeAnn Arave, Laramee Fox, Sheila Windley Staley, Shayla Y. Riley, Ashleigh Hourihan, Carol Howell, and Michelle Martin. I am so grateful for my friends who have been so kind to read and share my books: Jennie Ferguson, Dawn Mangum, Irene Clegg, Susannah Holden, and Debbie Welch.

"I wish Jane success with all my heart; and if she were married to him to-morrow, I should think she had as good a chance of happiness as if she were to be studying his character for a twelvemonth. Happiness in marriage is entirely a matter of chance. If the dispositions of the parties are ever so well known to each other, or ever so similar beforehand, it does not advance their felicity in the least. They always continue to grow sufficiently unlike afterwards to have their share of vexation; and it is better to know as little as possible of the defects of the person with whom you are to pass your life."

—Jane Austen, *Pride and Prejudice*

CHAPTER 1

Manderfield Estate, England, 1805

Every room in Manderfield Hall was haunted by memories from Lady Sarah Denham's past. It was more than a beautiful ancestral building; it was her home.

Her lips quirked up into a reluctant smile as she looked at the scratches she had made with her cousin Ralph on the main stairs banister. Her throat felt thick as she walked one last time through the grand entry with the black-and-white-checkered floor. She and her mother had once played a very large game of chess upon it. Oh, how she wished she could go back and relive each moment spent with Mama!

Sarah's breath slowed as she recalled dancing with her mother and playing hide-and-seek in the parlors and drawing rooms. Mama pretended she didn't know where Sarah was, even though she did. At the age of six, Sarah had always hidden in the same spot, the cabinet in the blue parlor. But still her mother would search loudly behind every curtain and under each chair. Sarah was five and twenty now, and she could no longer hide.

Her eyes ached with unshed tears. Saying goodbye to Manderfield Hall was like saying a final farewell to her mother. The familiar ache in her chest returned, and Sarah rubbed it, even while knowing there was no balm for such pain.

Manderfield Hall and estate no longer belonged to her father, and now she would never inherit them. They had been sold to pay off her father's gambling debts, and Ursula Yardley, the woman he'd lived with for the last six years and who called herself Sarah's "stepmother," would not give a guinea to save it, although she had inherited a fortune from her first husband. Sarah's father, the Earl of Manders, was now the earl of nothing. He held the title but no land. He would now be a permanent resident of London in Mrs. Yardley's house.

Papa had begun the process of having Sarah's mother declared dead so that he could marry Mrs. Yardley.

Sarah walked unhurriedly one last time through the gallery, running her fingers over the frames of every portrait. Her ancestors and relatives looked down upon her, some stern, others smiling. All dear and familiar faces. Even the paintings had been sold to the new owner, who presumably had no esteemed ancestors of his own to oversee him and his family.

With an unfocused gaze, Sarah stopped at the painting of her mother, Lady Louisa Denham, Countess of Manders. Around her neck was her golden locket engraved with the Denham family crest; Sarah could not remember a time when her mother had not worn the necklace. Mama had been a beauty with dark glossy locks, bright-blue eyes, and a rosebud mouth. The portrait was from her youth, but time had been kind to her mother and only softened her appearance. Mama had still looked youthful seven years ago.

That evening at dusk, in her crimson riding habit and matching bonnet with dyed red plumes, her cheeks had been red from excitement for her ride—or from her fight with Papa. She had kissed Sarah on the cheek and said she would be back in a little while. Then Mama had walked out of the door, never to return.

More time than a "little while" had passed, but Sarah still searched every dusk for her mother to return. She feared that if her mother came back after Sarah vacated the premises, she would not know where Sarah had gone to.

Sniffling, Sarah realized that she regretted the imminent loss of her mother's portrait more than that of the entire house. Unfortunately, Sarah looked nothing like her mother. Her hair was an ordinary shade of light brown, as were her eyes, and her mouth was a trifle too large. She would never attain the title of beauty, but Mama had taught her how to be striking. She darkened her eyelashes with kohl and skillfully brightened her lips with rose lip salve. Sarah sparingly used carmine for rouge and powder to cover the thirteen freckles that had taken possession of her nose. Luckily, her hourglass figure was shapely, and she spent nearly all of her pin money dressing it to perfection. What she could not afford to purchase, she sewed herself.

"Goodbye forever," she whispered as she caressed the edge of the portrait frame. Her eyelids felt heavy, and her chin trembled.

"Lady Sarah," Mrs. Harmony, the housekeeper, bellowed from the other end of the gallery. She was a small woman with a surprisingly loud voice and an abundance of yellow curls that were always escaping her white cap. "You ought to be in the carriage by now. It's not like you to keep people waiting, and poor Mr. Phipps has been walking the horses up and down the lane for the last half hour."

"I am sorry, Mrs. Harmony," Sarah said in a resigned tone. "I shall come at once."

She had known for months that this day was coming, but that didn't make it any easier. Walking slowly down the gallery, she heard her boot heels click on the marble tiles with every step. She tried to think of any excuse to linger, anything that needed attending to before the new owner took possession of the place, but she and the servants had made sure that every inch of Manderfield had been scrubbed and dusted from the basement to the attic. Even the outside windows had been washed, and not one weed could be found in the gardens, nor a pebble out of place. Since her mother's disappearance, Sarah had been mistress of Manderfield Hall, and as loath as she was to leave it, she wanted to leave it in the best possible condition.

Mrs. Harmony cleared her throat.

Sighing, Sarah knew she needed to go. All of her possessions had already been transported to Westbrook Park. The park was home to her mother's sister, Lady Venetia Randolph, and her husband, Sir Oscar Randolph, Baronet, and their son, the Honorable Ralph Randolph. Her aunt had kindly allowed Sarah to send her belongings to Westbrook Park, for Sarah no longer had a home of her own. She was now trespassing.

Her first friend and former lady's maid, Nelly Mills, came out from the servants' quarters and took Sarah's hand. "No one has ever loved or cared for Manderfield like you, but it has been sold. You must leave, Sarah. And perhaps this is for the best. It is time to let go. You deserve to marry and have a home of your own."

She forced herself to smile at Nelly. Her maid had declined to accompany her to Westbrook Park because of a very handsome footman. "The only person who is about to marry is yourself. Has Guy proposed yet?"

Nelly nudged Sarah's shoulder with her own. "He will soon if he knows what's good for him."

A laugh escaped Sarah's lips. The footman would find himself in front of the parson before he knew it.

Tapping her foot, the housekeeper sighed loudly. "Mr. Phipps is still waiting, my lady."

Sarah knew Mrs. Harmony meant well. There wasn't an unkind hair on the woman's head, and she had a great deal of hair. But Sarah didn't wish to marry or to move to another house. Manderfield Hall was her home, and someday her mother would return. She knew it in her heart. Mama loved her. She would never have abandoned her daughter.

Nelly tugged Sarah's hand, and together they walked to the front door, where a footman, Tom, opened it. Mrs. Harmony followed them. They walked out into the bright sunlight of the morning. Sarah squinted to see Mr. Phipps driving back up the lane toward her. She did feel sorry for her thoughtlessness, but goodbyes and endings could not be hurried.

Mr. Phipps tipped his hat to her, his usual pipe hanging from his lips.

Sarah nodded and smiled. His was another familiar face she would miss. Tom opened the door and waited to assist Sarah into the carriage, but her legs would not move. Nelly released her hand and gave her a small shove in the back. Having grown up together, her maid had never learned to show Sarah any deference for her station.

Manderfield belongs to another, Sarah reminded herself.

Mama was gone.

There was no reason to stay.

And every reason.

But she could not remain with the new family unless—the most outrageous idea popped into her head.

She couldn't. Could she?

Mrs. Harmony cleared her throat and put a gentle hand on Sarah's shoulder. "My lady, you need to get into that carriage. The butler expects Mr. Moulton to arrive at any moment."

Sarah's mind still whirled with possibility. "Is he married, Harmony?"

The housekeeper straightened her cap, but more curls escaped from it. "Not that I've heard. Just himself and his two younger sisters."

Sarah shook her head and pulled her arm away from Mrs. Harmony's touch. "Mr. Phipps, my deepest apologies, but would you please stable the horses?"

"Aye, Lady Sarah," he said and tipped his hat to her again before flicking the reins to start the horses toward the stable.

Nelly stepped so close to Sarah that their dresses brushed each other. She grabbed Sarah's arms in a tight grasp, her expression stern, and said, "I love you, Sarah, but you cannot stay. This is no longer your house."

"I wish to meet the new owner."

"But, Your Ladyship—" Mrs. Harmony protested from behind Nelly.

"I only wish to welcome him to the neighborhood," Sarah said with one of her bright smiles. "Prepare tea for us and have it served in the sitting room. I will await him there."

"But—"

"No buts."

Breaking out of Nelly's hold, a sense of rightness settled over Sarah. She walked back into the house and entered the sitting room. All the original furniture remained; like the paintings, her father had sold them with the house. Sarah had already packed all the knickknacks, and without them, the room appeared barren. Her old harp stood in the corner, looking sad and neglected. She had decided to leave it at Manderfield. She had not played it since her mother's d—she hadn't played it in years, and it would have been cumbersome to move and store.

Sarah paced back and forth the length of the room, glancing out the window. When would the man arrive? She did not care what he looked like or how old he was. She was going to marry Mr. Moulton. Manderfield Hall would be hers, and no one could ever take her home away.

A few minutes later, the butler, Mr. Wigan, brought in the tea tray. He was a short man with a swarthy complexion and thick dark eyebrows. Sarah told him to put the silver service on the coffee table. He bowed low, a hint of a smile on his lips. Wigan had always been her ally.

She lowered her chin to him. "Thank you, Mr. Wigan. I do not know what I would do without you."

The butler bowed again before leaving. Sarah turned back to the window.

Where was that dratted Mr. Moulton?

Her mouth felt dry, and her stomach was like an empty pit. Sarah fastened and unfastened the top button of her crimson pelisse. It was a fashionable piece of clothing with puffs at the tops of her sleeves. She had improved upon it by adding braided ribbon and matching tassels. Her fingers moved to the closest tassel, and she pulled on it nervously.

At last, she saw a man ride up on a brown mare. She had been expecting a post chaise, but still, if Mr. Moulton could afford to purchase Manderfield, he was no pauper. He wore a plain black coat and a black hat. She couldn't discern any of his features from the angle of the window. Taking a deep breath, she released it slowly and sat on the sofa, tucking one foot behind the other. She folded her hands demurely in her lap and put on her best smile. She was going to need it.

Mama's words repeated in her mind: *A lady is only as beautiful as she believes herself to be.*

Sarah had always thought it was a rather unfair phrase, for her mother was naturally beautiful and Sarah had to work very hard at it.

A few minutes later, Mr. Wigan opened the door and announced, "Mr. Moulton, Your Ladyship."

Sarah stood gracefully, turning slightly to show her best side, her left.

Mr. Moulton strode into the room, a cane in his hand. He paused when he saw her and took off his hat. If the man had suffered from smallpox, his face was not pocked. In fact, he was the most ruggedly handsome man Sarah had ever beheld. His features looked as if they had been carved roughly from stone. He was tall with broad shoulders and a muscular chest. She was uncertain of his age but guessed him to be somewhere between twenty-five and thirty. He had thick blond hair that curled slightly at the ends, with sideburns that connected to a tidy beard that emphasized his strong jaw. His cold gray eyes peered at her penetratingly.

Other ladies might have quaked in their boots from such a stare, but not Sarah. The nervous tingles in her hands and toes stopped. Her mother had taught her that she was descended from royalty. She did not cower before anyone. Not even the new owner of Manderfield Hall.

"Thank you, Mr. Wigan," she said to the butler. "I will pour the tea, and you may go."

Mr. Wigan bowed and left the room, closing the door behind him.

Sarah gave Mr. Moulton a polite smile and, tipping her head, pointed to a chair. He sat stiffly on the edge of it, and she took her own place on the settee.

Picking up the teapot by the handle and spout, Sarah poured two cups of steaming tea. She handed the first to Mr. Moulton across the table. His gloved hands were large. They had probably known physical labor, unlike those of any of the gentlemen she had previously claimed as suitors.

He accepted the tea with a firm "Thank you." There was a roughness in his manner that Sarah found quite intriguing and not at all unattractive.

She picked up her own teacup and sipped delicately. "I suppose you are wondering why I am still here."

"I understood from my solicitor that the hall was vacated," Mr. Moulton said and added a gruff, begrudging, "my lady."

Sarah liked the sound of his deep voice and cockney accent. She felt herself flushing. "I stayed to ensure that everything was in order for you, sir. And I hope you will find all at Manderfield Hall to your satisfaction."

Mr. Moulton looked around the room. "I am sure I shall."

"May I ask an impertinent question?" Sarah said, taking another sip of tea.

He set his teacup on its saucer and placed it on the coffee table. "I do not know why you are still here."

"I want to know why you have bought Manderfield Hall," Sarah said, ignoring his previous comment and bad manners.

The stranger grunted. "I don't know what business it is of yours."

"Are you married?"

"No, I—"

"Do you mean to enter local Society?"

He gripped his cane tightly and said through clenched teeth, "My business is *my* business."

Shaking her head, Sarah smiled. "Do you mean to join the *ton* in London as well? I suppose you must, for you have bought a fine house and estate."

She took a long sip of her tea and watched Mr. Moulton's face as he struggled to answer her civilly. If he had held his teacup as tightly as he did his cane, he would have shattered the delicate porcelain.

"Your Ladyship," he said at last, "I promised my father I would find good matches for my sisters, and I mean to keep my word. If that requires entering local or London Society, then I will do so."

Sarah nodded and nibbled a biscuit. She chewed it slowly before saying, "Wealth and a fine estate will take you only so far, Mr. Moulton. What you really need is noble family connections, which I have in abundance. I am the daughter of an earl and the granddaughter of a duke, with the additional benefit of being related to half the aristocracy of England."

"Bully for you."

She crossed and then uncrossed her legs; her hands were jumpy in her lap. "I propose we marry. I will be a perfect chaperone for your sisters, and I can introduce them to the highest members of Society. I can even ensure they are presented before Queen Charlotte—my mother was one of her ladies-in-waiting. No door in London, nor all of England, for that matter, is closed to me."

His expression changed from shock to incredulity, his eyes wide and his mouth slightly open.

Sarah took a long breath and then released it. Glancing at the door, she knew that she could not afford to lose her nerve now. Mr. Moulton examined her with a familiarity that she would have resented in any other circumstance. Her neck felt hot. She hated when people found her flaws.

Rubbing his beard, he said, "I do not know what to say, Your Ladyship. I do not even know your name."

She tried to smile but faltered. "My name is Lady Sarah Denham, and you need not answer right away. Actually, I would prefer that you didn't. One should not make such an important decision without some thought."

He nodded and then looked at her again with those penetrating gray eyes. "Why me?"

"Why do I wish to marry you?" Sarah clarified.

Mr. Moulton grunted. His free hand curled into a tight fist.

Sarah's heart beat rapidly as she bounced her knee. "I want Manderfield Hall. It is my home, and I love it. You and your sisters wish to enter good Society, and I can make that happen. It seems like a good bargain on both sides. We both get what we want."

He tapped his cane against his boot for a few awkward moments before saying, "I will consider your offer, Lady Sarah Denham. But I make no promises. I never planned on making a grand marriage for myself."

"Your consideration is all I ask," Sarah said, getting to her feet. She wished she could slow her heartbeat and stop her limbs from shaking. "I will be staying indefinitely with my aunt, Lady Venetia Randolph, at Westbrook Park. It is a little more than a half hour's coach ride away. You are welcome to call on me at any time convenient."

Mr. Moulton stood as well. At least this uncouth man had some manners.

Sarah held out her trembling hand. "I will go now. Thank you for your time, Mr. Moulton."

He took her hand in his own large one and bowed over it. "Lady Sarah."

She found that despite his brusque manners and his size and strength, he made her feel safe rather than intimidated. When her hand hit her side, she realized he had let go. She gave him a small smile and attempted to retrieve her dignity. She left the room with her head held high and asked Mr. Wigan to call for the carriage.

"I already have, Your Ladyship." The butler walked with her to the front of the house. "Mr. Phipps will be here with the carriage any moment."

"Mr. Wigan, should—should anyone come looking for me," Sarah said, her voice unsteady, "will you let them know where to find me?"

The butler gave her a sad, pitying look underneath his dark eyebrows. "Of course, Lady Sarah."

She heard the sound of clomping hooves. "Goodbye, old friend."

He assisted her inside the carriage, and the vehicle began to shake as it propelled forward. Sarah released a breath. She placed her hands on her chest in an attempt to slow the rapid beating of her heart. She had just proposed marriage to a complete stranger.

CHAPTER 2

Christopher felt as if all the air had been knocked out of him. A stunning woman, nay a *lady*, a complete stranger, had just proposed marriage to him. He sat back down on the chair—his chair. In his house. *His* estate. It was all so much to take in, but all he could think about was a pair of light-brown eyes and a beguiling smile. She was not beautiful; she was better than that. Lady Sarah Denham was unforgettable. Her clothing was the very finest and her figure perfection.

He pulled at his neckcloth. He had stared at her much too long.

What she proposed was preposterous!

Or was it?

He tugged at his neckcloth again and the knot came untied. In his father's wildest ambitions, he never would have believed that his eldest son could be the child to make a grand match. All of Papa's dreams had been for Christopher's late brothers and his younger sisters. Christopher had always been an embarrassment, the child his father had sent away to work at an early age to hide the scars beneath his nose. A social climber needed a perfect family.

Christopher sighed. Papa was dead. Christopher no longer needed to beg for his father's approval by marrying a grand lady. Besides, his sisters would be here at any moment, and he needed to prepare the house for their arrival. Standing up, he determined to think about Lady Sarah Denham another time. He opened the door of the sitting room and found every servant in the house standing in a row, as if they were soldiers. He swallowed, and the swarthy man, presumably the butler, who had brought him into the house came forward.

"Allow me to welcome you to your home, Mr. Moulton."

"Thank you," Christopher said and glanced again at the line of servants, who were watching him surreptitiously from where they stood.

"I am Mr. Wigan. I will be your butler, if you will it. This is Mrs. Harmony," he said and pointed to a thin woman of grim aspect and numerous blonde curls. "She has been the housekeeper for fifteen years."

Christopher held out his hand, and the butler bowed his head before taking it and shaking it. Christopher did not offer his hand to Mrs. Harmony; clearly the servants were not used to handshakes. He could not picture Lady Sarah grasping anyone's hand. He winced, realizing he had made a vulgar mistake within minutes of entering the house. He tried to keep a blank face as he nodded to the servants as Mr. Wigan introduced all thirty-seven of them. Christopher had no idea what most of them did; his house in London ran very well with only eight servants. Although his town house was large for London, it was small compared to the grandeur of Manderfield Hall.

The butler bowed to him again. "We can make any adjustments you think necessary, sir."

"I am sure your current arrangements will work very well for me," Christopher said, waving his hand. "You may all return to your work. Thank you for your time."

The servants filed off in every direction, leaving only the housekeeper.

Mrs. Harmony curtsied, her corkscrew curls bobbing up and down. "Mr. Moulton, sir, might I have a few moments of your time to discuss household matters?"

"Of course."

She reached into her apron pocket and took out a paper written in perfect copperplate script. "Lady Sarah prepared the dinner menu for the rest of the week. If it meets with your approval, I will let the cook know. If not, we will do our best to accommodate your wishes."

He accepted the paper from her and read the menu. At least half of the dishes' names he did not recognize. His stomach churned in discomfort.

Handing the paper back to Mrs. Harmony, he said, "Everything appears to be in order."

The housekeeper bit her lower lip and pulled a large brass ring full of keys from her pocket. "These are the housekeeping keys, sir. Usually the lady of the house holds them in her possession."

Christopher accepted the brass ring. "My sister Margaret will be keeping house for me. I will see that she receives these."

"Very good, sir," Mrs. Harmony said, holding up a finger. "There is just one more thing."

"Yes, ma'am?"

The older woman thrust both of her hands into her apron pockets and looked at the floor. "Lady Sarah selected rooms for your sisters; would you like to see them or pick your own?"

Christopher cleared his throat; he was half-impressed, half-exasperated. Lady Sarah seemed to insert herself into every aspect of the running of the house. Yet he had never seen a cleaner, better-run establishment. "I should like to see them," he said and followed Mrs. Harmony toward the grand staircase.

Mr. Wigan opened the main door, and Christopher's two sisters walked into the house. They had traveled separately in a post chaise. Christopher didn't particularly care to be boxed into a stuffy carriage. He had avoided tight spaces ever since the time his father had locked him in a dark cupboard to hide him from his business associates. Christopher had been scared, but mostly he'd been hurt to realize how embarrassed Papa was of his face. Unconsciously, he rubbed the mustache that mostly covered the scars. But it couldn't cover years of stares and scorn.

"Christopher!" Deborah, his youngest sister, bounded toward him and threw her arms around his neck. Her blonde curls framed her heart-shaped face. At sixteen years old, she was the baby of the family and, because of her pretty face and exuberant spirits, received the bulk of the attention. "Manderfield Hall is amazing. I am so glad you purchased it. How fancy we will be!"

He swung her around and set her down, patting her head. "Deb, you're a whirlwind."

Margaret did not run to him but walked more sedately. She was two years older and an almost watercolor version of her sister. Margaret's eyes were as light as an afternoon sky, her blonde hair nearly white. Her face was long and oval, rather than heart-shaped, and it didn't possess the same animation as Deborah's. She also embraced him and said in a quieter voice than her sister, "It is a lovely house, Chris. I can hardly wait to see my bedchamber."

"Mrs. Harmony, the housekeeper, was just about to show me your rooms," he said. "Shall we go together?"

"Yes!" Deb exclaimed and headed up the stairs without waiting for the rest of them. She burst through the first door she encountered, and he heard her say, "Golly! I've never seen anything like this!"

He and Margaret trailed behind Deb, and the housekeeper took up the rear. They followed Deb into the room, and even Christopher's mouth opened in surprise. The bed's canopy frame was nearly ten feet high. The ceiling was tiled with gold. The floors were covered in a sumptuous golden patterned carpet. The walls were decorated in a gilded and celestial-blue paper with carved crown-and-base moldings. The windows were dressed with tasseled gold curtains. There was a pair of overstuffed wing chairs, an antique table, and a set of Queen Anne wardrobes, large as a curricle, next to a door with a golden knob.

"This room is usually reserved for the master of the house, and its adjoining rooms are for the mistress of the house," the housekeeper said primly.

Christopher nodded and tried not to think of Lady Sarah or her preposterous proposal. It was difficult. He could picture her here. With him.

"I want to see them!" Deb exclaimed, opening the door, which led to a dressing room and another entryway that led to the mistress of the house's rooms.

Again Christopher was stunned by their sumptuousness. The mistress's room was a mirror of the master's, everything exactly the same, from the golden carpet to the golden tiled ceiling to the furniture. The only difference was that the coloring of the paper on the walls was a pale pink and gold instead of blue.

Margaret's eyes were wide. "It looks like it should belong to a princess."

"No, a queen!" Deb flung her arms out and spun around in a circle. "It is so large, my arms do not touch anything."

Christopher opened the door that led back to the corridor. "Let us go see your rooms. We will follow you, Mrs. Harmony."

The housekeeper walked down the corridor and opened a door to a much smaller bedchamber. Unlike the formal grandeur of the master's apartments, this room looked almost homelike. The carved oak furniture was older. The walls were papered in a yellow pattern, and the floor was covered in a net rug. There was a reading nook by the window, and on the table was an arrangement of fresh flowers. Like everything in the house, each flower was placed perfectly, with corresponding colors of yellow and blue.

"Chris, it is simply beautiful. I claim this for my room. Oh, look at all the fresh flowers!" Deb said enthusiastically, bobbing up and down on the balls of her feet.

"Mrs. Harmony, they are very lovely," Margaret said in a quieter tone. "What a thoughtful gesture."

The housekeeper stiffened and sniffed. "It was Lady Sarah who picked them from the gardens and arranged them for you this morning,"

"Lady Sarah herself?" Deb said, her eyes wide and sparkling. "Bully!"

Margaret twisted her hands together, a nervous habit. Her blue eyes studied the carpet. "Is she still here?"

Mrs. Harmony shook her head, and more corkscrew curls escaped her white cap. "No, Lady Sarah has left. It is your home now. Shall I show you the other room she has prepared for you?"

"I suppose that room will be mine," Margaret said, looking up at Chris and smiling.

They followed the housekeeper into the adjacent chamber, which was very pretty too. Its walls were papered in a green pattern. A great white canopy draped over the headboard of the bed. The dark-stained cabinets and tables looked to be antiques. Again there were fresh flowers, beautifully arranged, this time in pink and green. Deb nearly ran into the room and went straight to the three windows that let in the light.

"Oh look!" she said. "You can see the river and the forest from your windows! How beautiful! Oh, Margaret, can I have this room instead?"

"Of course."

"Are you sure, Margaret?" Christopher asked. "Deb already claimed the other chamber."

She lowered her head. "They are both nice rooms. I do not mind taking the one she doesn't want."

Margaret always gave Deb whatever she wanted, as did Christopher. Sometimes he wished his middle sibling would stand up for herself more. Deb was becoming quite spoiled and harder to control. She was the reason his sisters had gotten into trouble at boarding school and Christopher was forced to remove them. It was unfair to Margaret, since he was certain she had never made even one false step.

Deb danced around the room and touched every piece of furniture. "What would the girls at school say if they saw us now?"

Margaret sat on the edge of the bed, folding her hands demurely in her lap. "I am sure they would be happy for us. Thank you, Mrs. Harmony; that will be all for now."

The housekeeper curtsied and left the room, closing the door behind her. Christopher was finally alone with his two sisters. He exhaled a breath he hadn't realized he had been holding.

"Phew!" Deb said in a loud voice and fell back onto the bed next to Margaret. "I am glad she's gone. Your housekeeper's face is positively Gothic, and her hair is frightful. You ought to pension her off and get a smart, new, young one."

"Deborah," Margaret hissed in a whisper. "Speak softer. She might have heard you."

Christopher swallowed. "Yes, quiet, Deb. We have not even been here a day. It is much too soon to make changes."

Deb sat up and stretched out her arms as she yawned. "I do not see why that is. You are the owner of this estate. You can do whatever you would like. And since you are our brother, we can do whatever *we* would like."

He scraped his fingers through his hair and sighed. "It does us no good to set up these people's backs. We want to be accepted by the local community."

Deb took off her bonnet and stuck out her chin mulishly. "She is only a servant. Their feelings and opinions do not matter."

"Servants have both ears and mouths," Margaret said in a low tone. "And you know how damaging malicious words can be to a lady's reputation."

His youngest sister kicked her feet impatiently against the wooden frame of the bed. "But that is all forgotten now."

Margaret placed an arm around her sister. "I sincerely hope so. We can start fresh here, if you would only learn to behave with some semblance of proper manners."

Deb clenched her teeth and wrenched out of her sister's hold, standing up and walking toward Christopher. "You are neither my mother nor my guardian. And you are not as perfect as you think you are, Margaret, despite the airs you put on."

Christopher glanced from one angry sister to the other. They both looked at him to support their side. Deb was only two years younger than Margaret, and he could see how having an elder sister boss her about could be irritating. On the other hand, she needed an older woman to guide her through the change from girlhood to womanhood. Too often she behaved like a spoiled child. "Stubble it, Deb. You two settle into your own rooms. I need to meet with the steward."

He left the room with the housekeeping keys still in his hand. Giving them to Margaret would only fan the flame of rivalry between his sisters. Deb would be jealous if Margaret asserted any authority over the house or the servants. How different his sisters' manners were from Lady Sarah's poised ones. He reassured himself that she was also probably five to seven years older than Margaret, but the difference was stark. But he was not going to think about her anymore.

And he didn't, not until he sat down with his steward and the man presented him with yet another list written in a beautiful copperplate hand.

"Lord Manders hasn't been in residence for nearly seven years," the steward said, stroking his brown beard. "Not since before the tragedy of the late countess. But Lady Sarah has run the estate effectively. She created a catalog for you of repairs that need to be made. She prioritized them by necessity."

Christopher looked at the long inventory. It felt daunting. "This is quite the list, Mr. Pryce."

The steward nodded, continuing to stroke his beard. "Aye. Lord Manders took nearly every farthing the estate made and put nothing back into it again."

"It looks like we have our work cut out for us," Christopher said, holding out his hand.

Mr. Pryce shook it readily, smiling. "Aye, sir. A young, strong man like yourself is just the one to do it too."

Christopher smiled politely, but he had his doubts. His business was canals, not agriculture. He glanced down at the paper. It would seem that Lady Sarah was very knowledgeable about estate business. She had ranked the improvements needed from the most immediate to the least, and she had notated the costs of each item. It was well thought out and efficiently planned; still, Christopher felt like a drowning man. He'd wrongfully assumed that owning an estate was similar to running a business.

He tucked the catalog away and determined not to think of the beautiful stranger again that day. But when he sat down to luncheon, he could not help but realize that all the dishes were delicious and paired beautifully together. Lady Sarah certainly knew how to run a household well. And even though he didn't know the names of the dishes, they were very fine indeed. Unfortunately, his sisters quarreled through most of the meal, although Margaret always gave way to Deb's stronger personality in the end. He realized that what they needed, and what he required, was a wife. Someone who could guide both of his sisters in the way of Society.

A woman like Lady Sarah.

CHAPTER 3

It took nearly the entire carriage ride to Westbrook Park for Sarah to compose herself, and even then, her pulse still raced through her veins. When she saw the familiar iron gates and the lovely yellow-stone house in the distance, she felt the tightness in her chest ease.

As they passed through the gates, she saw her cousin Ralph riding toward her on his gray mare. He pulled up beside the carriage window and waved. Sarah was a year older, but they had been best friends forever. Although they were first cousins, they did not resemble each other in the slightest. Ralph was tall with curly red hair, bright-blue eyes, and a chin that pointed ever so slightly. His figure appeared quite slim compared to the muscular form of Mr. Moulton.

"Where have you been, Sarah?" he demanded, speaking to her through the carriage window. "Mama is in a state. She expected you hours ago. She made me mount up to look for you. She was certain something was terribly amiss."

Aunt Venetia was a dear, but she did tend to allow her imagination free rein. "I was proposing marriage to a stranger—what else?" Sarah let out a crow of laughter, or hysteria, when she realized she did not even know his given name. She hoped it wasn't Hubert. She hated all Huberts, and Humphreys weren't much better.

Ralph grinned as if it were all a great joke. "Really? Was he tall, dark, and handsome? A duke with an abandoned manor and a mysterious past? And I hope he had a fortune sufficient to meet your sartorial needs."

"No, Mrs. Radcliffe, he was not a hero, nor a villain, from one of your novels," Sarah said, shaking her head. "He was more of a blond Hercules, the sort that would show to advantage in the boxing ring. And I am afraid he is not noble at all."

Her cousin curled his clean upper lip in disbelief and mockingly lifted his hat to her. Ralph must have decided to lose his mustache after she had called it a rodent underneath his nose. "You shock me. I thought only a duke would do for you since you turned down an offer of marriage from the Marquess of Ingress last year."

Sarah felt the heat rise on her neck again. "Hush, you! I told you about that in the strictest of confidences."

"Mr. Phipps won't tell anyone. Will you, sir?" Ralph called, placing his hat back on his head.

"No, Master Ralph. I know how to keep my mouth shut," Mr. Phipps said from his driver's seat.

The carriage came to a stop at the front of the house. Westbrook Park looked like an Italian villa, with a row of pilaster pillars and a second-story balcony. The stones were a creamy yellow, and there were several pointed arches. Ralph dismounted from his horse and opened the carriage door for Sarah. She accepted his hand and stepped out of the carriage.

"Are you sure you didn't forget anything, Freckles?" Ralph asked, raising one red eyebrow. "I believe you have only taken up the entire west wing with the boxes you've already sent. I am sure we could find space in the east wing as well."

Sarah laughed and released his hand. She despised the nickname Freckles, particularly because Ralph was covered in freckles himself. "Poor Flames. Did you have to toss a few of your cricket trophies into the rubbish pile?"

Before Ralph could reply, Aunt Venetia swept out of the house in a flourish of purple skirts and a mass of red curls. Her loquacious aunt loved to dress in bright colors that clashed horribly with her shade of hair, which was a color Sarah suspected was now dyed.

She threw her arms around her niece, squeezed her tightly, and said dramatically, "I thought you were stolen by vagrants! Or that your carriage had overturned. Or that you had a grievous injury. My dearest Sarah, niece, daughter of my beloved sister, what took you so long?"

Sarah returned the embrace, then stepped back. Her aunt never said one word when she could say ten. She glanced at Ralph, half expecting him to tell his mother about the marriage proposal he'd assumed was a jest.

"My cousin was simply making sure she didn't forget anything," Ralph explained, taking off his hat and kissing his mother's cheek. "But how there could possibly be anything left at Manderfield Hall to forget is beyond me. I believe she brought it all here with her."

Sarah playfully shoved him. "I am sorry that I worried you, Aunt."

Aunt Venetia gave her a loving smile that showed the lines around her blue eyes and her rosebud mouth. She took Sarah's hand and placed it in the crook of her own elbow, patting it. "How happy I am to have you, Sarah. How I have missed my own girls since they've married. I've had no one at all to keep me company. Not a soul to talk to. Not a one."

Ralph grunted and raised an eyebrow.

"Sons are not at all the same," Aunt Venetia said and drew Sarah inside the house. Ralph followed behind them. "Men are not half as good company as women. Except, of course, your uncle Oscar, who has always been most excellent company. He is always in possession of the latest gossip about town, and did you know, this very morning, he was telling me the most interesting story about Lady Jersey. He said . . ."

Sarah looked over her shoulder and grinned at Ralph's chagrined face, but she knew her aunt was only being kind. Sarah was the worst kind of visitor—the sort without a specific end date—and she felt fortunate to have such caring relatives to welcome her into their home.

CHAPTER 4

Early the next morning, Christopher called for his horse. He needed to leave immediately before he changed his mind again. He asked the head groom, Mr. Phipps, for directions to Westbrook Park since he'd driven Lady Sarah there only the day before.

Mr. Phipps looked at him speculatively but told Christopher to follow the village road until it reached the pike road and then turn onto the path near the manmade river. "You can't miss Westbrook Park," he said, scratching his cheek. "It's a big yellow house in the middle of a valley, styled after an Italian villa. Sir Roger even imported trees all the way from Italy at great expense, sir."

"Thank you, Mr. Phipps."

His heart beating abnormally fast, Christopher mounted his horse and kicked his heels into the animal's flank. He usually enjoyed riding, but this morning his mind was weighed down with indecision, and he nearly turned back to Manderfield Hall. What if his sisters didn't like Lady Sarah? What if *he* didn't like Lady Sarah? What sort of woman would marry a stranger for a house? It was a great estate, but in the end, it was merely stones and mortar. A foolish thing to love.

Christopher wondered what sort of man he'd become. Was he truly willing to accept a proposal of marriage from a stranger? Lady Sarah would manage the house and estate beautifully, far better than a London businessman could. She would also chaperone his sisters and allow them entrance into higher Society—the sort his father had always craved to be a part of but was continually excluded from. It was everything his father had wanted and nothing that Christopher did.

He pulled his horse to a halt when he caught a glimpse of the yellow house only a mile away. His muscles twitched, and his mouth was dry. Once his sisters married, *he* would be stuck with Lady Sarah for the rest of his natural life. The daughter of an earl and the son of a canal man. They were mismatched in every way. How could they possibly be happy together? Tugging on the reins, he turned the horse to return home. His sisters would be waiting for him, possibly squabbling.

Christopher had no idea how to handle them. How to gently rein in Deb's exuberance and encourage Margaret to stand up for herself more. He needed a wife. And surely one of the richest men in England deserved the very best. He could think of no better wife than Lady Sarah. She was elegant, well-mannered, intelligent, talented, and beautiful. And she had asked *him*!

Turning the horse once again, he prodded the beast into a canter toward the yellow mansion. Pulling the horse to a stop in front of the house, he dismounted and handed the reins to a groom, who seemed to have nothing to do but wait for someone to come by. Christopher gave the man a nod and walked toward the house, but before he reached the door, he heard a voice from behind him.

"Mr. Moulton, what a delightful surprise," Lady Sarah said in her cultivated tones.

He turned to see her carrying a basket full of freshly cut flowers in one hand and her bonnet in the other. She was wearing a blue dress, and the color contrasted with her lovely brown eyes. She was so striking that Christopher blinked, as if not quite trusting his own sight. After a moment of hesitation, he walked toward her. She set her basket down and held out her hand, palm down. He paused. He was pretty sure he wasn't supposed to shake it, but what should he do? Touch it? Kiss it?

Before he could make up his mind, she dropped her hand. Color stole into her cheeks. Relief swept over him; he was not the only one who felt nervous during this odd interview.

"Lady Sarah Denham, I have come to discuss your proposal."

"Excellent," she said, giving him another beautiful smile that caused butterflies in his belly. "Shall we take a turn around the gardens? They are lovely, and we shall have privacy there."

He nodded.

Lady Sarah picked up the basket and handed it to a footman, instructing him to see that the flowers were put into water. She turned back to Christopher and pointed the direction they were to go. They walked next to each other in silence until they reached a large oval fountain with a high-arching spray. As a man who, until recently, had worked with water all day, Christopher was intrigued with what mechanism was used to shoot the water so high.

Stopping, Lady Sarah turned to him, and all thoughts of fountains fled his mind. She was more beautiful than he'd remembered, and there was a pretty pink in her cheeks. Perhaps she felt as embarrassed as he did. "Have you come to a decision, Mr. Moulton?"

"Yes. Yes, I have."

"And?" she prompted, biting her lower lip.

"I believe our union would be beneficial for both parties, and I am agreeable. If, that is, you haven't changed your mind about marrying a stranger?"

She shook her head. "I have not."

"Then, we have an agreement," Christopher said, and without thinking, he offered his hand to shake as if this were a business matter. He recollected himself and was about to drop his hand when Lady Sarah placed her slender hand in his. She seemed frail and delicate, like the flowers she'd picked. A real lady.

"We do," Sarah said and gave him a most beguiling smile.

If he wasn't careful, he could lose his heart to such a woman, and that would be a disaster. No fine lady like her would ever have tender feelings for a scar-faced canal man. He squeezed her hand automatically, but she returned no pressure. He found his neck feeling hot. He released her limp hand and pulled at his neckcloth.

"I did not mean any disrespect, Lady Sarah," he said quickly. "A handshake is commonplace after an agreement in business."

"I should have thought a kiss would be more commonplace in this situation," she said with a saucy wink.

Christopher should not have looked at her mouth—her beguiling lips. He was better at kissing than conversing, and Lady Sarah had suggested a kiss to bind their agreement. Leaning forward, he waited for her to move away. She did not. In fact, she lifted her mouth to meet his. Her lips were soft and tasted sweet, like spun sugar. He put his hands on her shoulders to bring her closer to him, but her body stiffened. He broke the kiss instantly.

Embarrassed, he stepped back. She was a gently bred lady, and he had been too bold.

Touching her flushed cheek with her hand, she gave him a tremulous smile. "Thank you, Mr. Moulton. A kiss *is* far more satisfactory than a handshake. Our deal is struck."

He swallowed and was grateful that he was not forced to apologize to her for his uncouth behavior. "I suppose you ought to call me Christopher, if we are to be married. Or Chris, as my sisters do."

She laughed; it was a sweet, airy sound, like a delicate bell. "Chris-topher," she said slowly. "I should like to call you Christopher, and you must call me Sarah."

"Very good, Sarah," he said. "How soon should you like to be married?"

Smiling, she shrugged her shoulders. "Tomorrow. Or as soon as possible. We could be married by a special license."

The hairs on his arms stood up. Why was she in such a rush that the banns could not be read? Was she hiding something?

"I do not see the need to rush."

"And I do not see the need for delay," she said, sticking her chin out slightly. "I want to go home to Manderfield Hall, and I cannot until we are married."

Christopher sucked in a quick breath. "I could write to my solicitor and have him purchase a special license, but there is the little matter of marriage settlements. And your father's permission."

Sighing, she shook her head slightly. "I do not need, nor do I desire, my father's permission. I am five and twenty, and my maternal grandfather, the Duke of Aylsham, has already settled ten thousand pounds on me, which will become yours upon marriage. However, I should like to make one request: in addition to whatever money you mean to settle on me as your wife, I want the title of Manderfield Hall to be legally mine if, by chance, you should die before me and there are no children from our union."

Christopher was not surprised by her request. Sarah was willing to marry a stranger for the house; she would not wish to lose it upon his death. But did she mean she didn't desire to bear children? Or that she wanted a marriage in name only? "Do you not wish for children?"

"I want at least a half dozen babies," she said with a bright smile. "But one never knows. My mother wished for many children and was only able to have one daughter."

Relief flooded over him like a broken dam. He wanted a real marriage with Sarah and several children too. His betrothed was simply being cautious, something he respected, from his business experience. "Very well. I will ensure that both my will and the marriage settlements are clear on that matter."

"Excellent," Sarah said. "Then, we can marry as soon as you obtain the special license."

Christopher was about to speak when he heard a man's voice.

"Freckles, there you are." A young, redheaded gentleman walked to them, eyeing Christopher, and then angled himself so that he stood between Christopher and Sarah. He was several inches taller than Christopher and looked down on him in more than just height. The slender man was dressed elegantly and clearly thought he was much better than Christopher.

He flexed his arm muscles without thinking. The gentleman may be taller, but Christopher was broader in the chest and much stronger than this frippery fellow. Christopher had dug more than a hundred canals and was more than willing to sport his canvas.

The man touched Lady Sarah's arm, and Christopher saw red. "Is this man bothering you, Sarah?" the odious man said.

"Mr. Moulton, this is the Honorable Ralph Randolph, my cousin," Sarah said, stepping to the side of her cousin to give Christopher a reassuring look. "Mr. Moulton is the new owner of Manderfield Hall and my b-betrothed."

"Sir," Christopher said curtly, nodding. Resentment crawled up his spine. Christopher was not a lord or an honorable. His family wasn't aristocracy or gentry. They were as common as bread. His fortune had been made in the digging of canals.

The Honorable Ralph Randolph looked from Sarah to Christopher and back, then shook his head. "I don't believe it."

"You don't have to," Sarah said, crossing her arms. "It is none of your affair."

Ralph's eyes bulged. "My mother is waiting for you inside, Sarah. You should go to her."

Sarah pushed back her shoulders in apparent defiance. "You are not my keeper, Ralph. I will come into the house when I am ready. And you have yet to acknowledge Mr. Moulton, whose manners, might I add, are much better than your own."

"My mother is waiting for you," Ralph said sharply, his grip on Sarah's arm tightening. "And for the second time in two days, she is sure that you are lost. After what happened to *your* mother, I would think you would be more considerate to mine."

Christopher wondered what had happened to the late countess. By the sound of it, something terrible.

Sarah jerked back from her cousin as if she'd been slapped, and the *dis*-honorable Ralph Randolph released his viselike hold on her arm. She recovered her countenance enough to smile at Christopher. "I look forward to seeing you very soon, Mr. Moulton. Thank you for calling on me."

She curtsied and then took her cousin's arm and dragged him away from Christopher, as if to prevent the two of them from fighting. "Come, Ralph. Let us go assuage your mother's doubts about our safety. She's probably worried about you too."

Ralph glared over his shoulder at Christopher, but Sarah did not let go of his arm.

Alone, Christopher walked slowly back to the front of the mansion, where the groom from before was waiting with his horse. Christopher swung up into the saddle and prayed that he would not regret today's decision.

CHAPTER 5

Ralph tried to pull his arm away, so Sarah tightened her hold and pinched his bicep with her other hand. She got mostly coat, but she was happy to see him squirm. She had never been so furious with her cousin. A footman opened the door to the morning room, a bright calico-striped parlor with comfortably stuffed furniture.

Aunt Venetia stood and opened her arms to Sarah again. "Oh, my dearest niece, you were not stolen by bandits."

"I am certain the bandits would have returned her after a few hours and have gladly paid us a ransom to keep her," Ralph said sardonically.

Groaning, Sarah gave Ralph one last pinch before releasing his arm and embracing her aunt. Her cousin always brought out her most pettish behavior. Aunt Venetia's hug was nearly as tight as Sarah's grip on Ralph's arm. She felt her throat closing up, as if all the air was being squeezed out of her.

"Sarah, I do not mean to keep you wrapped in cotton," Aunt Venetia said, hugging her a second time. "I just get so worried when I don't know where you are."

Forcing herself to smile, Sarah stepped back. "I appreciate your concern, Aunt, and I am sorry if I caused you any anxiety, but I simply wanted to arrange some flowers in your hall."

Aunt Venetia nodded, placing a hand on her chest. "They are beautiful. I saw your flower basket, but I couldn't find you. And then this dreadful premonition came over me, and I sent Ralph to find you. I thought you had vanished like my sister."

"Your premonition was partially correct," Ralph said caustically. "Sarah's gone and engaged herself to a perfect stranger. A cit, of all things. I've heard around Town that this Moulton fellow is some sort of canal worker—a manual laborer."

Aunt Venetia's already expressive features seemed to enlarge at this statement. Her eyes bulged, her mouth gaped, and even her nostrils flared. "Engaged to be *married*? Our Sarah?" She turned her incredulous face from her son to her niece. "Well . . . isn't that wonderful!"

Sarah tried to force a smile again, and she nearly managed it. *Wonderful* was not quite the right word for marrying a stranger; *resolved* was a better one. "I had hoped to break the news to you more gently, dearest Aunt. But my cousin is correct. Mr. Moulton and I are engaged. I believe the union is in both of our best interests."

Tipping her head to the left, her aunt asked, "Whoever is this Mr. Moulton?"

As usual, her dear aunt had missed half the conversation and nearly all of its meaning. Sighing, Sarah prepared to explain it to her in the plainest words possible. Her aunt often muddled things up. "Mr. Moulton is my betrothed."

Ralph clenched his hands and scowled at Sarah. "A complete stranger to us. If Moulton really is his name. But how can we know for sure? The only thing for certain is that he smells of the shop."

Sarah felt her own nostrils flaring. She turned from her confused aunt to her seething cousin. Mr. Moulton was a ruggedly handsome man. Even if he didn't dress to the nines, his clothing was still well made. And he didn't smell of the shop. He smelled like leather and musk, which was quite an attractive combination, in her opinion. "I don't see why he would lie about his name. It would only invalidate his legal contracts. And I know that he is a man who keeps his word. He promised his late father that his sisters would make good marriages, and he is fulfilling it by marrying me."

Her cousin pointed his finger at her, his upper lip sneering. "You don't know anything about him. He could be a criminal for all you know."

"I know all I need to know," Sarah said, puffing out her chest and pointing her thumb at herself. "He is the owner of Manderfield Hall, and when I am his wife, I shall be its mistress."

Aunt Venetia looked back and forth from Sarah's angry face to her son's, as if trying to keep up with their conversation. She was the kindest woman imaginable, but her intellect was not very sharp. She nodded as if comprehending the main part. "Then, Mr. Moulton is the new owner of Manderfield Hall. Well, that is quite promising, I think. I've always admired the house and the surrounding land. I often believed that my sister loved Manderfield more than her own husband. But perhaps I should not say that aloud. Your poor father has been through a great deal these last seven years, Sarah. I have heard more than one rumor amongst the elite of the *ton* that he had something to do with your mama's disappearance, which we both know is not true. He adored her. We all did. There was no kinder or lovelier woman than my sister Louisa."

Gulping, Sarah tried not to think of her mother. Or her father. She had *not* known that such gossip existed about Papa. But it shouldn't have surprised her. The *ton* thrived on rumors and was not particular about their veracity. She felt a small pang of sympathy for her father but quickly buried it. Papa might have mourned his wife initially, but his one true love would always be gaming. He had diced away her security and treated his responsibilities like a house of cards. Several months after her mother's disappearance, her father had begun a relationship with the wealthy widow Mrs. Yardley so that she could pay his gambling debts. And he'd abandoned his only daughter, with nothing but the clothes on her back, to the charity of her mother's family.

Aunt Venetia took Sarah's hands into her own. "Perhaps, dearest Sarah, you ought to become better acquainted with this Mr. Moulton before your uncle writes to the papers to announce your engagement. And I really should ask my papa—your grandfather—for permission. You know how dictatorial the duke can be. He always seems to want a say in everything."

Sarah took a deep breath, trying to calm her agitated heart and soothe her angry mind. Her maternal grandfather was the Duke of Aylsham, a white-wigged, gouty-footed aristocrat who was used to getting his way. Sarah adored her surly grandpapa, but she would not be ruled by him. "I don't need anyone's permission, dearest Aunt. I am of age, and I mean to be married and back at Manderfield Hall where I belong by the end of the week."

"You would sell your soul for a house?" Ralph said.

Manderfield Hall held her heart and soul.

"Do not attempt to judge me," Sarah said in a much louder voice, her heartbeat thundering in her ears. "You have a home, and I do not. I am entirely dependent on my family's generosity, and I do not want to end up like Aunt Belinda, at the beck and call of the family, always visiting and never with a home or a place of her own."

Shaking her head, Aunt Venetia sighed. "My poor sister Belinda; I do feel for her. I've invited her to stay here at least a handful of times, but she is always needed somewhere else. I declare all twelve of Beatrice's children once got the chicken pox at the same time. Or was it the measles? And then another time, Belinda was supposed to visit and Papa came down with a terrible cold and she couldn't leave him. And then—"

"Yes, Mama," Ralph said, interrupting her reminiscing. "You have invited Aunt Belinda many times, and she has never come. But Sarah is hardly a spinster yet; she is only five and twenty, and the Marquess of Ingress proposed to her last year."

How dare her cousin betray her confidences thus! Sarah's insides felt like a teakettle about to explode with steam.

Aunt Venetia's hands flew to the sides of her face. "You don't say! Oh, Sarah, that would have been a most excellent match. I've always loved the title *marchioness*. Doesn't it just roll of your tongue so beautifully? Mar-chion-ess. Say it and you'll see."

A moment before, Sarah had been so angry that she was shaking, and now the shaking became uncontrollable laughter. Her shoulders shook, and finally she could no longer hold in her mirth.

Reluctantly, Ralph joined in her laughter.

"What is so funny?" Aunt Venetia asked, blinking at Sarah and Ralph.

"Mar—mar—chion—ness—ss," Sarah tried to say between giggles.

Ralph guffawed loudly. "Rolls right off the tongue, doesn't it?"

Wiping at her eyes, Sarah nodded. "Just like bar-ron-ess."

"And coun-tess," Ralph added with another snicker.

Raising one eyebrow, Aunt Venetia shook her head at her son and niece. "I don't see what is so funny about any of the titles. Had I not fallen madly in love with your father, I might have married a peer just to become a marchioness or a countess."

Or a baroness, Sarah added in her mind. Uncle Oscar was only a baronet, and as his wife, Aunt Venetia would only have been Lady Randolph; however, her own title as a duke's daughter was higher, so she was referred to in Society as Lady Venetia. Uncle Oscar did not have an aristocratic title, but he had a great fortune that had made him worthy in the duke's eyes.

The aged Duke of Aylsham had needed to marry off nine daughters—a daunting task for any widower. He'd found husbands for eight of them. All except for Aunt Belinda, who was now an old maid—a frightening role for any woman. No home of her own. Continually dependent on the whims and wants of her family members. Poor Aunt Belinda was little better than a drudge.

Spinsterhood was the fate staring Sarah in the face if she did not marry soon. She had already lost her home. She would be devastated to lose her position in Society. To be relegated to the corners of the room. The edges of the table, by the unwanted guests. To be nothing more than an unpaid servant to a married cousin or aunt.

Mama had always said, *"Marriage is the greatest gamble of all."* No matter how much or little one knew about their intended spouse, a person was always different once they were married. One could no longer hide their flaws or foolish propensities. Her mother had not known that Papa was a hardened gambler who was addicted to both cards and dice. What could Mother have learned from their courtship, aside from Papa's favorite jig, preferred ice, and opinions on the weather? They were never alone together. They never spoke about the topics that really mattered. Mama had married a stranger—an extravagant earl with feet of clay.

Sarah had probably learned more about Mr. Moulton in their two private conversations than her mother had about Papa in their first year of marriage. Sarah knew that Mr. Moulton was a devoted son and brother who would keep his word no matter what. She knew from the size of his shoulders to the roughness of his hands that he knew how to work hard and knew the value of money, something her father still did not understand, having never labored even one day in his life. It had been Sarah who had scrambled to keep Manderfield estate going after her mother's disappearance. Sarah who had visited the tenants and cared for her home with her own hands.

Returning her attention to Aunt Venetia and her cousin, Sarah attempted to further lighten the tense situation with a jest. "Had I only known how lovely it was to say marchioness, I might have accepted the marquess last year. Alas. A lost opportunity."

The laughter fell from Ralph's face, and he sneered at her sally.

Aunt Venetia clapped her hands as if she'd come up with a magnificent idea. "Do you think I should have Oscar write to the Marquess of Ingress and tell him that you've changed your mind? He has a very pretty property. In fact, I believe he has several estates. He is a little old for you, Sarah, but I do not think you'll mind that too much. He still has a very fine figure. I believe he's closer to forty than thirty. What think you of his age?"

Sarah sobered quickly and took her aunt's arm, leading her to a settee, where they both sat down. "He is thirty-seven years of age, Aunt, and I still do not wish to marry him. Please do not instruct Uncle Oscar to write to him. I am quite content with Mr. Moulton."

Wrinkling her nose, Aunt Venetia tipped her head to the side. "Are you sure? Because I believe Capability Brown himself designed the gardens at Ingress Abbey, and I don't think you could find a finer house in all of England.

Well, maybe Blenheim Palace is quite its equal. And, of course, we should not forget Chatsworth or—"

Sarah took her aunt's hand to stop her rambling. Aunt Venetia closed her mouth mid-sentence.

"Those are all fine houses, but they are not *my* home."

And they are not where my mother will come back for me.

Aunt Venetia nodded absentmindedly. Sarah could tell that she was about to start a catalog of all the nicest estates in England, when Ralph stomped across the room and towered above them. "This isn't about Manderfield Hall at all, is it, Sarah? How could I be so blind to your true reason? I know you better than anyone in this world."

She stood to meet his gaze. She still had to look up to Ralph, and that irked her. "What do you mean?"

"This is about your mother."

Aunt Venetia made a whimpering sound and gave Sarah a pitying look. "Poor, poor Louisa. My loveliest sister."

Swallowing, Sarah stuck out her chest like a rooster attempting to appear larger. "And what if it is? Mama said that she would come back, and she will."

"Aunt Louisa's gone, Sarah," Ralph said in a voice barely above a whisper. "Your mother is gone . . . and marrying a stranger to remain at Manderfield Hall for the rest of your life is not going to bring her back. You need to accept this and move on. Marry someone of your own class and social standing."

Her cousin wasn't the first person to say that to her. Her father had said it months after her mother went missing, when the Bow Street Runners had been unable to turn over the smallest of clues as to her whereabouts. *"It's no use pining for what is gone. We each must look to our own futures."* In that same year after her mother's disappearance, Papa had put on a black armband and declared himself a widower, even though Mama wasn't declared legally dead.

A year after her mother's disappearance, Sarah's grandfather, the Duke of Aylsham and a loving autocrat, had settled a respectable dowry on Sarah and encouraged her to find a husband. Grandfather had said that her mother was never coming back. He'd even commanded her aunt Venetia to drag Sarah to London for two months every year to participate in the Season. But as soon as it was over, Sarah always rushed back to Manderfield, anxious for news about her mother.

Over the years, one by one, each servant in her home, and even the tenants, had all gently encouraged her to let go. To move on. But she was stuck, like she was six years old and still hiding in the same cabinet, waiting for her mother to find her. She couldn't leave until she knew where her mother was or what had happened to her.

She huffed and sat back down by her aunt. "I don't need to accept anything. I know in my heart that she is coming back. My mother would never have left me."

"I believe she would not leave you willingly, but she is gone, Sarah," Ralph said quietly.

The door to the room opened, and Uncle Oscar walked in. Like his son, Uncle Oscar was a tall, spare man. Unlike his son, Uncle Oscar had black hair, though it was now mostly gray. His intelligence was as sharp as his wife's was vague. However, it was usually turned to improving the "capabilities" of his estate and making it "picturesque." He was a great admirer of Capability Brown's work.

"What is all the commotion?" Uncle said.

Ralph pointed at Sarah. "Papa, tell Sarah that she cannot marry a complete stranger for a house."

Her uncle breathed in deeply and then slowly exhaled. Walking over to his son, he put a hand on his shoulder. "My dear boy, never tell a woman she cannot do something. Nothing is more certain of setting up her back and encouraging her to do the exact opposite of what you wish."

Sarah's shoulders and back were up, but she could not help but smirk at this excellent advice. Her uncle had a sly humor that many people missed, including her aunt. The tightness in her body eased a little. Uncle Oscar was everything that her father was not: reliable, sensible, and dependable. Even if he had spent the last five years designing and building a fake ruin to add ambiance to his estate.

"Now, Sarah," Uncle Oscar said, "why don't you tell us all about your betrothed."

She shook out her hands in her lap. "Mr. Moulton has earned his fortune in the canal business. He is the new owner of Manderfield Hall and wishes to find a wife and chaperone for his two younger sisters, to usher them into good Society. He is a hardworking family man, whom I believe will treat me with respect and consideration. I shall have a home and family of my own. No woman could ask for more."

Nodding, Uncle Oscar widened his stance. "Ah, I have heard of Moulton. He is well respected in the city. I have even invested in several of his canal projects. He is a good businessman and as wealthy as a nabob. Our Sarah could do far worse."

Aunt Venetia made a yipping sound, much like her favorite little Pomeranian puppy. "Our Sarah could do much better. A marchioness, Oscar! Can you imagine? Ingress asked for her hand in marriage. He is not yet forty and a fine figure of a man. I daresay he could still father several children."

Sarah wanted to box Ralph's ears for breaking her confidence. Aunt Venetia did not have a great deal of wit, but once an idea found purchase in her brain, it was hard to move her to a new subject. She clearly wanted her niece to be a marchioness. Sarah was not a title-hunter, nor was she mercenary. As much as she liked the Marquess of Ingress, she did not love him. She did not love Mr. Moulton either, but she loved Manderfield Hall and her mother, and they were worth any sacrifice. She gave her uncle a beseeching look.

He nodded slightly, as if understanding her silent entreaty. "I wonder if Mr. Moulton could redirect the river on our estate and make a lake for Westbrook Park, dearest. I know you've always wished for a larger water feature, and Capability Brown always created the loveliest serpentine lakes."

"Oh, how beautiful that would be!" Aunt Venetia exclaimed, touching her cheeks and apparently forgetting all about her niece's approaching nuptials. "Do you think this Mr. Moulton could ensure our new lake reflects the house like all the best artificial lakes do?"

Uncle Oscar moved forward to put a hand on his wife's shoulder as she sat bouncing in her seat. "We will not accept anything less than the best, dearest. Sarah, you're looking a bit peaky. Why don't you go and rest before dinner. I think we could all use a little time on our own to think."

Standing, Sarah thanked her uncle and left the stuffy room. Once she stepped onto the gray marble tiles of the entry hall, she ran to the stairs and took them by twos to the bedchamber where she was staying. It had once belonged to her elder cousin Amanda, who had been married for ten years now. This chamber would never be Sarah's. Even if she stayed in the family rooms, she was still only a guest. The furniture was not hers; it was too new, too shiny. And there was no window seat for her to sit on and ponder.

She pushed a chair to the window and sat on it with her knees tucked against her chest. The view was not the same as the one from home. She could not see the forest and the lovely peaks of the mountains. Only her uncle's imported Italian evergreens and the top of his fake castle ruins.

Sarah sighed. She and Ralph had not been in such a row since the summer she'd accidently broken his cricket wicket when she was twelve. How long ago that seemed now. Her mother had been there to hold her then, to tell her that everything would be all right, while she cried. Sarah did not cry anymore. She had not wept since that night.

The last night she'd seen her mother alive.

***

That evening, Sarah looked a little pale in her mirror, so she carefully applied a little extra rouge to her cheeks. Her dinner dress was made out of organdy with white ribbons that she had added herself. She smoothed out a wrinkle with her hand. She missed her maid, Nelly, but without any steady income, she could not afford to hire a new one. Nor did she wish to further financially impose on her aunt and uncle.

She heard a knock on her door. She got to her feet and opened the door a crack to see Ralph, his expression still stern. She hoped he had not come to renew their argument. Weariness clung to her like a set of too-tight stays.

Her cousin did not meet her eyes, but said in a low voice, "May I come in?"

Sarah felt the tightness in her stomach loosen a little, and she opened the door wider. "I suppose so. Have you come to apologize?"

"No. I've come to propose," Ralph said, kneeling before her. "Sarah, will you marry me?"

Feeling dizzy, Sarah took two steps back from him. "Are you foxed?"

Ralph shook his head, looking more serious than she ever had seen him. "No, I am not inebriated. I have come to you with a clear mind. You are my best friend, and I love you better than anyone else. Will you marry me, Sarah?"

The anger that had consumed Sarah all afternoon dissipated instantly, like dew in the morning sun. She walked forward and knelt beside him, taking his hands. "Oh, Flames, that's the loveliest thing anyone has ever said to me. But you know we would not suit at all. One of us would murder the other before the first year was out."

Ralph smiled a little at this sally. "I'm serious, Sarah. You would have a home. You would not be an old maid. You would have security. You could be close to Manderfield Hall. Everything you want."

Squeezing his hands, Sarah gave him a lopsided smile as an expansive feeling of warmth grew inside her chest. "But not anything that you'd want, my dearest cousin. I love you too, but not in the way a wife should love her husband. And you do not love me the way a man should love a wife. Let us stand up. I'm wrinkling my gown, and it is one of my favorites."

Huffing, Ralph helped her to her feet, and Sarah pulled her hands away. She took a deep breath. She often used her love for fashion to cover her emotions. That her cousin was willing to make such a great sacrifice for her meant everything. The only other person who had ever put Sarah's needs before their own had been her mother. She loved Ralph better in this moment than she ever had before.

"Just consider it, Sarah," Ralph insisted, raking his hands through his messy red curls. "My parents would be delighted. They've hinted for over a year that it was time for me to settle down and get married. And our mothers always wanted us to make a match of it."

Tears filled her eyes and she shook her head. "Not anymore. Your parents want you, quite rightly, to marry a young lady of fortune and position, which I no longer am."

"You're not penniless. Grandfather settled some money on you."

"But I am the daughter of a disgraced earl who has lost his inheritance, and you wouldn't be making this declaration if I weren't already planning to marry Mr. Moulton."

"That cit," Ralph spat out.

"Ralph, I do love you better than anyone. But I am not the least bit *in* love with you, nor you with me. Only conceive how terrible it would be if we get married and you finally fall in love—but with someone else. All of us would be made miserable."

"You're not in love with Moulton either. What if you were to fall in love?"

Sarah shrugged. "I thought I was in love with my French dancing master when I was sixteen. He had the most dashing mustache."

Ralph guffawed. "You couldn't understand half of what he said."

"That made it all the better," Sarah said with a grin. "But seriously, Flames. I will not ruin your life to secure my own comfort."

"You'll ruin your own, Freckles."

"No, only Mr. Moulton's comfort, and you don't like him anyway," Sarah said with sly humor. "But I mean to make it such a lovely ruin that he never notices. Now, go to the village and carouse with your friends until the wee hours of the morning. And when you wake up tomorrow, you will be ever so grateful that I said no."

"Are you sure?" Ralph asked, almost smiling. His whole countenance lightened, as if he'd been relieved of a great weight.

"Entirely. Go and celebrate your freedom. I'll make your excuses at dinner."

"All right then," he said and left the room.

The warmth in her heart faded, and her chest felt empty without the anger. When she had been frustrated with Ralph for trying to spoil her plans, she didn't have to focus on her own apprehensions. Was she making a grave mistake marrying this stranger? Her hands began to shake, and she held them together, trying to stop them from trembling. Despite her bravado with her aunt and uncle, she knew very little about her bridegroom. Only his name. What if she was making a terrible choice?

Shaking her head, she knew she could not afford to lose her nerve now. She was going to marry Mr. Christopher Moulton. She was going to live out the rest of her life at Manderfield Hall, and when her mother came home, Sarah would be there waiting for her.

CHAPTER 6

MR. WIGAN CARRIED IN A silver tray with a single white letter. Christopher's pulse quickened as he picked up the post and thanked the butler. With a swift slice of his penknife, he opened the letter. He instantly recognized Sarah's perfect copperplate handwriting. The lady seemed to do everything well. He had not seen her for three days, but he could not stop thinking about the kiss they'd shared.

> *Dear Mr. Moulton,*
>
> *Thank you for your letter. I shall be ready and waiting for you tomorrow morning at nine o'clock to go to the church. I appreciate the speed and the delicacy you have shown in this matter.*
>
> *Yours Sincerely,*
> *Lady Sarah Denham*

He liked that the missive was short and to the point. Also that she didn't pretend to possess any warmer emotions than either of them felt. He folded the letter and placed it in his coat pocket. His pulse slowed to a normal rate. He would tell his sisters about the marriage after dinner. That was soon enough.

Opening his desk drawer to put away his penknife, he saw the household keys. He had never given them to Margaret. Somewhere in his mind, he must have known they'd always belonged to Lady Sarah. The estate needed her and so did he. His sisters wandered the house and gardens listlessly. They had no acquaintances or friends in the area. And they no longer had school or a governess to arrange their studies and occupy the long hours of the afternoon.

Deb, in particular, became quite fractious when she had nothing to do and took out her sour mood upon Margaret. Christopher had chided Deb more than once, but he did not know how to solve the problem without causing more conflict. And Margaret avoided conflict at all costs.

Christopher sat down to dinner at the head of the table. Margaret took her usual seat at his right, but Deb did not sit at his left.

She put her hands on her waist and stomped her foot. "Why does Margaret always get the best spot at the table? It isn't fair."

"Because you get the best of everything else," Christopher wanted to retort. But that would hardly defuse the situation. "Custom and tradition, Deb. Now, stop acting like a child and sit down. You are making another scene in front of the servants."

Deb scowled and slumped into her chair. Christopher ignored her and focused his attention on the delicious dinner that the footmen brought out in several courses. They ate together in an uncomfortable silence. Deb was sulking again. She needed a mother. She did not remember Mama. He could not provide her with a mother, but he would give her a lady that could guide her, help shape her, and teach her the manners required for Society. His youngest sister wasn't a bad girl, but she behaved like an unbroken colt.

His sisters left after the last course, and Christopher sat alone, drinking a glass of port. What an odd tradition the nobles had of drinking after just eating an enormous meal. Still, the butler faithfully brought the port after dinner and expected Christopher to drink it. He had not known how limited his meal selections were in London. He wondered if his city servants thought he was common. There was no book on how to become a gentleman. The closest thing, he supposed, was a peerage, which only told the names and ranks of the members of the aristocracy.

He believed that gently born sons were taught in their homes the social graces required. That was why, when his father died nine years before, Christopher had sent his sisters to a select girls' seminary. Nineteen at the time, he'd felt like too old a dog to learn new tricks. His sisters hadn't been, only they hadn't seemed to learn as much as he'd hoped. Then again, this thought was not fair to Margaret. She always sat up straight in her chair and ate as neatly as a princess. Whenever he did not know which utensil to use, he watched to see which one she picked up.

She had certainly learned how to be a lady in school; he wondered why Deb had not. She was the stronger willed of the two girls, and unlike Margaret, she didn't remember their three late siblings or their mother, who had all succumbed to an unknown plague thirteen years ago. She'd been a child of only three. Both she and Margaret had been removed from the house so as not to contract the illness. Christopher had not been at home in London either. He had been sent away when he was eleven. Papa had said it was to learn the canal trade by laboring with the employees, but Christopher had always thought he was sent away because of the scars on his face.

Mr. Downman, the foreman, had been a kind man and had watched over Christopher as a young lad. Canal workers were a rough lot who moved from job to job. A construction site usually held between two hundred and three hundred workers. There were few safety measures, and there was a great deal of gunpowder. It had been no place for a boy, and his father had never once visited him there in Gloucestershire. Once completed, the Sapperton Tunnel was the longest canal in England at over two miles. It linked the Severn River to the Thames. He'd carted stone and sledge until his body was no longer that of a boy's but a young man's. Christopher had been proud of his part in the canal.

Until he'd learned that several members of his family had died whilst he'd been away. Papa had not sent for Christopher until six months after the funeral of his little brothers and his mother.

John, age 12.

Fred, age 9.

Francis, age 7.

Mama, age 35.

Mama had been only seven years older than he was now.

Christopher had never gotten the opportunity to tell them goodbye. At the time, Papa had explained that he couldn't risk the health of his three living children. The plague was extremely contagious. Even the nurses his father had hired had succumbed to the disease. Nearly all their possessions were burned to stop the infection. The house was left vacant for over a year before Papa sold it. Neither Christopher, Margaret, nor Deborah had set foot in it again. Either the deaths of his wife and children or his own contact with the disease had weakened Papa's heart. He was never the same hale and hearty man again. Perhaps that was why he'd finally accepted his eldest son—or perhaps it was only the growth of a mustache that covered the scars Papa was so ashamed of.

Slowly, Christopher began to take over his father's duties. He'd made arrangements with the foremen and planned the routes with the engineers. He'd taken over all the finances and turned his father's prospering canal business into the largest and most respected canal-building company in England, Wales, and Scotland. With his own hands, he'd carved out his place.

But Papa had never gotten to see the fruits of his eldest son's labors. He would have loved Manderfield Hall and Lady Sarah even more. Christopher wondered if Papa would have finally been proud of him. He prayed his sisters would be.

Leaving the table, he wandered through the corridors until he found his sisters playing cards in the sitting room where he'd first met Sarah. Their shadows were illuminated by the generous fire in the hearth. Both sisters turned to look at him as he entered the room.

Deb gave him a glittering smile, her earlier sulks apparently forgotten. "Shall you join us at cards, Chris? I have already lost so much money to Margaret that I have had to apply to her for a loan to keep playing."

"Yes, please come play," Margaret said, giving him a gentle smile and an arched look. "I should like to have some competition."

Deb stuck out her tongue at Margaret and threw her cards down on the table. "If I am bad at it, you've only yourself to blame, for you are the one who taught me how to play."

Christopher was certain Margaret had only meant to tease and not to wound, but handling Deb was like holding gunpowder in one's hands—it could explode at any time. Christopher had carried enough dynamite into the Sapperton Tunnel to know how dangerous and volatile it was.

He took a seat at their table. "I would actually like to speak to both of you about something of a serious nature."

Groaning, Deb put her elbows on the table and rested her head in her palms. "Not another lecture."

He glanced at Margaret and saw the surprised look on her countenance. He hadn't meant to alarm either of them. Christopher held up his hands. "Nothing bad, I assure you. Quite the reverse, actually. I am getting married."

Gasping, Deb sat up in her chair. "To who? Do we know her?"

"To *whom*," Margaret corrected softly.

Deb scoffed at her sister and then snapped her fingers. "I know! Our particular friend, Miss Adkins. She's been throwing her cap at you for ages, and what a fine wife she will make. Thanks to her father's factory, we shall never want for beeswax candles again."

Had Christopher felt the smallest flicker of attraction to Miss Adkins, he may have asked her to become his wife. She was nearly his same age and the heiress to her father's beeswax candle factory. It would be a good match with a woman of his own rank, but it would not propel his sisters into the *ton* like he'd promised his father. If anything, such a marriage would harm their chances of marrying a man with a title.

Shaking his head slightly, he said, "It is not Miss Adkins, nor anyone else of your acquaintance."

Margaret touched his shoulder gently. "Don't keep us in suspense, Chris. Tell us at once."

Taking a deep breath, Christopher said, "Lady Sarah Denham."

"Bully! A real lady?" Deb exclaimed, clapping her hands.

Margaret pursed her lips and appeared thoughtful. "Isn't that the young woman who used to live here? I believe every servant has mentioned her name at least a dozen times since we arrived. She is much beloved."

He nodded slowly. "Yes, she is the daughter of the Earl of Manders."

"How exciting! Was it a whirlwind romance, Chris?" Deb asked eagerly, her hands resting on her bouncing knees. "When did you meet her? Where did you propose? Tell us everything. Was it terribly romantic?"

Christopher sighed. His sisters would not appreciate the truth, nor the sacrifices he was taking upon himself to make way for their welfare and his own stupid pride. For half a moment, he contemplated prevaricating, but the truth always came out in the end. "I have only met Lady Sarah twice; however, we decided that a union between us would be in both of our best interests."

"Oh," Margaret said, slumping back in her chair. "I suppose you know what is best, Brother. But should you not have some warm feelings for her? Some affection before marriage?"

"Ours will be a marriage of convenience, which is quite normal among the upper classes."

"I hate her already," Deb declared, standing up and stomping her foot. "How could you be so stupid as to marry without love?"

"I am not being stupid," Christopher said between clenched teeth. "I am being practical, and if we want to join the *ton*, to be a part of the highest echelons of London Society, we need a family connection to the nobility. Lady Sarah's connections are among the highest in all of England. She can arrange for you both to be presented before Queen Charlotte. It is everything and more than Papa hoped for, for all of us."

Margaret stood too and placed a hand on his shoulder. "I know you promised Papa you would find us grand matches, but I am sorry you are to be sacrificed for our father's social pretentions. Deb and I only want you to be happy."

"It's not a sacrifice," Christopher said, getting to his own feet and twisting out of his sister's hold. "Lady Sarah is an accomplished and beautiful woman with great deal of countenance and exquisite manners. Any man would be honored to call her his wife. I believe we will be very happy together. I look forward to marrying her."

"Then, why is she marrying you?" Deb asked, her hands on her hips.

Christopher had received many slights in the city, especially by men of the aristocratic class that his father had been so eager for them to join, but he wasn't used to insults from his sisters. Deb's words stung. Did she not think him worthy of a proper lady?

Before he could reply, Margaret answered for him. "Lady Sarah is marrying Chris for Manderfield Hall, of course. All the servants talk about how much she loves it. Mrs. Harmony even showed me the portrait of her mother that hangs in the picture gallery. She said how sad Lady Sarah was to leave it but that the earl had sold it with the rest of the estate."

Christopher wondered which painting it was. Had he only known, he would have given it to her. When Lord Manders's solicitor offered to sell the furniture and paintings with the house, he'd happily paid the additional price. He hadn't wanted a mansion with nothing on the walls. But he would not have missed one portrait of a woman he never knew. How he wished he had a painting of his own dear mother to place in the portrait hall. Her face was becoming shadowed in his memories, and he could no longer remember her clearly. Had her eyes been more like Margaret's or Deb's? Both of his sisters had Mama's fine complexion—a daintiness that he most certainly hadn't inherited. His skin was a warmer olive shade, and he'd always been a big lad. Now he was a large man.

He shouldn't allow himself to be cowed by his little sisters. "That is correct," he said, confirming Margaret's words.

Deb gritted her teeth and stomped her foot again, like a child throwing a temper tantrum. "You're making a mistake. And I refuse to go to your wedding! You might as well call it your *funeral*. A lady who would marry for her own gain will never love or respect a man like you, and she will look down on all of us for the rest of our lives! We shall all be miserable!"

Breaking into sobs, she spun on her other foot and ran out of the room. Christopher watched Margaret look at the open door, then back at him. She stared at the fire with Christopher without speaking for several minutes. As much as Deb's words had cut him, Christopher had thought the very same things. Lady Sarah would probably always look down on his gruff ways, coarse accent, and common background, but he wouldn't allow anyone to treat his sisters poorly, lady or not.

Margaret clicked her tongue. "Perhaps Lady Sarah will have a calming influence on Deborah. She doesn't do a thing I tell her to, and she hates it when I correct her. I fear if she makes the same mistake here that she did in school, she will be scorned and shamed again. I tried to warn her over and over again, but she never listens to me. Perhaps she will pay attention to a real lady."

Turning his head, he met his sister's concerned eyes. "You *are* a real lady, and I hope you will both be happy with Lady Sarah's companionship."

Margaret nodded, exhaling slowly. "I am sure we shall be. When are you to be married?"

Her gaze penetrated his very soul, and he had to look away. "Tomorrow morning, by special license."

"So very soon?"

"Yes." *Before either of us loses our nerve and changes our minds*, Christopher thought. His limbs tingled, and he focused his gaze on his hands. The large and rough hands of a laborer. A trickle of sweat dripped down the back of his neck.

"May I come to the wedding?" Margaret asked in a small voice.

Not looking up, he said, "I should like that."

***

Christopher much preferred riding, but one could hardly expect the ladies to ride a horse to the wedding. Margaret sat beside him in the carriage, dressed in her finest cambric dress. Her eyes rested on her hands, which were folded in her lap. She rocked back and forth in her seat, and not to the same movement of the carriage. His family had never socialized with the nobility, not even with the gentry, and he felt nervous too. His muscles no longer tingled, but his insides quivered uncomfortably. When Margaret looked up at him, he stared out the window, eager to escape her all-too-seeing eyes.

The carriage pulled up to the large yellow mansion of Westbrook Park. Experiencing a bout of dizziness, Christopher tugged at his neckcloth with his finger, needing more air.

A footman opened the double front doors, and Sarah walked out. For a few moments, Christopher forgot to breathe. He'd never seen anyone so beautiful. Everything about her spoke to her excellent taste and refined manners. Over her face she wore a thin white veil, which was attached to her bonnet, but he could still see all her perfect features. She was smiling.

Relief washed over him like a waterfall. He felt lightheaded and giddy; Sarah hadn't changed her mind. He stepped out of the carriage and held out his hand. It shook a little. She placed hers on top of it and allowed him to assist her inside the conveyance. She sat on the forward-facing seat next to Margaret. Christopher climbed back in and sat across from them.

"Your dress is exquisite," Margaret said in awed tones.

His sister was not wrong. Christopher had never seen a more lovely or ethereal garment. It was white, the color that only the wealthiest people wore. The gown was all one shade, but there was nothing simple about it. His bride wore a silk chemise with a pattered silk gauze with small white dots. The puffed sleeves resembled flower cups with gauze petals. He had never seen the dress's equal.

Sarah gave his sister an enchanting smile. "Thank you, dear girl. I should have worn a pelisse over it, but I didn't wish to smash the sleeves. I hope a bride is allowed a little leniency on her wedding day."

Margaret stared at Sarah with unabashed admiration.

Sarah fingered one flowerlike sleeve. "I shan't deny that I worked very hard to make it lovely, and I woke with the dawn and have been busy getting ready ever since."

"You sewed it yourself?" his sister said.

Christopher was surprised too. The gown was the sort of garment he'd seen only in one of his sister's fashion plates.

Sarah's gaze moved to him, and she gave him another smile that made it difficult to breathe. "I am quite good at needlework. It is my best talent. Would that I had something clever and more accomplished to display, alas. Now, Christopher, please introduce me to your beautiful sister. I have been longing to meet her."

Taking in a sharp breath, Christopher tried to recollect himself. He was acutely aware of his own heartbeat and the hairs rising on his arms and the nape of his neck. "Sarah—I mean, Margaret—may I introduce you to Lady Sarah?"

The person of lower rank was always presented to the person of higher station, Christopher recalled. He'd learned a few things about the aristocracy through his business associations. Including that a gentleman was always presented to the lady.

Lady Sarah inclined her head. "I am delighted to meet you, Miss Moulton. May I call you Margaret?"

"If you wish to, Lady Sarah," Margaret said shyly, her gaze downcast.

"I do," Sarah said, her eyes alight. "And you must call me Sarah, for we are to be sisters by the end of this morning, are we not?"

Margaret blushed and repeated, "Sisters."

"I hope you do not mind, Christopher, but Lady Venetia, my aunt, would like to see our marriage," Sarah said in her beautifully cultivated voice as she turned her body to look directly at Christopher. The sensation of lightheadedness returned. "She is going to follow in a carriage behind us with my cousin, Mr. Randolph. If agreeable to yourself, he will serve as one of the witnesses."

Christopher flexed his arm muscles when she mentioned her cousin. It put a damper on his attraction to her. The Honorable Ralph Randolph was the last person on earth he would want at his wedding, much less witnessing it, but he dared not say or do anything that might cause her to change her mind. "Whatever you wish."

"Thank you, sir," Sarah said and pointed out her window. "Margaret, if you look just there, you will see the most impressive ruins of a castle."

His sister leaned toward Sarah and gazed raptly at what she pointed at. Christopher also looked out the window. A historic-looking building with several stone archways but no roof was situated near a forested area, and he had not noticed it during his last trip to the Westbrook estate. Although, that day he had been weighed down with a great deal on his mind.

Margaret's eyes widened, and she smiled becomingly. "How very beautiful! It must be a very old castle."

Sarah laughed; it sounded like the tinkling of a bell. "I am afraid it is not. My uncle Oscar just recently completed overseeing its construction."

"He built a ruin?" Christopher asked in surprise before he could stop himself.

"Yes," Sarah said with another tinkling laugh. "He needed ruins to add some picturesque antiquity to the grounds, and now he wishes to create an artificial lake. I thought I should tell you, Christopher, that he means to ask for your advice in diverting a river to make one at the earliest opportunity. And once my uncle has an idea in his head, he is like a dog with a bone. He will not let go of it and can think of nothing else, much like his wife."

Raising a gloved hand to her mouth, Margaret giggled. "How can one create a lake?"

At least this conversation was about something Christopher was an expert on. "A surveyor would have to ensure the area has sufficient slope and depth for the lake. Otherwise, the land or a retaining wall would have to be built up around it. Both are costly but not impossible processes. One would try to find the shortest route from the river to the proposed location. It costs around seven pounds a yard and a crew of over a hundred strong men and skilled laborers."

Sarah leaned back in her seat, as if she were not nervous at all about their impending nuptials. Christopher could not say the same. He was wound up tighter than a clock. All of his movements felt jerky and unnatural. He blabbed on about canals.

"What a fascinating subject, Christopher. I had no idea the process was so complex or costly. I am glad that I warned you about the lake before our first dinner at Westbrook Park," she said, her lips tilting upward into a slight smile. "It would not surprise me if halfway through the fish course, my uncle drags you out to show you where he wishes to put it. His estate is his passion."

His head jerked back a little. "Are we to receive social invitations from Sir Oscar?"

Sarah nudged Margaret with her elbow. "Or, rather, from Lady Venetia. My aunt adores having company over. I am sure she will take you and your sister underneath her wing, Margaret. She misses her own daughters, who have all married and moved away. They have children of their own but none old enough yet for matchmaking, which my dear aunt believes she has a talent for."

Margaret's cheeks turned a pretty pink, and she gave Sarah a shy smile. "I would be honored by her interest."

Sarah's brown eyes focused back on him. "And, Christopher, you will receive invitations from Uncle Oscar to go hunting, but I feel I should also delicately hint that when my uncle says 'hunting,' he truly means birdwatching."

Christopher didn't have much experience shooting for sport. He was either overseeing the construction of canals or handling the business side in London. He was flattered that a baronet would include him in any sort of invitation. But all of that dimmed every time Sarah said his name. He liked how it sounded in her aristocratic voice. And he liked how his chest felt warm when her eyes focused on him.

"Now, tell me all about yourself, Margaret," Sarah said, turning her attention back to his sister. "Do not leave out the smallest of details, for I want to know it all."

At last Christopher was relaxed enough to be able to lean back and listen as his shy sister spilled all of her secrets to Sarah. Sarah listened raptly and asked several clarifying questions. Margaret blushed and talked more than Christopher had ever heard her speak. He learned more about his sister in these few minutes than he had in the last few years. He had not known how much Margaret loved music, nor that she was interested in learning how to play more instruments. He was amazed at how quickly Sarah had seemed to win his reticent sister over. Deb would not be so easily swayed.

When they arrived at the church in the village of Eden, he assisted both ladies out of the carriage. They were also met by clusters of flowers and clumps of rushes on the porch of the chapel. He wondered who had provided them. The wedding was small and private.

The vicar opened the door of the church in his ceremonial robes and came out to greet them. He was a young man. Christopher supposed that he must be younger than Sarah and only a handful of years older than Margaret. He was tall and handsome with dark skin and curly black hair that was cut close to his head. From his features, Christopher guessed that he was of both African and English descent. The young vicar must have attended Cambridge or Oxford for his degree, which made him more educated than Christopher. He hoped the young man would not hold Christopher's lack of scholarly attainments against him. It would be nice to have a friend near his own age. He had employees and business acquaintances but few friends. And he was quite certain that the Honorable Ralph Randolph was *not* going to become one of that small number.

"Lady Sarah, how charming you look," the young vicar said. "I do not know if I have ever seen a more beautiful bride."

Smiling, she bowed to him. "Since I believe this is the first marriage you have ever performed, Mr. Robinson, I shall try not to become too conceited."

Margaret giggled and then covered her mouth with her hand. Her cheeks flushed with embarrassment when the vicar's eyes landed on her.

"Where are my manners?" Sarah asked, drawing the attention away from his flustered sister. "I hope you will all forgive me. Miss Moulton and Mr. Moulton, may I present Mr. Brian Robinson? He is our new vicar and is recently come to us from Oxford. His father has a delightful estate nearby. Mr. Brian Robinson is quite the best addition to the neighborhood that we've had in years, with the exception of yourselves."

Christopher held out his hand to Mr. Robinson.

The young man hesitated only a moment before shaking it and smiling at him. "It is wonderful to meet you, Mr. Moulton. And your sister."

Poor Margaret's face was as red as a cherry. Christopher's sister had been at school for many years, and he supposed she had not come into contact with many handsome young men, nor a person of a darker skin tone. Christopher had worked on docks and in canals. He'd employed men from all over the world. He'd learned that the color of a man's skin had nothing to do with his intelligence or his ability to work. A prime example was Mr. Sinclair, his best foreman, whose father was from India and his mother from England.

A fine carriage with a family crest on the panel pulled in front of the small church.

Sarah clapped her hands. "Ah, my aunt and uncle are here, as well as my cousin Ralph. He promised me he would behave, but if he doesn't, can you all pretend you didn't see it?"

"Or hear it?" Christopher quipped.

Sarah winked at him, and he felt strangely warm all over. "Precisely." She linked arms with Margaret. "My dear soon-to-be-sister, would you be willing to be my attendant?"

Margaret stared down at her boots. "I should like that very much, Sarah."

A footman opened the carriage door, and Christopher had no difficulty recognizing the tall, redheaded young man from a few days before as he alighted.

Mr. Randolph gave Christopher a cold nod of acknowledgment and assisted his mother out of the carriage. At least this time he'd not given Christopher the social cut. The young man held a bouquet of flowers. Were they for Sarah? Should Christopher have brought a nosegay for her?

Lady Venetia was elegantly dressed in a dark-blue pelisse and matching bonnet. Her bright-red curls, a shade lighter than her son's, framed her face. She stepped forward and hugged her niece.

Christopher heard the older woman speak in a loud whisper to Sarah. "Well, at least your Mr. Moulton is handsome. Not quite as handsome as the Marquess of Ingress, but he is quite a bit younger, which is to be preferred for the siring of children. And you should not wish to be a widow for a long time. How lonely that would be! And your fellow is broader in the shoulders, I think. Do you not think so?"

He did not hear Sarah's reply to this long speech. She obviously knew how to whisper much quieter than her aunt.

"Mr. Moulton, I believe we have met before in London."

Christopher turned to see a tall, spare man with a shock of graying black hair poking out from underneath his beaver hat. He was dressed as fashionably as his son, but there was a relaxed air about him. He bowed to Christopher, and Christopher returned the gesture.

"Yes, Sir Oscar. You invested in my canal near Clapham."

"And a tidy dividend it earned me, sir. I look forward to getting to know you on a more personal basis. Lady Sarah is precious to me, like a daughter. I would ask that you be gentle and patient with her. Despite her rank, life has not been kind to my niece."

All Christopher could do was nod. He supposed this uncomfortable interview was what it felt like to ask for a father's permission to marry his daughter. "I will do my best, sir. I know how fortunate I am to soon be her husband."

Sir Oscar patted him on the shoulder. Christopher flinched. He was not used to being touched by a stranger.

"You don't know how fortunate you are yet, but you will. I am sure of it. Sarah is a rare jewel," Sir Oscar said and then turned to the others. "Well, Mr. Robinson, shall we go inside the church and proceed with the marriage?"

The vicar and the Randolphs walked into the church through the large wooden door. Sarah entered the church with Margaret, their arms still linked. Taking a fortifying breath, Christopher followed them inside. Mr. Robinson stood in the front, with Sir Oscar and Lady Venetia seated on the front row on the right side—the bride's side. There was no one on the groom's. Sarah escorted Margaret to the front of the church and showed her where to stand as her attendant. Christopher was the last member of the group to walk down the aisle, which was usually the role of the bride.

Sarah cleared her throat, and the Honorable Ralph handed her the beautiful bouquet of flowers and then sat down beside his parents. She cleared her throat even louder a second time and tipped her head toward Christopher. Her look was stern, and she seemed to be communicating with her cousin without words.

Sheepishly, the Honorable Ralph's face turned red, and he got back to his feet, bowing his head to Christopher. "Mr. Moulton, might I stand as your attendant? My cousin Sarah is my oldest and dearest friend in the world. I should very much like to be a part of her wedding."

The man's words were clipped but not cutting. Christopher assumed it had cost the young buck of the first water a great deal to ask anything of a canal man. A cit from London.

"I would be pleased, Mr. Randolph."

"*Ralph*," Sarah hissed, giving her cousin another stern glare.

Her tall, skinny cousin's face turned even darker, until it was the same bright red of his hair. "I would be honored, Mr. Moulton, if you called me Ralph. We are to be family."

Out of habit, he held out his hand. "Christopher."

They awkwardly shook each other's hands before Ralph stood behind Christopher in the position of best man. Christopher stood across from his bride, and she gave him a beaming smile. He was not particularly pleased to have the fashionable young buck stand as his best man, but he could not help but return her smile with a small one of his own. There was something magnetic about Sarah.

Mr. Robinson began the ceremony, and Christopher's nerves continued to be on edge. When the vicar said, "If any man knows of any impediment as to why these two may not be joined in marriage, let him speak now or forever hold his peace," Christopher looked over his shoulder at Ralph—who still looked angry, but he did not speak a word.

The vicar continued with the marriage ceremony, and when he asked Lady Sarah if she would take this man to be her lawful husband, she said, "I will" in a strong, clear voice.

She did not hesitate for even a moment, but Christopher realized he had been holding his breath. He still couldn't quite believe that the accomplished and beautiful lady standing in front of him was his bride. He'd worried that she would change her mind even now. That she would realize how far below her he was on the social scale. Glancing up at the stained-glass window, he saw the Virgin Mary holding her babe. He wondered, if he and Sarah were blessed with children, which society would accept them? The elite of the *ton* or the merchant class? Would either?

CHAPTER 7

"Wilt thou have this woman to be thy wedded wife, to live together after God's ordinance in the holy estate of matrimony?" the vicar repeated in his pleasant baritone voice. "Wilt thou love her, comfort her, honor, and keep her, in sickness and in health, and forsaking all others, keep thee only unto her, so long as ye both shall live?" Mr. Robinson was a very welcome replacement for the elderly and often crotchety Mr. Stephens, the previous vicar. The young man was pleasant without pushing. His sermons were thought-provoking but not so theological that his audience did not understand them.

Sarah looked at Christopher expectantly. He only needed to speak two little words and their bargain would be complete, but he did not utter a syllable. His focus was on the stained-glass window above the vicar. With her free hand, Sarah smoothed out a tiny wrinkle in her skirt. She felt light-headed, and there was a tightness in her chest.

What should she do?

What could she do?

Nothing.

A shiver of panic crawled up her spine as she stood with her head held high; her face grew hotter with every second of silence. Had he changed his mind? She dared not look at the young vicar or her cousin, who was likely grimacing worse than ever, nor at anyone else but Christopher Moulton—the man she was supposed to marry.

She swallowed. She could not allow her plans to fail now. Sarah needed him to marry her so that she could return to Manderfield Hall. She had to be there if—*when*—her mother came home. She swallowed a second time; her throat was dry and gummy. She forced her strained mouth muscles to form the largest and brightest of smiles. Hopefully it would encourage him to come to the point.

"I will," he said at last.

In relief, Sarah's grin faltered, and she released the breath she was holding. Mr. Robinson pronounced them man and wife. They exchanged rings. Then the vicar led them over to a table and had them sign the marriage license and then the parish register. She signed her name twice, and it was done. She was now the wife of a stranger.

Christopher avoided her gaze, so she turned to see the small audience. Margaret's eyes were focused on Mr. Robinson, and her cheeks were tinged a pretty pink. Sarah guessed that she found the vicar attractive—she was not the only young woman in their parish to think so.

She glanced at her family. Uncle Oscar gave her a half smile and a reassuring look. He took the quill from the vicar and signed his name as a witness, then gave it to his son. Her cousin scratched his signature onto the paper and dropped the quill as if it were on fire. Ralph then folded his arms, and his expression was not unlike a petulant child caught in the larder. Two tears slid down Aunt Venetia's cheek, and she dabbed at them with her handkerchief. Aunt had once told Sarah that crying at weddings was fashionable.

"If only Louisa could have been here," she said, coming to Sarah and enfolding her into her arms.

Sarah did not wish to think about her mother now or the fact that she had missed another important day in Sarah's life. Mama had been absent for many of Sarah's accomplishments at school. Not that it had been her mother's fault; Papa wouldn't let her visit Sarah. All she'd received from her mother were letters. But she hadn't received even one note from her father. Sarah sometimes wondered if he forgot about her very existence. She'd tried to be an ideal student and perfect young lady to impress him. It hadn't worked. Papa had only two loves: his wife and the dice. Everything else was secondary. Mama had no choice but to obey him. A wife was little more than the legal property of her husband—and now Sarah herself was a bride.

"She would have been so—"

Ralph, thankfully, cut off his mother. "Felicitations, Sarah. Or should I call you Mrs. Moulton now?"

She half-wondered what her aunt was going to say. Sarah didn't know if her mother would have been pleased by her marriage. Like Aunt Venetia, she probably would have pushed the suit of the Marquess of Ingress. She'd wanted Sarah to make a grand match. Mama had been disappointed that Sarah hadn't received an offer of marriage in her first Season and had insisted that she would receive several in her second—only, her mother had disappeared before they could go to London that year. Sarah might not have married a man with a title, but she still had a title of her own.

"Lady Sarah, if you would, *Cousin*. Like your mother, I retain the title I was given at birth."

"I suppose there will not be any wedding cake," Aunt Venetia said, shaking her head. "I don't think I've ever been to a wedding where there wasn't cake. When I was a young girl, we used to put pieces of cake underneath our pillows so that we would dream of our future husbands. At my dear sister Louisa's wedding, we broke the cake over the earl's head and hers. Some sort of local custom, I believe. I wouldn't mind breaking a little cake over his head now. Your father ought to have been here. He should not have abandoned you for that vulgar Mrs. Yardley."

Aunt Venetia's well-meaning but tactless words cut at Sarah's already thin skin. Her father had left her alone. He had not cared for her at all, nor for the home of his ancestors. He'd squeezed every farthing from Manderfield Hall and then sold it.

Uncle Oscar picked up Sarah's hand and kissed it. "The earl's loss is our gain. I have never seen a lovelier wedding. I wish my own dear daughters' weddings had been as simple."

Aunt Venetia touched her cheek with her hand. "That reminds me: at my daughter Mary's wedding, they broke the wedding cake and threw it into the crowd. Another local custom. And at Arabella's—"

Ralph interrupted his mother again. "Sarah was at both of those weddings, and I daresay her memory is as good as yours. We had best get back home, Mama. Sarah's new family is waiting for her."

Glancing over her shoulder, Sarah saw Christopher and Margaret standing a little apart from them and watching. Bridging their two worlds was going to be tricky.

Aunt Venetia raised her handkerchief to her eyes once more and dabbed at imaginary tears. She gave Sarah another embrace. "I will throw a party for you and your Mr. Moulton. And I will have Cook bake you a wedding cake. I feel that you need a proper wedding cake, Sarah, even if Mr. Moulton is a cit. And all of your friends and neighbors will expect to be given a slice of cake as well."

"I am sure they will all be delighted to receive it, my dear," Uncle Oscar said.

"A wedding party is a wonderful suggestion, Aunt Venetia," Sarah said and kissed her aunt on the cheek. Then she hugged Uncle Oscar and would have embraced Ralph, too, if his arms hadn't been folded across his chest. At least he'd been willing to stand as a part of the wedding party. She touched the side of his arm. "I'm sure that I will see you soon, Flames."

His features softened a little. "Take care of yourself, Freckles."

Smiling, she released her hold. "I will. And everyone else."

Shaking his head, Ralph smirked. "The poor Moultons have no idea what is about to befall them. I suppose when I next clap eyes on them, the entire family will be unrecognizable. No one loves a project more than you do."

Sarah laughed at the truth of his sally and turned to face Christopher and his beautiful sister. Ralph hadn't been far off. Sarah meant to help her new husband and sisters fit into higher Society. That would require better manners and new wardrobes. Sarah didn't think she would have any difficulty marrying Margaret off to a member of the *ton*. She had the freshness of a country girl with her blonde locks, wide blue eyes, and petite mouth (how Sarah wished her own mouth were smaller!). And, luckily, Margaret was possessed with good manners, albeit a bit too shy. Sarah would have to bring her out a bit more. The girl did not have much countenance, but Sarah could teach her that. Her mother had once said, "It is amazing what a large dowry can fix." And she was certain that Christopher would give his sister a considerable portion.

"Well, Husband," Sarah said in a rallying tone. "Shall we go home?"

"Yes, of course," he said and began to walk out of the church.

He should have offered Sarah his arm. She quickly linked her arm with Margaret's and said in a falsely cheerful voice, "We are now sisters by law, and you are stuck with me."

Christopher shook hands once again with Mr. Robinson at the door and thanked him for performing the ceremony. He was not completely without manners, but he did lack social niceties. Sarah would have thanked the vicar as well if Christopher hadn't opened the door to the carriage and all but lifted her inside. Then he assisted Margaret in. He sat across from them, silent. Was he already harboring regrets? His current silence reminded Sarah of the ceremony, when he'd kept her in suspense of his answer. It did not raise him in her esteem. She looked at Margaret's lowered gaze. Sarah did not like silence.

"I hope you do not mind, Christopher," Sarah said, forcing him to pay attention to her. "I instructed my aunt Venetia's servants to send over my possessions. I believe they will arrive before we do, or, Margaret, I shall be obliged to borrow a dinner dress from you and possibly a nightgown."

Margaret blushed again and assured Sarah that she was welcome to any of her dresses.

"You are too kind, Mar—" Sarah began to thank her but was distracted by what she saw outside the carriage window. Workers were standing on the roofs of the cottages on the Manderfield estate. The old, rotted thatched roofs were being scraped off and new ones put on. Her heart warmed for the first time that day. Her eyes flitted back to the stranger she had married. "You did it."

"What?" Christopher asked, turning in his seat to see what Sarah was looking at. "Oh yes. The rethatching. It was the top item on your list, and they were in bad repair. I had Mr. Pryce find workers at once."

All the frustration she'd felt toward him at the ceremony evaporated. He had not only read her suggestions; he had begun to implement them. Her father had ignored her the dozen times she'd asked him to repair the roofs of the tenant cottages. He'd said that she was a foolish young woman who didn't understand business. Yet Christopher, a successful and wealthy businessman, had followed her advice. A surge of hope filled her heart. Perhaps their marriage could grow into something more than one of convenience. "You're doing all the improvements I suggested?"

Raising one eyebrow, he gave her a wry smile. "They were suggestions? I thought they were demands."

Sarah blanched but then realized he was not trying to offend her but to tease her. She laughed and then gave him her first genuine smile. Her limbs felt light, and she had an overwhelming feeling of weightlessness. "I am so glad. Although, probably not as glad as your tenants, who will no longer have leaks when it rains. Have you met the tenants yet? They are most excellent people."

Christopher shook his head. "Am I supposed to?"

Taking a deep breath, Sarah explained, "It is a good idea. And I am sure you will be the most popular landlord in the county after these new roofs. If you'd like, I could accompany you and introduce you to everyone."

"Very well," he said, folding his arms and leaning back against the carriage seat. "If you think it is a good idea."

She did. Sarah knew all the tenants very well. Her mother had taught her that although women did not always have control over their lives, they could carve for themselves little "pockets of power." Mama was never allowed to go or stay when she wished to. By law she had to obey her husband's wishes and receive his permission before traveling to London or visiting Sarah at school.

Her mother had not wanted to send Sarah to a boarding school. She'd wished to keep Sarah close to her at home by hiring a governess. Papa had ignored his wife's feelings and sent Sarah off to Bath at the age of eight. Children, like wives, were legally the property of the husband. There was nothing Mama could do, except teach Sarah how to find her own little pockets of power. At school Sarah had learned all the girls' names and what they liked. She'd even curried for her teachers' favor. A good student received more privileges than a naughty one. And a popular girl needn't worry about what people said behind her back. What *she* said was what mattered.

Both Sarah and her mother had carved a pocket of power by knowing, respecting, and serving their tenants. Mama had always brought a gift when a tenant had a child. She was attentive when someone was sick and generous with holiday baskets. The tenants had loved her and despised Papa. If Mama asked them to do something, they did it, whether or not the steward required it of them.

The mistress held all the keys of the house, symbolically and physically. Her mother had poured all the love that she had not found in her marriage into Manderfield Hall and its inhabitants. She had taken great care of it and always ensured that each room was filled with flowers.

She had also been a powerful figure in London Society. She was a well-connected countess and a lady-in-waiting to Queen Charlotte. Her beauty was much admired, and she liked to set fashions. It was perhaps her favorite pocket of power. She had loved when other ladies mimicked the style of her hair or the cut of her gown. One time she'd worn a single white daisy in her hair to a ball. By the next day, nearly every woman of the *ton* had a daisy in her hair. Silly? Perhaps. Influential? Definitely.

Sarah would need to use all of her pockets of power to bring the Moultons into fashion and Society.

Christopher did not speak again for the rest of the trip to Manderfield Hall. Sarah was busy with her own thoughts, and his silence this time did not bother her. He seemed to speak only when he had something to say, and he felt no need to utter polite nothings to keep the conversation moving. She would have to teach him the social niceties and how to speak cleverly about nothing at all.

When at last they arrived, he assisted Sarah and Margaret out of the carriage and then went into the house without a word to either of them. He did not bid Sarah farewell, nor tell her where he planned to go or what he was doing. Resentment blossomed in her chest like a rose. She had been beginning to think upon him favorably again, but she realized that bringing him into Society was going to be a much larger job that she had previously anticipated. He had a beard and behaved uncouthly.

Sarah spun around to see the grounds. She'd been gone only a fortnight, and yet she could identify the smallest of changes brought by the turning of the seasons. On the west side she was relieved to count no less than three wagonfuls of crates and Mrs. Harmony standing by one of them, ordering the servants to take Sarah's trunks inside. The only sign that the housekeeper had seen her was by the slight upturning of her lips as she continued to direct the lower servants.

Margaret gasped. "You must have a great deal of clothes."

Chuckling, Sarah shook her head. "Those crates are full of trinkets, fine china, and the silver I inherited from my mother. Only the trunks have clothing in them. Most of my gowns have been made over at least once. My funds have been tight for the last few years."

Margaret's eyes were still wide. "I should like to see them. They must be very fashionable."

"If that is the case," Sarah said with a wink, "you can help me unpack. But let us have some tea first. I'm famished. I had no idea that getting married could make one so hungry."

Mr. Wigan held the main door open for them, and if he was surprised to see Sarah, he did not show it by so much as raising his thick eyebrows. Sarah wondered if Christopher had told the servants, or if he'd not bothered to speak to them about something he thought was not their business. He would soon learn that in the country, everything was the servants' business.

"Dear Mr. Wigan, could you have tea sent to the sitting room, please?"

Placing a hand on his stomach, he bowed. "Of course, Lady Sarah."

Sarah held out her left hand with the gold circlet around her fourth finger and smiled.

Mr. Wigan bowed to her again. "Allow me to offer you my sincerest congratulations, my lady."

"They are much appreciated, my old friend," Sarah said, beaming at him. "Do let all of the servants know and see that a bottle of wine is served to them with their dinner. I should like everyone to be a part of the celebrations."

"Very good."

Sarah took off her poke bonnet and handed it to him. Margaret did the same. They linked arms and walked toward the sitting room. A young lady was already in there. She stood and gave Sarah an awkward curtsy. She was obviously Christopher's other sister. There was a marked family resemblance between the three siblings. They all had the same blonde hair, predominant blue eyes, and small mouths.

This sister wasn't as classically beautiful as Margaret, but her countenance was much more expressive. Her face was heart-shaped rather than oval, and she was shorter and thinner than her sister as well. But something about the tilt of her chin and the obstinate line of her pouty mouth told Sarah that this sister would be much more difficult to guide than Margaret. Not that Sarah doubted her own abilities to find a high match for the younger sister. She had run a large estate for years.

"Deborah, may I present Lady Sarah?" Margaret began, gesturing to the other young woman.

"Simply Sarah." Sweeping a perfect curtsy, Sarah bent her knees only a few inches and lowered only her eyes. She gave the girl her most ingratiating smile, but the tilt of the schoolgirl's defiant chin did not lower. Sarah was going to have to work very hard to win this stubborn chit over to her side. "What a pleasure to finally meet you, Deborah."

The younger woman huffed. "I am not sure why you say *finally*, since you have been acquainted with my brother for less than a fortnight."

Her mother had always said that bad behavior should be ignored or isolated. Sighing, Sarah chose to ignore Deborah's comment and sat down on her favorite chair. "Margaret and Deborah, you both have such lovely names."

"They're from Christian martyrs," Margaret said as she sat near Sarah on a sofa. "Our mother was quite religious."

Sarah's mother had been only fashionably pious. Sarah knew most of the biblical stories, but the previous vicar's sermons had been dull enough to put the most devout person to sleep. And he'd rarely preached of women at all, except to focus on Eve's transgression and how Rebecca had fooled her husband into giving the wrong son the birthright. He'd used them as examples of why women were not trustworthy.

"I know the story of Margaret of Antioch," she said, "but I confess I do not know the story of Deborah."

"She was a prophetess in the Bible!" Deb said loudly and then pinched her lips shut.

Raising her eyebrows, Sarah said, "A prophetess. How very interesting. What great miracles did she perform?"

She could see that Deborah wanted to tell her but was fighting her own stubbornness. The young woman was clearly determined not to be civil to

Sarah. And, truthfully, Sarah was interested to know. She'd been unaware that women *could* be prophetesses. Deborah's need to boast must have overcome her desire to snub Sarah. "She led an army to victory."

This was intriguing. Perhaps a little flattery would help the younger sister put down her defenses. "Then you were named well, Deborah, for I perceive that you are brave enough for anything."

Deborah stuck out her chin again and gave Sarah a mulish look. "Don't think you can flatter me."

Sarah touched her chest in mock humility. "I would not dream of it. At least, not with such a small compliment."

Margaret stood and walked toward where the harp was, in the corner of the room. "Do you play the harp, Sarah?"

She was obviously anxious to change the conversation and perhaps prevent her younger sister from being uncivil. Yes, Sarah did play the harp. Or, at least, she had played it when her mother was still there to hear her. After seven years, her musical talent was probably very rusty, like an unused door.

"My mother taught me," Sarah said at last.

Deborah walked to the harp and plucked a string, then jumped a little at the noise it made. "I've always wanted to learn. So has Margaret."

This was Sarah's opportunity to win over Deborah, and she was not such a fool as to let it pass by. Margaret, too, had spoken of her interest to learn to play more instruments on the ride to the church. "Then I will teach you—both of you—if you'd like."

Mr. Wigan brought in the tea tray, and Sarah was surprised at just how hungry she was. But she poured her new sisters-in-law their tea before filling up her own plate with sandwiches and biscuits. It was no fancy wedding breakfast with her family in attendance, nor was there a cake with several tiers and sugar icing. It was not at all the sort of meal she would have expected on the day of her marriage. They ate in relative silence, and what little conversation they had was strictly on the weather. It had started to rain quite hard. The drops pelted loudly against the windows.

Margaret set down her teacup and dabbed her napkin against the edges of her mouth. "I do hope the servants got all of your things inside before it began to rain."

Getting to her feet gracefully, Sarah took a deep breath. "Shall we go see?"

"I should like that," Margaret said and walked to stand by Sarah. "Are you coming, Deb?"

Deborah stuck her chin out again, but Sarah saw her curiosity overcoming her stubbornness. "I suppose. There is nothing else to do in the country but twiddle your thumbs."

Sarah didn't take them outside, but up the stairs to the mistress's rooms. Mrs. Harmony and Nelly would have ensured that the crates and trunks were inside before the downpour. The housekeeper also knew where all the trinkets and knickknacks had been positioned only a fortnight before. Sarah didn't need to oversee every little detail. She knew it would upset the servants. They had earned their positions through their hard work.

When she opened the door to the mistress's rooms that had once been her mother's, she felt the familiar pang of loneliness. How she missed her mother! Even the smell of her perfume. The touch of her hand. The sound of her laughter. Over time Sarah's memories had lost the senses. Only vague images remained.

Her previous lady's maid, Nelly Mills, was already in the room, putting dresses away in the wardrobe. When Sarah had left only a fortnight before, Nelly had been demoted to an upper maid, but she had reclaimed her old position now that Sarah was back. Nelly set down the dress she was holding and curtsied to Sarah and the sisters. Sarah tried to hide a smile. Nelly had never curtsied for her benefit. Having grown up together as friends, not as servant and mistress, their relationship was less strict than most. Nelly rarely bothered to show Sarah any deference at all in private.

Her old friend had the darkest shade of black hair that Sarah had ever seen. It was braided back and tucked neatly underneath her mobcap now. She had hazel eyes, a small but pointy nose, and a mouth with a sharp tongue.

"Miss Mills, may I introduce you to Miss Moulton and Miss Deborah?"

"Pleased to meet you," Nelly said and went back to putting away Sarah's clothes. If she wanted to say something to her mistress, she would wait until the others were not present. Overfamiliarity could get them both into trouble.

Sarah walked over to the closest trunk and unlatched it. Margaret and Deborah followed and marveled at her silk stockings and the number of slippers she had perfectly tinted to match specific dresses. She allowed herself to enjoy their praise. Fashion was one of her favorite things, and she had an eye for colors. Her ability to transform gowns into looking new was her greatest talent, and a crucial one for a lady with a small purse.

"I was an attendant for a girl from school last year," Margaret said, hiding her hands in her skirts. "After the ceremony, the bride and groom sat on the bed, and we stood at the bottom. Then we turned our backs to them and tried to throw our stockings at her. If your stocking hits the bride, it means that you will be married next."

Her story reminded Sarah of Aunt Venetia's recitation of local cake customs. "Did one of your stockings hit the bride? Should we start purchasing your trousseau?"

The ever-ready blush was back in Margaret's cheeks as she shook her head.

Sarah walked over to her bed, then sat down and scooted back until she reached the upholstered headboard. "Let's see which one of you will be married first."

To Sarah's surprise, it was Deborah who first went to the edge of the bed and sat down and took off her stockings. Margaret followed after her sister, her blush blooming like a rose.

Sarah sucked her teeth. "Miss Mills, you should come too. You have a beau, after all. Who knows? You may be the first of the trio to wed."

Nelly closed the latch of an empty trunk with a click. "It's not my place, Lady Sarah."

"That's never stopped you before," Sarah said. "And don't tell me that you don't long to throw something at me, for I will not believe you if you do."

Nelly laughed. "Too right."

Her maid stood as far from the sisters at the bottom of the bed as possible to take off her boots and pull off her stockings.

"Are you ready?" Sarah asked.

They all said yes.

She held up a finger. "Now, no cheating. Keep your backs turned, and on the count of three, throw your stockings at me. One, two, three!"

Deborah's first stocking landed on the coverlet below Sarah's feet. Both of Margaret's stockings landed on the pillows next to Sarah. Nelly threw her stocking so hard that it flew over the bed and onto the floor. Deborah tossed her last stocking, and it landed on Sarah's lap. Sarah picked it up. "Well, Deborah, it appears that I will require my sewing needle. Who is the lucky man?"

The younger girl laughed, and it was a charming sound. Her whole countenance changed from stubborn to happy. She smiled and took her sister's hands. "I am to get married before you, Margaret."

"I don't mind," Margaret said, but Sarah could tell that she did mind, for she didn't smile. There seemed to be a sort of competition between the two sisters. Sarah had no siblings of her own, so she didn't precisely understand the dynamic. The closest thing she had was her cousin Ralph, with whom she was still put out.

Nelly turned her back to Sarah and threw her other stocking. It hit Sarah square in the face. Sarah laughed and lifted it up. She scooted off the bed and picked up Nelly's other woolen stocking and held them out to her. "I will have to inform Guy of his good fortune."

Nelly blushed and grabbed the stockings from Sarah. "If you say a word to Guy, I'll burn a hole through your favorite silk dress. You know which one."

This was the saucy Nelly whom Sarah knew and loved. Sarah scooted to the edge of the bed and stood up. "I'd better take off my wedding dress. It appears it may be needed by any one of you in the very near future."

CHAPTER 8

Christopher looked out the window at the darkening sky. He was now a married man, but he didn't feel like it.

He sighed.

A marriage for social aspirations may never be more than pretense, he reminded himself. As much as Lady Sarah fascinated him, she had married a stranger for a fancy house and an old estate. He'd do well to remember that before laying not only his property and wealth at her feet but his heart as well. He took another drink from his decanter before placing it on the table. He picked up a candle, left the room, and was about to climb the stairs when he saw Mr. Wigan hanging lanterns by the windows that faced the forest.

Surely the butler was not involved in the smuggling of port and wine.

"Are we expecting anyone, Mr. Wigan?" Christopher asked, trying to keep his tone even to allay possible suspicion.

The swarthy butler did not look at all nonplussed. He bowed formally to Christopher. "No, sir."

Christopher pointed at the lanterns. "What are those lights for?"

The butler raised his thick eyebrows. "I thought you knew, sir."

"I do not."

Mr. Wigan pointed at them. "We light lanterns every night for Lady Sarah's mother, Lady Louisa Denham, so that she might find her way home."

Christopher nodded, but he did not understand. "Why? I understood from my solicitor that the late countess is dead."

"We do not know if Lady Manders is dead," Mr. Wigan said in a tone of no emotion. "She disappeared one night seven years ago. The current earl has begun the process of having her declared dead."

"Disappeared?"

The butler bowed his head. "I do not wish to gossip, sir. But the Earl of Manders and his lady got into a rather heated argument, and then she left the house near dark. She ordered her horse to be saddled and rode toward the forest without a groom. Her mount returned to the stables without her. By that time, it was pitch-black outside and had started to rain. We lit lanterns and searched for hours, but we never found her. The rain washed away any tracks we might have used to locate her in the daylight."

"Were there no further efforts to find her?" Christopher pressed.

Mr. Wigan sighed heavily. "The earl hired Bow Street Runners and even an American Pinkerton detective, but there was no trace of Lady Manders anywhere. The earl rode up and down the forest for weeks. He finally gave up after six months and went to London. Lady Sarah stayed and waited for her mother to come back home. She had—*has* us light the lanterns every night so that if Lady Manders is out there, she can find her way back to Manderfield Hall."

His first impression that she was a materialistic snob faded, and Christopher felt only sorrow for his new bride. It appeared that none of the servants believed the countess would ever return.

"Thank you for telling me, Mr. Wigan."

The butler bowed, and Christopher carried his candle upstairs to his bedchamber. His mind was reeling with new ideas. Perhaps Sarah had not married him for his money or for Manderfield Hall. What if she had married him in hopes of finding her lost mother? If so, she was not a beguiling and mercenary creature of the higher class but a heartbroken human being he could relate to. Someone he could sympathize with.

He'd never gotten to say goodbye to his own mother, nor his three little brothers. Nor did they have proper graves with stones, because of the extent of the outbreak. His beloved family members had been cast into a common grave, and Christopher did not wish to speak to bones. He missed his mother. She had never been embarrassed by his scars or made him feel unworthy to be a part of the family. He had loved his mother with all his heart.

How awful it must be for Sarah not to know whether her mother was alive or dead. With that sobering thought, he knocked gently and opened the door that led from his room to hers. He didn't know what he expected to see, but it wasn't what he found.

Sarah was sleeping, and her candle was still burning. A dangerous thing. She must have been waiting for him. He leaned forward to blow the candle out but was transfixed by the way the candlelight lit up her face. Even sleeping, Sarah was a study of perfection. Her hair parted into two loose braids that framed her face. With her eyes closed, her long dark lashes rested against her cheeks. And, for the first time, he saw freckles on her nose. He counted them. There were thirteen.

She murmured something unintelligible, and Christopher stepped back, embarrassed to be caught staring at his own wife. But her eyes were still closed. She mumbled something about flounces and rolled over onto her side. Christopher leaned down again and, this time, blew out the candle. He walked back to the door that led to his own bedchamber, but before he closed it, he could not resist looking back at her one last time. From the dim light of his own candle, he saw her outline and thought how little he truly knew about the woman he would spend the rest of his life with.

Then he smiled. He did know one thing—that she mumbled in her sleep.

CHAPTER 9

The next morning Christopher again knocked on the door that led from his apartments to hers. He would respect her space and privacy.

"Come in," she said.

He opened the door cautiously. Sarah was still in bed, sipping a cup of chocolate. Her braids fell over her shoulders, and she was wearing only a pink silk robe.

She yawned. "Thank you for blowing out my candle. I am sorry I fell asleep before we could talk. It was rather an exhausting day, and I had awoken very early."

Christopher shifted on his feet and focused his eyes on the fancy carpet on the ground. He felt embarrassed and unsure of himself, like a lad of fifteen and not a successful businessman of eight and twenty. "That is why I came this morning."

"Then, let's talk," Sarah said with her most beguiling smile.

"Should you like to get dressed first?" he asked, still not looking at her directly.

Sarah laughed, and he heard her step out of the bed. "If you insist."

A young servant woman came into the room. Christopher felt his face redden but glanced at Sarah, who showed no discomposure.

"Ah, Mills, would you bring both of our breakfasts to my room, please?"

Miss Mills, presumably, bobbed a quick curtsy. "Yes, my lady."

The servant left the room, and Sarah walked to the windows and pulled back the gold brocade curtains, letting in the light. Then she entered her dressing room and closed the door. A few minutes later she came out dressed in a fetching white day gown with little pink flowers. She sat down on a chair by the window and gestured with her hand to the chair on the other side of the table. Christopher pulled at his neckcloth before sitting.

"A married lady always has breakfast in her bedchamber, but you are welcome to eat it with your sisters in the breakfast room," she said. "Today, however, I thought it would be a trifle awkward for you to be obliged to eat with them the morning after your wedding."

His heart thumping, Christopher pulled so hard at his neckcloth that it came untied.

"What would you like to talk about?"

Anything.

Everything.

Nothing.

His carefully prepared speech completely vanished from his mind when her beautiful brown eyes focused on him. Her hair was still down in two braids from when she was sleeping, and they made her look younger and more vulnerable. More like a person he could know. Like a young woman he could fancy and love.

Christopher sucked on his teeth nervously, then said, "You mentioned that you wished to introduce me to the tenants. I thought we could go today."

She. Laughed. At. Him.

His face flushed red like Margaret's always did when she was nervous. This high-and-mighty lady was mocking him. Sarah continued to laugh so hard that tears rolled from her eyes, and she brought a hand to cover her mouth. Wincing, Christopher had never been so mortified in all his life.

Sarah held up a hand and took a deep breath. "Forgive my mirth. It is not directed at you, I promise, but rather at the ridiculous situation we find ourselves in. I only found it amusing to go visiting the morning after a wedding day. Particularly this early. We would be making ourselves figures of fun."

Christopher's face grew hotter. He had not thought of that. She was right. A newly married couple was not supposed to be out and about in the early morning the day after their marriage. His mortification eased to a gentle amusement. His lips tugged upward only a little, but it was enough to send Sarah off into another peal of laughter. She was still giggling when Mills and a footman, whose name Christopher did not remember, brought in two trays of food and set them on the sitting table between them.

"Thank you, Mills. I shall ring the bell for you should I need your assistance."

The maid bobbed a curtsy. "Yes, my lady."

"And thank you, Guy," Sarah said with a bright smile, her face still glowing from her laughter. "I am sure that you can find *something* to do to keep our Nelly busy for a little while."

Guy grinned back at her. "I am sure I can, my lady."

Nelly grimaced. "*Sarah.*"

Christopher was not used to servants speaking with such familiarity to their employers.

His wife continued to smile. "You're wasting valuable courting time remonstrating with me, Nelly."

With a reluctant second curtsy, the young maid left the room, the grinning footman trailing behind her.

Sarah took off the silver lid of her tray and set it on the side of the table. "I am sure you are wondering why Nelly spoke to me so informally. She is my oldest friend, and it is actually much stranger for me to hear her call me my lady. She's never bothered to in the past. And I should really call her Miss Mills or simply Mills, since she has the exalted position of lady's maid in the household. Shall we eat?"

She picked up her fork and took a bite of egg before Christopher took the lid off his own tray. He was surprised and pleased that Sarah cared for her maid as a friend and, even more so, that they treated each other like equals. Setting down the lid, he noticed the food had been arranged artistically on his plate. It looked almost too pretty to eat, but his stomach growled, and he overcame his scruples. The eggs benedict were cooked to perfection.

Sarah took a drink from her juice glass. "We should definitely make some calls to our neighbors after luncheon and our tenants another day. But I should like to spend this morning getting to know you better."

A small spark of hope lit in his chest. Perhaps a lady and a canal worker could become friends. For the success and happiness of his marriage, he prayed it was thus. "I should like that."

She shrugged and gave him a gamin grin. "Shall we start at the very beginning? Where were you born and when? I should hate to miss your birthday. Like my Aunt Venetia, I am very fond of cake, and I like making atrocious birthday hats. Be prepared for a sparkling confection."

Christopher almost smiled as he remembered Lady Venetia's recitation of the different local customs of wedding cakes. "The third of April 1777. In London."

He watched Sarah tap her delicate fingers on the table, as if doing the math.

"Then you are three years older than me. I was born on the thirtieth of August 1780, and I feel obliged to warn you that I like a great deal of fuss made over my birthday. More *is* always better. My mother would start celebrating the week before my birthday and at least a fortnight after. Something small every day that made me feel special."

This was the first time Sarah had mentioned her mother to him. It was no wonder that she missed her. No one celebrated Christopher for even one day, let alone for over three weeks. Birthdays were often marked with a small gift, but nothing special for the meal or any parties. His own mother had grown up very poor as the tenth daughter of a carrier, and her housekeeping had been quite plain. Christopher did not remember ever eating cake, and the only sweets had been Christmas puddings. The food was simple and hearty. Mama had never put on any airs. Not even when Papa had made his first fortune. She liked her small and tidy house in London with only two servants. A house that Christopher had never seen again after he'd been sent to work on the Sapperton Tunnel.

"I seem to have lost you," Sarah said, watching him closely. "Have you fallen into a memory? Can you take me with you?"

His eyes fell to his plate, and he picked up his fork. "I was thinking of my own mother. She liked things plain and simple."

"Oh dear. I do not like anything plain or simple."

Christopher could well believe that. Every piece of clothing he'd seen Sarah wear had been ornate and eye-catching. And nothing about Manderfield Hall was plain. Especially not her room, which was sumptuously decorated in pink and gold. Like a beautiful butterfly, Sarah fit perfectly in it. If only Christopher could fit half so well in his own room of blue and gold.

He cleared his throat. "Mama led a simple life. She was never taught to read or write. She didn't have her first servant until after my younger brother Francis was born. Papa insisted that she needed the help with the children."

The sunlight that was in Sarah's face dimmed. She must have realized that Francis had died. She reached her hand across the table and grabbed Christopher's thick wrist, squeezing it gently. Her delicate hand didn't reach even halfway around it. "Oh, Christopher, I am so sorry to hear about your little brother and your mother."

He did not meet her eyes. "My three little brothers. A plague was rampant in the neighborhood and claimed all four of them in a matter of a fortnight. My father was wise enough to send my two sisters away from the sickness."

Sarah did not release her hold on his wrist. "And where were you?"

"Digging a canal near Gloucester. I did not learn about it until long after. My father didn't bother to tell me."

She squeezed his wrist again. "How devastating. I am so sorry, Christopher. To lose so many beloved members of your family in such a short amount of time—I cannot comprehend such sorrow. What were the names of your other brothers?"

"John and Fred."

"And Francis," Sarah said.

She had been listening closely to what he said. Christopher nodded, his heart heavy. "My father was never the same after. He became obsessed with joining the highest echelons of Society." For his two youngest daughters. Not Christopher. Never for his scarred eldest son.

Sarah let go of her hold on him. He instantly missed her warmth and the silklike touch of her skin. "Terrible things happen even to members of the *ton*. Misery doesn't care about one's position in Society or whom it leaves alone."

Despite the difference in their classes, he truly felt that his new wife did understand the pain that he carried. That he would always carry. It was a rather somber subject to base their relationship on, but grief was something they shared. Something that only other grievers could understand.

Christopher took a few bites of his breakfast. "Still, I intend to make all of my father's dreams for my sisters come true."

Tilting her head to one side, Sarah eyed him closely. "Did your father not have any dreams for you? And do you not have dreams for yourself?"

As the head of his business, no one had dared asked Christopher such searching questions. He'd never had the time to create dreams of his own. Over the years, he had learned every position involved by first doing it himself. He was a decent drafter, a fine foreman, and an even better land engineer. He'd been taught how to read and to write and to run a company. He'd been too busy taking care of his father's legacy to dream.

He glanced up at Sarah's dancing eyes, and he knew he could not give her that answer. "Friends. Family. Children of my own. The usual things."

"I wish for the usual things too," she said in a soft voice, and there was no trace of arrogance.

"If you'd like, I can start new inquiries about the disappearance of your mother." The words were out of Christopher's mouth before he'd even had time to go over them in his brain.

Sarah flinched in her seat, but then he saw the smile build on her face. The way to Sarah's heart was through her mother. Not even her position in Society. Nor her title. Not Manderfield Hall—even though she cared a great deal for the estate and its tenants. "That would be wonderful, Christopher. I can give you all the initial reports from the original inquiries. I kept everything."

"Thank you. That would be most helpful. I have many connections at the English docks and with merchants all over the world. I will have them scour every manifest and list for the last seven years."

If Lady Manders had abandoned her daughter for the Americas or Australia, it would be painful for Sarah to learn, but it would still be better than her being plagued by not knowing.

"And there is a portrait of my mother. Perhaps a likeness could be made and copied to be sent out."

Christopher drained the juice from his cup. "Do you resemble her?"

Her eyes were full of tears as Sarah shook her head. "No. Mama was a great beauty."

"So are you," he said and meant it. The more he saw her and got to know her, the more beautiful this striking woman in front of him became.

Shrugging, she gave a little laugh. "I work very hard to be presentable."

"You needn't, I assure you."

"I resemble my father's family. And you? Do you favor your father or mother? I can see the resemblance between you and your sisters. You're all very blond and attractive."

He set down his glass. "Margaret resembles Mama the most. Mama's hair was the palest shade of blonde, nearly white. Her eyes were the lightest-blue shade of an afternoon sky. She was quiet-spoken and very shy."

"Then, I take it Deborah does not resemble your mother in personality or appearance very much."

Shaking his head, Christopher chuckled. "No. Deb takes after my father and must be at the center of attention at all times. She's determined, like he was, and twice as stubborn. I find her almost impossible to lead."

"You said that your sisters have been at school. Might I ask which one?"

He flushed, remembering that Deb's actions had caused his sisters' hasty exit. "Miss Mason's School for Gentry in Bath. They were there since my father died nearly nine years ago."

Sarah took a bite of her fruit and nodded. "Margaret's table manners—in fact, her manners in general are perfectly pleasing. Perhaps a little animation in her countenance would do her some good to attract more male attention. Otherwise, I can find no fault with her. She is intelligent, thoughtful, and extremely beautiful. I do not think we will have any difficulty finding her a fine match, when she's ready."

Christopher dropped his napkin. "You do not think she is ready?"

"For Society?" Sarah said. "Definitely. I think we will have a most lovely little Season in the fall and push for her to be presented to the Queen in the spring. I only meant that I do not think that she is eager to marry yet. I believe she wants to have a home before she becomes the mistress of one."

He felt his hackles rise. "My sister has always had a home with me in London."

"The Christmas holiday and a couple weeks in the summer is not the same. From what she confided to me yesterday afternoon, she has no close friends. And she and Deborah do not always get on comfortably."

Gripping his fork tighter, Christopher said, "Deb's not the type to get along comfortably with anybody."

Sarah raised her eyebrows. "That I can well believe. However, all that I am suggesting is that we not be in a rush to lose Margaret. If and when she finds a gentleman she holds in high esteem, then we shall approve of the match."

"You do not think my sister could marry a titled gentleman?"

"Oh, I think Margaret is sweet enough and beautiful enough to marry anyone. I only caution you that there are very few aristocrats with titles and even fewer whom you'd wish for her to marry. I would not want her to be matched with a lord who is old enough to be her father, nor to a young buck living a life of dissipation, waiting upon his expectations to inherit a title or property."

Christopher dropped the fork onto his plate with a clatter. "Like your cousin, the Honorable Ralph Randolph?"

"Oh no. Ralph is not a part of the fast set. All his friends are gentlemen of good reputation, for which we, his family, are all most grateful. But he would not do at all for Margaret. She is too timid, and he would ride roughshod over her feelings. No, if you were interested in the heir to a mere baronet, I would say he would do very well for Deborah. They both have such strong personalities and outgoing natures. I daresay they would come to either loath or love each other."

Christopher's brow furrowed. He'd assumed Sarah did not think his sisters were well-born enough to marry aristocrats or members of her esteemed family. He'd jumped to conclusions and judged her wrongly once again. His wife was more worried about his sisters' happiness than their social aspirations. Something his own father should have thought more of. Something that he himself needed to remember. Something that made his chest warm and his blood thrum in his body. "Then, Deb . . . ?"

"I do not think she should marry for several years at least," Sarah assured him with an airy wave of her hand. "She is only sixteen, and between you and me, she has a great deal of maturing left to do. Her behavior is often childish, and she can be carelessly cruel to Margaret. If we do not nip it in the bud, she will become a mean woman."

He squirmed. "She isn't a bad girl."

"Of course not. She is merely a young lady who still needs to learn when to hold her tongue and how not to throw a tantrum when she doesn't get her way. Mostly, I think her outrageous behaviors are a plea for attention. The poor child has lost both her parents, and she resents when her elder sister attempts to mother her. I am hoping that if I shower her with the right kind of attention, she will be less likely to seek the negative type. I think Deborah is simply bored and will blossom nicely when she finds friends of her own age."

Picking up his napkin, Christopher wiped at the corners of his mouth. He was impressed and a bit flabbergasted by how easily and *accurately* Sarah had been able to assess his sisters. What surprised him more was that she seemed to genuinely care for their welfare and finding them good gentlemen to marry, rather than just making them a good match.

"Are there many young ladies in the area?"

Sarah placed the lid back on her tray. "Several. Not as many as we will find in London, of course. There are the three Lake sisters, who are Mr. Robinson's stepsisters. I would guess their ages to be close to those of your sisters. Miss Lily is not yet out, but she has the same boisterous spirits of Deborah, and I think they would get on swimmingly. I can see them as a very tight pair. There are also the misses Whitman and Miss Iphigenia Wentworth. Her mother is a bit pretentious, but the daughter is quite charming."

Christopher leaned back in his seat, his worries concerning his sisters lessening a little. He was right to find a wife to oversee them. "And will they all welcome friendship with my sisters, despite their lower origins?"

Sarah waved one of her delicate hands in the air. "They will all welcome friendship with the sisters-in-law of Lady Sarah. I am still the highest-ranking lady in the neighborhood, and my grandfather is the Duke of Aylsham. The young ladies will like your sisters, and their mothers will follow my lead.

And, as I told you when I proposed marriage, my family is one of the most prominent and well-connected in England. Only a fool would try to snub one of its members."

"And me? Will they accept a businessman as your husband, or shall I be treated like a poor relation?"

Shaking her head, Sarah chuckled. "I should hardly describe you as poor, Christopher, and you are my husband. I would never countenance anyone treating you with anything but the highest of respect. It would reflect poorly on both of us."

"But I am not your equal."

"In what way? Birth? I had nothing to do with that. Education? I can assure you that I am your superior at sewing and needlework; I've had to be since I make most of my own gowns. However, a lady's education is not very deep. I can read and write and have a passable knowledge of history and geography. I am also learned on the pianoforte and the harp. If pressed, I can speak a few phrases in French and Italian. But you are an intelligent and capable businessman. And fortune? No, indeed. I am not your equal. My father gamed away my dowry, which forced my maternal grandfather to settle some money on me so that I would not be completely destitute. And a lady is not allowed to earn her own way in the world, as you have done so brilliantly. In that way, I would say that you are my superior. In fashion, however, you are quite a bit behind me. And probably always will be, for I am a trendsetter."

Sarah winked at him, and Christopher again fought to keep himself from smiling. Maybe they were not as different as he'd originally supposed. His heart lightened at the thought. His formal education was sparse, but he'd traveled a great deal. "I also know a phrase or two in French and Italian that I learned from dockworkers—none of them, I believe, are appropriate for mixed company."

She laughed the light, bell-like sound that he was growing to love. "Perhaps do not speak them at Almack's assemblies."

"Shall I receive a voucher?"

Shaking her head, Sarah touched her neck. "Christopher, Christopher, Christopher, you will have to tie your cravat, which I see has come undone, and possibly shave off your handsome beard, but yes, you will receive a voucher. I am an intimate friend of all the patronesses, as was my mother. They would never dream of snubbing you, or me through you. I am closely related to too many powerful people."

He sighed, dropping his shoulders. He hadn't shaved off his mustache and beard since they'd first grown in. If he looked carefully in the mirror, he could see the scars behind the hair. He never wanted his wife to see them. "If I were to go, I would stand out like a sore thumb. A goat amongst the sheep."

"Not if I had the dressing of you."

Christopher's neck felt hot again.

A slight pink stole into Sarah's cheeks. "What I mean to say is that with a few alterations to your wardrobe, you could take your place amongst the pinks of the *ton*."

"And the tulips of the turf?"

"You would outshine the out and outers."

Resting his elbow on the table, he leaned his chin against his hand. "You could make me into a Bond Street Beau?"

Sarah smiled. "I could make a Bond Street Beau envious of the way you tie your cravat, the cut of your coat, and the style of your boots. Society is truly a silly bunch of people trying to outdo one another. Once you realize this, you can manipulate the game to your own advantage."

Christopher exhaled in relief. He was rather good at business games. "When do we start?"

She elegantly rose to her feet, and Christopher stood as well. "First, let us go to your room. I will need a freshly starched cravat if I am to tie it in a fashionable style. And, if you do not mind, I should like to go through your wardrobe with your valet."

He fiddled with his shirtsleeve. "I have a batman."

"I daresay he will do just as well."

Rubbing his beard, he said, "But I won't shave."

"Brava! You are a clever pupil. You are already starting a new fashion."

Christopher smiled as he followed her into his own room.

CHAPTER 10

The batman, a Mr. Harris, was a young man probably closer to Margaret's age than Sarah's. He appeared to be a sharp and intelligent young man, as well as patient. Sarah insisted on seeing every article of clothing that Christopher owned. The linens were in good condition; she merely instructed Harris to starch the collars with a recipe she'd learned from her friend Beau Brummell. Some dandies' collars were so high that they were unable to turn their heads from side to side. Such ostentatiousness, she knew intuitively, would make Christopher uncomfortable. But he could be stylish without being extreme.

She also showed Harris how to tie Christopher's cravat in the style of the scholar. Her mother had tied her father's cravats, and after she went missing, Sarah had taken over for Mama until Papa had left for London. The tying of neckcloths was an art.

"Before the Season, we will have to come up with a unique style of your own, Christopher. All the dandies will then ask you what it is called, and we can invent a name, or you can simply reply in a haughty voice, 'I call it a style of my own.'"

Harris chuckled and then clapped a hand over his mouth. The edges of Christopher's reluctant lips quirked up. For a handsome man, he was entirely too serious, and smiles softened his rather rugged features.

Her new husband was not smiling when Sarah insisted that he try on all of his waistcoats and coats. The waistcoats fit well, and Sarah only suggested switching around which coats they were paired with. The coats, however, were too loose on his muscular frame. A fashionable man's jacket was contoured purposely to his figure, and he would not be able to take it off by himself because it fit so precisely. Christopher could easily shrug himself out of his coats, which would not do at all. A man of high birth could get away with a great deal in regard to fashion, but Sarah's husband had to be careful.

Too ornate and he would be mocked for trying to ape his betters. Not stylish enough and he would be scorned for his common background. The *ton* delighted in tearing one another down. She would give them no opportunity to treat Christopher poorly. Or his little sisters. Another reason to put off bringing Deborah out into London Society. Her connection to Sarah and her fortune would give her one chance—not more than one—and Sarah couldn't be certain that her new sister-in-law would not squander it with her headstrong and obstinate behavior.

"Harris, will you bring Miss Mills up to us and have her fetch my sewing kit? I believe a few well-placed darts would suffice to make Mr. Moulton's coat presentable until a tailor can be hired to bring them all in."

Christopher easily pulled off his jacket. "Must I wear my coats like a second skin?"

Raising her eyebrows, she shook her head slightly. "If poor Mr. Harris is not yanking for all he is worth, your coat is not fitting well enough."

Her bridegroom made a pouty face, and she chuckled as Harris left the room to get Nelly. Her friend and lady's maid helped Sarah sew the darts into Christopher's coat. They were both excellent seamstresses. Sarah couldn't resist adding a couple of furbelows to the garment as well, from her sewing collection. She'd learned that these extra little touches made the garment unique, and other people assumed she'd spent a great deal of money on her original wardrobe.

Harris helped Christopher tug on the newly tailored coat. Sarah walked around him and smoothed out the material over his shoulders. A warmth formed in her belly as she touched his muscles. Her husband was a very handsome man. And even more attractive when dressed to the nines.

"Now that you are presentable, I am going to need at least a half hour to make myself so."

"More like an hour," Nelly chimed in.

Giggling, Sarah nodded. "True. We will also need to see that my new sisters-in-law's dresses are up to standard. Harris, will you have a message sent to them? And, Christopher, can you have a carriage called in an hour and a half? I need to introduce you all to the neighborhood."

***

Unsurprisingly, Margaret was easily guided. Nelly rearranged her curls so that more of them framed her lovely oval face. The young lady even allowed Sarah to add the slightest bit of rouge to her cheeks and carmine to her lips. Heavy cosmetics had gone entirely out of fashion, but a clever woman could still use a little here and there to highlight her natural features. Margaret was a lovely young woman, but her paleness caused her to appear a bit washed out. Her white dress and celestial-blue pelisse were of the very finest materials and well-made, if not a bit basic. Sarah added some braided lace to the shoulders and a few tassels to the pelisse. She loved how a good tassel dangled. To complete the look, Sarah lent her new sister-in-law a pair of pearl earrings.

Deborah did not wish for Nelly to fix her hair, even though an entire section had fallen in the back. Nor did she want Sarah to add extra details to her pelisse to make it more customized and stylish. One worthy of a London modiste.

"Our old headmistress, Miss Mason, said that only a shallow young lady is obsessed with her appearance."

Sarah suppressed her smile. "Quite a set down, Deborah. However, my mother, a *countess*, taught me that a person's first impression of you can dictate your entire relationship and to always put your most polished slipper forward. Rarely do people in Society bother to get to know the young woman inside the dress—shallow or deep. Taking control of your appearance and how others perceive you is one of the few powers allotted to ladies. I would not forsake it for a trite principle."

Deborah huffed and said in a small voice, "I suppose Miss Mills might be able to repair my hair, and if you would like to add silly little hanging things to my pink pelisse, I care not."

"Come sit over here, miss," Nelly said with a wry smile on her lips.

Sarah did not add "silly little hanging things" to Deborah's pink pelisse. She did, however, add some blonde lace on the bodice and sleeves in a vine-like pattern. It was quite the loveliest creation Sarah had made in many a month. Deborah, whose hair was no longer falling in the back, turned up her nose at it. "I suppose it will have to do."

"Deb, you are being unconscionably rude," Margaret said, blushing for her sister's lack of manners.

"One might even say *shallow*," Nelly quipped and then curtsied as if she hadn't just called the daughter of the house a name.

Sarah pinched her lips together tightly to keep in her smile. How she loved her old friend's fiery personality!

Deborah's jaw dropped. "How dare a servant speak to me thus! I shall see you dismissed."

Folding her arms, Sarah shook her head. "You shall not, Deborah, for you are not the mistress of the house. I am. And Miss Mills is *my* friend and *my* lady's maid. She may speak freely in my presence, as I have allowed you to do. However, I do not recommend that you behave similarly on our visits today. As I have already said, you will not get a second chance to make a good first impression in the village. When in doubt, do not open your mouth."

The young girl gaped like a fish. Sarah supposed that she had not been forced to obey many people in her life. Not even the sage Miss Mason. Sarah did not wish to break her spirit, but good manners were fashionable in every class.

"Now, my lovely sisters-in-law, I need to dress myself. I shall meet you all in the carriage in a half hour."

Margaret took Deborah's arm and tugged her out of the room.

Once the door closed, Nelly said, "That Miss Deborah's going to be a handful, Sarah."

Sighing, Sarah held up her palms. "I am going to need both hands and yours too."

Nelly and Sarah used their four hands between them to change Sarah into her newest day gown, rose-colored pelisse, and trimmed-to-match chip bonnet. A large rose-colored plume gave it height and presence. Sarah carefully made up her face whilst her lady's maid convinced her wayward hair to form a low chignon and extra curls in the right directions. Nelly made the arranging of hair an art.

"Remember what your mother always said, Sarah," Nelly said, putting her hands on Sarah's shoulders as she sat in front of her vanity and mirror. "A lady is only as beautiful as she believes herself to be."

Taking a deep breath and then exhaling, Sarah got to her feet and left the room. She did not fear for her own acceptance in the neighborhood. She'd long reigned as the highest-ranking lady, the person whom others came to for attention and approval. And she had always tried to be gracious and welcoming, for her mother had another maxim: *Kindness is always in fashion*. She could only hope that the stanch matrons of Eden society would be equally gracious and welcoming to the Moulton sisters. She did not fear for Margaret, but she was terrified for Deborah.

Christopher and his sisters were waiting for her as she descended the stairs. They were a remarkably attractive trio. He offered his arm most gallantly to Sarah, and she did not hesitate to take it. She wondered if Mr. Wigan or Guy had given him a little hint that it was his responsibility as the gentleman to escort her. He helped Sarah first into the carriage and then his sisters. Both Margaret and Deborah sat with their backs to the driver, leaving the only seat next to Sarah. It felt a little odd sitting next to a man that she was not related to by blood, but Christopher was her husband. She would be sitting next to him for the rest of her life.

The carriage lurched forward, and Sarah grabbed Christopher's arm in surprise. She was about to remove her hand when he placed his opposite palm over hers. His fingers were large and surprisingly comforting. She relaxed against the back of the seat, still touching him. Still connected.

"We are going first to Hanford House, which is the second largest estate in the area and owned by Mr. and Mrs. Robinson," Sarah began. "They are hosting a garden party in three days, and we need to secure an invitation. It will ensure your welcome to the neighborhood. Everyone must be on their best behavior." She looked at Deborah meaningfully. "Also, their family situation is rather unique, so please do not speak without thinking first. Mr. Brian Robinson, our vicar, is Mr. Robinson's son. Mr. Robinson is, of course, very proud of him, as any father would be of such an accomplished, affable, and hardworking young man. Mr. Robinson married the current Mrs. Robinson nearly a decade ago. She brought three daughters with her to the marriage: Miss Cynthia Lake, Miss Olivia, and Miss Lily."

Deborah sniffed loudly. "Why haven't you already received an invitation if this garden party is so important?"

Swallowing, Sarah said, "I was invited nearly three weeks ago, but I was forced to send my regrets because I was moving to Westbrook Park. Hopefully, since I am returned to the neighborhood, Mrs. Robinson will be so kind as to extend another invitation and include you all as well."

"What sort of woman is Mrs. Robinson?" Margaret asked, lacing her fingers together on her lap.

"The sort of woman you would not wish to offend. She is the most prominent hostess in Eden society, and if she accepts you, everyone else will follow her lead."

Deborah clucked her tongue. "I thought you were the most prominent person in the neighborhood, *Lady Sarah*."

"Alas. I was a single young lady and could not entertain at Manderfield Hall since my mother's disappearance. Now that I am married, I can assure you that we will be good hosts and great neighbors. However, the tone will be set by Mrs. Robinson. She is a daughter of a squire and proud of her birth, but not haughty. Her daughters have pleasant, unaffected manners. I like them a great deal, and I am certain that you will as well. They even live close enough that you could walk to their house, if you chose to."

Her sour sister-in-law seemed to perk up at this. "And you think they'll befriend us?"

"If you are kind, I do not see why they would not be kind in return."

Deborah shrugged, but Sarah felt as if she'd gotten her point across. Her new sister-in-law resented Sarah, but she was not a fool. She would not wish to isolate herself from her new neighborhood.

"What are their names again?" Deborah asked.

"Miss Cynthia Lake, whom you will refer to as Miss Lake, Miss Olivia, and Miss Lily."

"They have pretty names," Margaret said.

"Just as long as they are not prettier than us," Deborah said in a serious tone, and Sarah once again had to fight her smile. The word *shallow* came to her lips, but she did not say it.

The carriage pulled up to Hanford House, which was a lovely white Georgian building with colonnades. It was not as large as Manderfield Hall, but it was newer and modern in its design. A grand staircase led into the house. A butler ushered them all inside and to a sitting room with several marble statues. She'd seen them many times before, so they were not of particular interest to her. Deborah, however, stopped to examine each one and exclaimed, "These are the works of masters."

After they were all seated, Christopher's hand moved to his cravat that Sarah had tied for him. If he touched it, he would ruin the style. Sarah grabbed his wrist and brought it down to her lap, covering it with her other hand. "You look very handsome, Christopher. Do not fret about your appearance."

"The collar is too tight."

"Never complain about your apparel being too tight to a woman wearing a corset."

A laugh escaped from Margaret's lips. Deborah snorted and laughed loudly. Christopher even managed a half smile. The Moulton family was at their very best when Mrs. Robinson and her three daughters entered the room. To be fair to Deborah, the Lake sisters were not as pretty as herself and Margaret. They were attractive girls with pleasing faces and figures, but not memorable ones. They all had rich brown hair and hazel eyes. Honestly, Sarah had difficulty telling them apart now that they were all nearly the same height.

Standing, Sarah curtsied to Mrs. Robinson, whose brown hair was now liberally streaked with gray. "It is lovely to see you again, Mrs. Robinson, and your beautiful daughters. Please allow me to introduce my husband, Mr. Moulton, and his sisters, Miss Moulton and Miss Deborah. They are new to the neighborhood and eager to make friends."

Christopher bowed and his sisters curtsied. Mrs. Robinson and her daughters returned the courtesy. "Won't you please be seated, my lady? I, too, look forward to getting to know our new neighbors. Where are you from, Mr. Moulton?"

He glanced briefly at Sarah, who gave him a reassuring smile. "London, ma'am. But I am happy to now consider Manderfield Hall our home."

Mrs. Robinson nodded politely. "And do you still have a home in London?"

"Yes, ma'am. In Kensington."

Not the most fashionable area, but a very respectable one. The Robinsons were well-to-do, but they did not own a London house. When they went for the Season next year, they would need to let a building. Sarah knew that Mrs. Robinson was deciding whether or not the Moultons were rich enough to be of interest to her.

"I shall, of course, be inviting you and Miss Lake to a ball there next Season," Sarah cut in, sweetening the pot. "Our dear Miss Moulton will be enjoying her first Season, like your daughter. All of my aunts and uncles are eager to be a part of her presentation. And my grandfather the Duke of Aylsham insists that he be there as well."

This was a slight prevarication. Sarah did not doubt that she could guilt her aunts into accepting her invitations and send notes to her uncles to ensure that her husband's name was put up in the best clubs. And her grumpy and beloved grandsire would not dream of missing any party that Sarah threw. She was his favorite grandchild, and he told everyone. She only hoped that he would not be disappointed when he received the letter about her wedding. It would be arriving at Hemsley Palace any day now.

"We would be honored to receive an invitation," Mrs. Robinson said in a sweet voice, "and we do hope that you all will be able to come to our garden party on Friday. I am afraid that it is short notice."

Relief filled Sarah's chest like a breath of fresh air, and she smiled. "We will be delighted to come."

They had gotten over the first social hurdle, but there would be many more to come.

CHAPTER 11

Christopher had survived the social calls two days ago—barely. He'd met only one gentleman, a Mr. Wentworth, who was older than his father. The man was bluff and genial but not the sort of friend Christopher wished for. He supposed he would meet Mr. Robinson again at the garden party tomorrow. He was not looking forward to the event, but his sisters were. Every time he saw them they were speaking of it or preparing for it. Margaret had told him that Sarah was remaking Margaret's dress so that it would be the prettiest at the party.

He was not one for fashion, but that did not make him unobservant. He'd noticed slight alterations to all of his sisters' clothing over the last pair of days. But the greatest change was to their hairstyles. He could see Sarah's hand in every aspect of his sisters' appearances, and he was certain he had made the right choice. Sarah had even invited the Lake sisters over for tea that very day to allow them to become better acquainted with Margaret and Deborah. He had simply sipped his tea, but he'd watched how Sarah drew out not only his sisters but their neighbors. By the end of it, Margaret was leading Miss Lake through the gardens and Deborah and the two younger girls were playing a game of tag. He'd never seen his sisters so relaxed before. So happy.

Exhaling, he wondered if he had not been a very good brother. He had provided them with a good education and fine clothing, but he had not spent a great deal of time with them. He was nearly ten years their senior and had already left home by the time they were in leading strings. He loved them, and he was fond of them, but he wasn't certain he truly *knew* them. Breathing in, Christopher realized that he'd never asked Margaret or Deborah if they even wanted to make grand matches. Or live in a fancy estate like Manderfield Hall. It had been their father's dream, but was it theirs?

There was a quiet knock on the door of the room he'd chosen to be his study. He set down his papers. "Come in."

The door swung open, and Sarah entered the room. He hurriedly got to his feet. He'd been expecting a servant. "Sarah. Is there something I can do for you, dove?"

The endearment had slipped out, but she didn't seem to mind it. His wife's cheeks turned a pretty pink.

"Nothing, dear Christopher," she said, and he wished that he were dear to her. That their marriage were more than a bargain for social advancement. "I am only here to inform you that we have been invited to dinner by the Wentworths next Sunday evening, and before you frown, Mrs. Wentworth has assured me that she has included Mr. Brian Robinson and Mr. Harry Whitman in the invitation. I know Mr. Wentworth speaks only of his port, but both of his young male guests graduated from Oxford University and are good conversationalists. I am sure you will enjoy their company."

How had she noticed that he missed male friendship? Sarah was uncommonly perceptive when it came to people's thoughts. After only one day in his sisters' company, she'd taken their complete measure. He wondered how many of his own secrets she'd already discovered.

Christopher frowned. He did wish to enjoy other men's company, only he was afraid that he would not. He had not gone to university, nor had he attended a public school like Eton or Harrow. Most of his learning had been on the job, and he did not wish for these young men to find him ignorant. "What a thoughtful invitation."

Sarah came closer to him, and he caught a hint of the lovely honeysuckle scent that she wore. She leaned against the side of his desk. "For someone who wishes to join local Society, you don't sound particularly pleased by the invitation. Are you worried about the forks?"

He gulped in surprise. "Excuse me?"

"Which fork to use. In our dinners together, I have seen that you are not always certain which utensil is the correct one for the course. You needn't be embarrassed; we can go over them together."

If Christopher wasn't embarrassed before, he certainly was now. His wife proposed to teach him how to use the correct fork, like a child.

Sarah continued. "A little utensil trick my mother taught me is to go from the outside in. The farthest fork or spoon first."

His toes curled and his chest tightened. "I do not need your help with forks."

She bit down on her lower lip. "If not forks, then friends. You are worried about how you will fit into the neighborhood."

Christopher had a twitchy feeling in his extremities and would have left the room if it hadn't been his study. "You are treating me like a child, and I resent it greatly."

Sarah surprised him by taking one of his hands in her own. "Do you fear that they will scorn you for your lack of formal education?"

He clenched his teeth. She'd even gotten the words in his head right. Never before had he felt so foolish in another person's presence. He was the boss. No one had ever questioned him like this. Knew him intimately like this—and in such a short time. His bride had seen through his facade as if he were as transparent as a newly glazed glass window. He could have dug his own grave and covered himself in dirt rather than face his new wife. She looked at him expectantly, as if waiting for his answer. All Christopher could manage was a curt nod.

Sarah sat on his desk, still holding his hand. "You silly man, don't you realize that they are worried too? You are a famous and wealthy businessman from London. You are older and more experienced in the ways of the world. If anything, they will be nervous to meet *you*."

Christopher hadn't thought of that. Perhaps his difficulty in making friends stemmed not so much from his lower-class background but from his own reticence. He squeezed her hand and attempted a joke. "Am I such an intimidating figure?"

With her free hand, she brushed his hair from his brow. His pulse leaped. "You are the strong and silent type. People will assume that you are uninterested or even rude. Mr. Brian Robinson, for example, is newly graduated from university, and this is his first position in the church. His knowledge is all theoretical; I am sure he would be grateful for the perspective of a man of the world."

"And Mr. Whitman?"

She placed her second hand on top of his. He liked the feeling of being touched by her. The shape and weight of her hands on his. The satin softness of her skin.

Exhaling, Sarah said, "Mr. Whitman's hair is brown, but his sideburns are as red as Ralph's curls. He is a shy man with a little stutter that he is very self-conscious about. I believe poor Mr. Whitman has felt very isolated in the neighborhood before now. He is the only gentleman of Eden society in his twenties, and he is also unmarried. He doesn't have much in common with middle-aged married men who have children nearly his own age."

Christopher's toes uncurled in his boots. The irritation that had tightened every muscle in his body loosened. Sarah wasn't trying to be condescending; she was trying to help him. And her words had lightened his concerns. Or, rather, her perspective of him. Christopher usually focused on what he lacked: high birth, education, and formal manners. His bride instead shined a light on what he had to offer in a friendship: experience, travel, and his reputation. He did have something to share with these young men.

"Besides being shy, what is Mr. Whitman like?" he asked.

Sarah tilted her head to one side. "I confess, I am not well acquainted with him. I know that he has a stud farm and raises horses. I have always felt that he was fonder of the animals he cares for than of people. But he is a kind man."

Christopher fought down the urge to smile at her wit. "And he is well educated?"

"His mother made sure that everyone in the neighborhood knew that he had received a first at Oxford and was awarded with the title Senior Wrangler. I can't recall whether it was for mathematics or something to do with the natural sciences. Mr. Whitman has never mentioned it himself. He is not one to boast, nor to speak above his company."

Christopher sighed. The man sounded like a clever cove. Christopher was decent at mathematics, but he left most of that to his bookkeepers. And as for the sciences, he knew nothing about them at all. At the moment, he'd rather dig a canal by himself than attend the garden party or dinner.

Raising one eyebrow, Sarah said, "You've grown silent."

"If I don't speak, then they won't know what I am lacking in education."

She released his hand and stood up, twirling around. "The answer is right in front of you—you're sitting in a library. If you feel that you lack knowledge, begin reading. Or ask questions. I have never met a man who didn't wish to explain some subject to me in great detail."

A reluctant laugh broke out of his throat.

Sarah grinned back at Christopher. "You think I jest, but the better listener you are, the better conversationalist people will believe you to be. Everyone loves to speak. Only a few people understand the value of listening."

Christopher was a good listener. Perhaps she was right. He did not have to worry about making conversation or appearing to be smarter than he was.

Coming to his side, she put a hand on his shoulder, and he jumped a little. "But you will have to make the first move toward friendship with both gentlemen. Even though you are new to the neighborhood, they will perceive you as holding a higher position than themselves because you are the owner of a grand estate. They will wait for you to speak to them and invite them. Don't be afraid to make the first step toward friendship."

Her hand was still on his shoulder, and he felt the urge to cover it with his own. He liked her touch and when she stood near to him. Sarah's presence had nearly made him forget what he'd been working on before she'd arrived. Christopher picked up the stack of papers and flipped over the first page. Mr. Wigan had shown him the portrait of Lady Manders. Christopher had done a sketch of her, adding shadowing to show her increased age. The woman would be double the age now that she was when she'd modeled for the painting.

Sarah dropped her hand from his shoulder and picked up the sketch. Her eyes searched it before she held it to her chest. "How?"

His drawing had reduced his loquacious bride to only a one-word sentence. He'd never thought to see Sarah speechless. She always seemed to have so much to say. Picking up his pencil, Christopher fiddled with it. "As a drafter, you have to make a pretty accurate map of the area for the building of a canal. I got to be rather handy with a pencil or charcoal. I thought perhaps that if I sent out a picture of your mother, we might have more success. I plan to commission an artist to carve a woodprint of it to distribute with the advertisement from the publisher."

Silently, Sarah held the sketch out and devoured it with her watery eyes.

Christopher feared it was not good enough or that it did not accurately reflect the missing countess. "I can make another. I was merely guessing how she might have aged, from her portrait. I don't need to send it to be made into a woodprint yet."

Sarah took a shuddering breath and attempted to hold in her tears. He'd tried to help her, and he'd only made it worse. He knew that finding her mother was the most important thing in Sarah's life.

"I only meant to help."

Sarah startled him by pressing a soft kiss against his temple and placing the sketch on his desk. "It is perfect. Might I have the original after the woodprint is created?"

"Of-of course."

She stepped back, her hands fisted. "I shall go and change for dinner. I heard from Mrs. Harmony that a tailor arrived this morning to bring all your coats in. I daresay you will be the best dressed at tonight's meal."

Christopher groaned and she laughed softly. He watched her walk to the door and pause when her hand touched the knob. She glanced back over her shoulder at him. "Helping me find my mother means the world to me. I cannot thank you enough, Christopher."

"You don't need to thank me. I am your husband. It is my duty and my pleasure to help you in any way."

Nodding, she left the room and closed the door behind her. Christopher's hand moved to his temple where Sarah had pressed a kiss. They had not kissed on their wedding day. Only the one time when they had sealed their bargain. But this gentle caress made him realize how much he wanted to kiss her again.

CHAPTER 12

"You don't need to thank me. I am your husband. It is my duty and my pleasure to help you in any way," Christopher had said. The words kept rolling around in Sarah's mind as Nelly tugged her hair with her brush and smoothed the back into a chignon. Sarah had never expected her husband to voluntarily help her. Even if she'd married the Marquess of Ingress or a different suitor. A wife was not considered to be a husband's equal in law or in marriage. A husband was the master in all ways. He could do with her what he pleased, treat her however he wished—even, sadly, beat his wife to "correct her behavior."

Papa hadn't physically injured Mama, but he'd been controlling in every other way. He'd wanted to know where she was at all times and whom she spoke to. Aunt Venetia had said that Papa had loved Sarah's mother greatly—but it wasn't love. It was obsession. If Mama was asked by a duke to waltz at a ball, her father wouldn't let her receive visitors for a week. If Mama spoke well of a footman or a groom, they were immediately dismissed.

Her father had even been jealous of the attentions Mama had shown Sarah. He didn't like when her mother had focused on any person other than him. That was the reason he'd sent Sarah to school at the age of eight despite Mama's tears and pleadings. And the more her father had tried to control every aspect of her mother's life, the more Sarah had grown to hate him.

She knew what her parents had fought over that fateful night when Mama had disappeared. Papa had used Sarah's dowry to pay off his gambling debts of honor. There was not even a farthing left of the thirty thousand pounds that had been set aside to ensure his daughter's future—money that had come from her mother's portion. Mama had been beyond livid. Sarah had never heard her raise her voice before, nor fight with Papa, despite the restrictions he had made on her every movement. It was only when he'd diced away his daughter's security that Mama had broken all of her rules. She'd yelled at Papa and told him that she would never forgive him. Then she'd left the house to go on a ride alone, something that Papa had never let her do. Mama was a capital rider. There had been no reason for Sarah to be worried, even after Mama had been gone for several hours. She often rode to release her frustrations. She'd once told Sarah that on the back of a horse was the only place that she felt weightless and free.

"There," Nelly said, tugging on a curl. "All finished. You're as pretty as a picture, Sarah. You'll have Mr. Moulton eating out of your hand."

"Like a horse?"

Nelly chuckled but then sobered. "I am glad you married him, even if he's not from the same class as you. I have missed you more than I can say. Manderfield Hall isn't home without you."

Turning in her seat, Sarah said saucily, "Yet you refused to come with me to Westbrook Park. Could it be that no place is home without a certain footman named Guy?"

Her old friend colored, which wasn't like Nelly at all. "He finally proposed to me last night."

Sarah placed a hand on Nelly's arm. "The stocking-throwing worked. Would you like to borrow my wedding gown, or shall we go into the village tomorrow and purchase some cloth from the shop?"

"I can't wear your dress. What will people in the village say?"

Sarah pinched her friend lightly. "Mr. Robinson will say that you are the most beautiful bride, but I should warn you that he says that to everyone and not to let it go to your head."

Nelly chuckled again. "Are you sure, Sarah?"

"Entirely," she said. "Shall I tell Cook to start doing the sugar-icing work for the wedding cake?"

Her lady's maid straightened the lace of Sarah's collar. "You may after the first banns are read on Sunday."

"And do I get to break the cake on Guy's head? My Aunt Venetia claims it is a local wedding custom."

Nelly gave Sarah a little push. "If anyone's breaking cake on Guy's head, it'll be me. Now, off you go, and teach those spoiled termagants some manners."

Sarah gave her old friend a mock curtsy, as if she were a queen and not a maid; then she left her room and met Christopher at the top of the stairs. He was dashing in his evening dress. The tailor had fitted his coat perfectly to his frame. Her husband would not have looked out of place at a St. James Palace levee. The corners of his lips tilted up, and he offered his arm. His words rattled through her head again: *"You don't need to thank me. I am your husband. It is my duty and my pleasure to help you in any way."*

She placed her hand on his arm and felt the strength there. "You are looking very handsome, Husband."

"As you always do, *my* wife."

Sarah thought she heard a slight emphasis on "my," and surprisingly, she rather liked it. Christopher didn't wish to own her or control her—he wished to help her. She smiled as they walked down the grand staircase together. His sisters were already in the dining room.

Deborah turned from where she was staring out the window and gave them a begrudging "Good evening."

Sarah still needed to win over the younger sister. Chaperoning her husband's sisters and ensuring they made good marriages was all that Christopher had asked of her in return for their marriage. He'd already kept his promise of making her the mistress of Manderfield Hall, and he was trying to locate her mother. He was doing more than she could have hoped for. Sarah needed to try harder.

After a delicious dinner, but with stilted conversation, Sarah stood. The Moulton sisters also got to their feet. Custom said that a man drank a glass after dinner by himself or with other men. The last two nights, she had not seen Christopher after the meal. She didn't know where he'd gone or how he'd spent his time. He was *her* husband, and she wished to get to know him better. She had to get to know all of the Moultons better. They needed to become a true family. Sarah wondered what her mother would have done. Christopher clearly loved his sisters, but he was not close to them. Margaret was reserved, and Deborah resented her elder sister's influence almost as much as she despised Sarah for marrying her brother for Manderfield Hall. Sometimes it made Sarah want to hide like she was still a small child.

That was it.

"Christopher," Sarah said as they reached the door. "Do not linger too long over your port. Your sisters and I will be hiding on the ground floor, waiting for you to find us."

"You wish to play hide-and-seek?" Deborah asked mockingly. "Isn't that a children's game?"

Sarah shrugged. "Are you afraid you will lose?"

"Never," Deborah said, pushing past Sarah and through the door.

Sarah winked at Margaret and lifted her skirts to make a dash for it. She heard Margaret's laughter behind her echoing in the marble entry hall. Sarah knew precisely where she was going to hide. Even though she was a great deal larger than when she had been six years old, she could still fit into the blue cabinet in the sitting room. Closing the double doors, her eyes grew accustomed to the darkness. A bubble of laughter grew in her chest, but she suppressed it. She could not make a noise, or Christopher might find her first.

Several minutes passed, and Sarah started to worry that he wasn't playing the game. She hadn't even asked him to. She'd told him. Placing her hand on the cabinet door, she was about to take a peek of the room when she heard footsteps. She moved her hand to her mouth to keep in her silent laughter. She heard Christopher check behind the tables, the furniture, and even the curtains, like her mother always had.

Then he opened both doors to her cabinet, and Sarah jumped in surprise, laughing. And then her serious husband began to laugh too. They laughed together, and that small moment seemed to create a bond between them. A memory to build their new relationship upon. Christopher held out his hand to her and helped her out of the cabinet. Sarah stepped onto the carpet, but he did not drop her hand. Like earlier that day in his study, Sarah discovered that she enjoyed holding Christopher's large, strong, and callused hand.

"Shall we find the girls together?" she asked, tugging him along and out of the room.

Together they found Margaret in the nook behind the main staircase and Deborah behind a sofa in the library.

Deborah dusted off her dress as she got to her feet. "It is not fair. Sarah has lived here all her life. There are no spots that she doesn't know about."

"You're right," Sarah agreed. "How about this time only one person hides on the first floor and everyone else comes to find them and then joins the person in their hiding spot?"

"You should hide, Sarah," Margaret said. "You know all the best places."

Reluctantly, Sarah let go of Christopher's hand. "Count to one hundred."

Picking up her skirts, she dashed up the main staircase and past hers and Christopher's rooms. She would be found too easily there. Out of breath, she also avoided the sisters' rooms and did not stop until she reached the farthest guest room. She closed the door carefully behind her and opened the wardrobe slightly before hiding underneath the bed. She was glad that she'd had the servants scrub Manderfield Hall from the attics to the basement, for there was no dust underneath the bed that might have made her sneeze and given away her perfect position.

Closing her eyes, Sarah couldn't remember the last time she'd had so much fun. Or behaved so silly. In her teenage years, the time with her mother had been so minimal that they hadn't played any games. Mama's attention had been on helping Sarah become the best version of herself so as to find a good match and secure a prominent place in Society. Beauty and kindness were important things, but Sarah wondered how her mother had felt about so many other subjects. Ones that they'd never had the opportunity to speak about. Even small things, like the foolishness of having nine utensils at dinner. What books she'd liked to read. What she'd thought about the class system and how a person's worth was measured. Sarah pondered what her mother would have thought of Christopher and his sisters. Would she have seen his worth beyond his wealth?

Despite her own disappointing aristocratic marriage, Mama had wanted Sarah to marry a man with a title. She and Christopher's late father had possessed the same goal. Sarah had been married for less than a week now, but she was already happier than she might have been wedded to any other man of her same rank, even the kind Lord Ingress. Like Papa, a titled peer would have expected Sarah to obey him. To be the beautiful wife on his arm. His political and social hostess, with no thoughts or opinions of her own.

The door to the room opened, and she saw a pair of slippers. It had to be one of the girls. She ran to the wardrobe and flung it open, only to find it empty. Then she left the room as quickly as she had entered it. Sarah had to cover her mouth again not to snigger. Her trick had worked.

A few minutes later, a pair of boots walked into the room—Christopher. His feet moved across the room as he methodically checked every nook and cranny, even the wardrobe that was ajar. She heard a shuffling of feet and then saw his knees before his handsome face peeked underneath the bed skirt. Sarah couldn't hold in a little laugh, and Christopher grinned at her for the second time that evening. She loved how happiness softened his rugged features and filled his serious countenance with light.

"Quickly, come underneath the bed," she whispered.

Christopher lay down on his back and wiggled underneath the bed until he was next to her. His lips brushed her hair and her cheek. She wondered how they would feel on her mouth again. Her marriage of convenience was turning out not to be so convenient after all. Sarah had only been kissed once before by Christopher, and she hadn't known how to respond. She had stiffened in surprise when he'd touched her, and he'd stopped immediately. How she wished he would try again.

His eyes met hers and Sarah could not look away. It was as if some invisible bond held them together and neither could turn away from it. Her mother had always said that love made one blind to another's faults. Sarah wasn't blind to Christopher's. He was stubborn and secretive, but he was also endearingly shy and a little lonely. She wanted to help him make friends, but more than anything, Sarah wished to be his friend. She could not drink with him after dinner, nor did she wish to go hunting with her husband. None of the activities of a male friendship. She wanted to walk with him. Talk with him. Share her secrets with him.

"Sarah, I—" he began in a soft voice, but she did not get to hear him complete his sentence, for another pair of slippers entered the room, and it did not take Margaret long to find them underneath the bed. Sarah scooted closer to Christopher to make room for his sister. Her arm was touching his, and everywhere their bodies met, she felt delicious tingles. Margaret started to giggle, and her mirth was infectious; soon all three of them were laughing, and Deborah found them easily. One by one they crawled from underneath the bed. Sarah was the last one out, and Deborah offered her a hand to help her up. It was the first sign of the stubborn girl receiving her, and Sarah accepted it gratefully.

"You know what children's game we should play now?" Deborah asked.

Margaret shook her head. "What?"

"Spillikins! I saw a set in the parlor." Deborah grabbed her sister's hand, and they rushed out of the room with the same boisterous energy with which Deborah had entered it.

Sarah gestured to the door. "Shall we?"

Christopher held out his hand to her, and Sarah did not hesitate to take it.

CHAPTER 13

A GARDEN PARTY IS NOTHING to be nervous about, Christopher assured himself. If anything, it was less formal than a ball or a dinner. It was just the sort of relaxed outdoor atmosphere that would be ideal for meeting new people. His hand moved to his cravat, but then he remembered that it had taken his batman no fewer than four tries to get the folds correct. Both Harris and Sarah would be upset with him if he mussed it up.

He also hated riding in a stuffy carriage. It reminded him of the two worst days of his life: being locked in the cupboard and when his father had come to collect him after his mother's and siblings' funerals and the carriage had driven through the night. The trip had taken several days, and Christopher had felt like he was in a cage. He couldn't get out. He couldn't cry. When his eyes had begun to tear up as he'd received the news, his father had told him to be a man. Men, it would seem, did not cry. And gentlemen rode in carriages to garden parties.

Christopher met Sarah and his sisters in an antechamber. He watched as Sarah straightened Deborah's bonnet and retied the bow so that it was swept fetchingly to one side. Next, she moved to Margaret and said, "Forgive me," before she pinched her cheeks.

His little sister yelped, but her usually pale face was no longer pale. A little more color was becoming to Margaret's complexion.

Sarah turned to face him with the smile that always set his pulse racing.

He held up both of his hands as if surrendering. "Please don't pinch my cheeks."

Deborah snorted with laughter, and Margaret giggled. It was only a small joke, but Christopher realized that he never teased or joked with his sisters. Particularly after the death of their father, Christopher had taken his responsibilities toward them seriously—perhaps a little too seriously. Laughter was good for the soul.

"I have no intention of pinching your cheeks," Sarah said, coming closer to him so that the skirt of her day dress touched his boots. "I know how to add color another way." She tiptoed and kissed one of his cheeks and then the other.

Christopher's face, neck, and entire body warmed. He did not doubt that his cheeks were suffused with color.

Deborah snorted again. "A kiss works better than rouge."

Sarah winked at her. "Our little secret."

Without waiting for him to offer his arm, Sarah tucked her hand into the crook of his elbow. Instinctively, he covered her hand with his opposite palm and smiled down at her. He had never been one to show his emotions on his face, but in Sarah's company, he found it difficult not to.

"I have a little surprise for you, Christopher," she said and led them out of the house and onto the gravel pathway.

He heard the sound of horse hooves and expected to see the formal, closed carriage. Instead there was a landau with no roof. It appeared to be considerably older than the barouche, but he didn't care. He was not going to be trapped inside a moving vehicle. He had ridden in a carriage with Sarah only twice before, but she must have noticed that he did not enjoy it. Nothing went unseen by her watchful eyes.

She tightened her hold on his arm, and he felt her touch all the way to his heart. "Girls, pull out your pretty parasols. It is time to show them off to admiration."

Christopher helped Sarah up and was not surprised to see her open a lacy parasol that appeared to be more fashionable than functional. Paired with her yellow pelisse and bonnet trimmed in yellow and white flowers, his wife looked like a picture on a fashion plate. He still could not quite believe that this beautiful woman was his wife and that she cared enough to notice that he didn't like to ride in closed carriages. He helped his sisters in and took his seat by Sarah. Again she placed her hand on his arm in the place that seemed to be made just for her. His sisters opened their parasols, and Christopher asked Mr. Phipps to begin their drive.

He half expected Sarah to give them a lecture on how they were to behave or what not to say in company, but her only remark was on the scenery. "I know it is unfashionable these days to prefer formal gardens over the picturesque wildness of a landscape, but I must confess, I love the order and symmetry of Manderfield's gardens."

"What about Capability Brown?" Margaret asked.

He was the famous garden architect known for designing the landscapes of many prominent estates. He liked smooth grass and clumps of trees or bushes. And, like Sarah's uncle, Mr. Lancelot "Capability" Brown created many artificial, serpentine-like lakes by damming rivers. The fashionable gardener had once compared the structure of a garden to that of a sentence: "There I make a comma, and there, where a more decided turn is proper, I make a colon; at another part, where an interruption is desirable to break the view, a parenthesis; now a full stop, and then I begin another subject." Christopher's father had tried to use Mr. Brown's philosophies in the creation of his canals. He had wanted them to add beauty to the landscape as well as a convenient way to move supplies and goods over a great distance in a short time.

Sarah spun her parasol. "He believed in improving on nature. I do not think anyone could improve upon Manderfield's formal gardens, but I will own that Mr. and Mrs. Robinson's landscape is delightfully untamed, unlike my poor uncle Oscar's style of gardening, which is nature at its most pretentious. We will have to explore the grounds of Westbrook Park farther the next time we are there."

"And when shall we go there?" Deborah asked.

Sarah stopped spinning her parasol's handle. "I received a note from my aunt this very morning. She has already sent out invitations for a party to celebrate our wedding in a month."

"Why so far away?" Deborah demanded.

Christopher had wondered as well, but he'd been taught his entire life not to question his betters.

His wife, however, did not seem at all discomposed. "Aunt Venetia wished to invite the entire family and thought some might need a little more time to make the journey. But never fear; she has tasked her cook to begin making different cakes so that the most superior-flavored one will be chosen for the wedding cake."

Christopher's hand moved to his collar, but he stopped himself once again from pulling it. He contented himself with rubbing his trimmed beard. He wasn't sure he was ready to meet all of Sarah's grand relations. He was just getting used to being married to a lady. He did not wish to be surrounded by lords and ladies and dukes and duchesses. Nor did he want his sisters to see how his grand relations treated him. He expected the same cool condescension he'd received from the Honorable Ralph. He knew that Deborah would fly to his defense and Margaret would be disappointed. He could only pray Sarah's toplofty family would be kind to his sisters.

Margaret wrinkled her nose. "One would not wish for an inferior flavor of sponge for a wedding cake."

Sarah grinned. "I don't know why the flavor matters at all. Aunt Venetia wants to break the cake over Christopher's head and my own. Supposedly it is a local custom and a superstition for good luck."

Dropping her parasol, Deborah shook her head. "You are pulling our legs."

His wife held out her right hand solemnly. "I assure you that I am not. And you will see for yourselves at Nelly and Guy's wedding in three weeks."

Christopher thought these names sounded familiar, but everyone in the neighborhood of Eden was still new to him.

Deborah closed her parasol with a snap. "You mean to attend your maid's marriage?"

Sarah leaned a little against Christopher's shoulder. "I hope to be asked to be her attendant. Nelly Mills is my oldest friend. I would not miss her wedding for any reason. And I am sure the entire village will come out to celebrate. Both Guy and Nelly are very popular amongst the younger set."

"The footman," Christopher said out loud as he realized who the groom was.

His wife nodded against his shoulder.

"We'll have to give them both a week off with pay as a gift and have Cook prepare a wedding breakfast for all their guests," he said.

Sarah pulled away from him, but only to look Christopher in the eyes as she smiled up at him in approval. "How very thoughtful you are."

In that moment, Christopher would have given the pair a year of paid leave.

"I should like to come too," Margaret said, blushing a little and looking down at her hands. Christopher wondered if his sister was just being polite or if she wished for another opportunity to see the handsome young vicar.

"I suppose I shall as well," Deborah said, kicking her foot against the seat. "I don't wish to be the only one left out."

Christopher hoped neither of his sisters would feel left out at the garden party.

The landau pulled up to the front of Hanford House, and a footman opened the carriage door. Christopher alighted first and then helped his wife and sisters. Sarah thanked the footman by name and again took Christopher's arm. She led him and his sisters to where the other guests were gathering. Several white tents had been set up on the south side of the house, with tables and chairs. Flowers in vases served as centerpieces, as well as towers of fruit and biscuits. It was lovelier than any tradesmen's ball he had ever attended.

Mrs. Robinson greeted them with a slight upturn of her thin lips. "Husband, may I introduce Miss Moulton, Miss Deborah, and Mr. Moulton? Lady Sarah you already know."

At first glance, Christopher did not think Mr. Brian Robinson resembled his father much. Mr. Robinson's hair was as white as a rabbit's pelt of fur. He had tired blue eyes, an aquiline nose, and thin lips. His height and form, however, were very like his son's, if a bit broader from time. He appeared to be near fifty but was still fit. Christopher also noticed that the shape of the man's face and the line of his jaw was identical to his son's, as was the man's smile. "Delighted to welcome you to the neighborhood, Moulton. I have seen your canal from the Dunkerton pits to Bath, a countryside as highly picturesque as any in the kingdom."

Christopher's lips twitched at the mention of the picturesque countryside. He was pleased with the comparison, even if his lovely wife did not approve of Capability Brown's landscapes. "We do our best to make the canals look as natural as possible, sir."

Mr. Robinson shook his hand warmly and suggested that they go hunting a morning next week. Pleased, Christopher agreed to it on the spot, even though he was not at all handy with a gun.

He watched Sarah speak to each of Mr. Robinson's stepdaughters: Miss Lake, Miss Olivia, and Miss Lily. They were standing near their mother and helping welcome the guests.

Why wasn't Mr. Brian Robinson beside them? Christopher spotted the tall vicar speaking to another young gentleman under the shade of a tree near the first tent. The other man was likely Mr. Whitman. His features met Sarah's description. His sideburns were very red, despite the brown of the rest of his hair. Sarah and his sisters seemed well occupied speaking to the other ladies, so Christopher set off to approach the young men. He meant to follow Sarah's advice and offer his hand in friendship first.

Halfway there, he was stopped by Mrs. Wentworth. "Mr. Moulton, how surprised I am to see you here."

Christopher did not quite know how to respond. Was the older woman surprised that he had been invited too? Or that he had accepted the invitation? Was she insulting him or pandering to him? "It is a lovely garden and an even lovelier party."

Mrs. Wentworth sniffed, sticking her nose into the air. "I confess I have never cared much for the outdoors. If a lady is not careful, her skin can become quite brown." She said these words as if acquiring tanned skin was the worst thing that could happen to a woman.

Christopher pointed to the tents. "I believe our hosts have provided those tents for just that purpose—to block the sun."

Not that he had any doubt that Mrs. Wentworth was able to block the sun in any situation.

The older woman touched the pearls at her throat, as if to call Christopher's attention to them. "Poor Mrs. Robinson. I quite feel for her. To be forced to accept her husband's by-blow at her party, even if he is a man of the cloth. And I worry for her daughters. What if the elder Mr. Robinson were to leave them nothing?"

Christopher was done with this conversation and this prejudiced woman. "Perhaps their own late father has left them dowries, Mrs. Wentworth." He touched the rim of his hat and walked past her without giving her time to reply. He did not wish to hear her bigoted opinion. He thought it must be hard enough for Mr. Brian Robinson to be singled out because of his background; how much harder must it be for the man to be judged by the color of his skin. If the man would accept his friendship, Christopher would be very pleased.

He walked up to the pair of gentlemen and held out his hand first to Mr. Robinson, whom he'd met before. "Vicar, it is wonderful to see you again."

Mr. Robinson shook his hand. "And you, Mr. Moulton. I was telling Mr. Whitman here that you had married our Lady Sarah."

Christopher released Mr. Robinson's hand and took Mr. Whitman's. Up close, he could see that the young man had a great deal of little reddish-brown freckles. "A pleasure. My wife told me that you breed horses."

Grinning, Mr. Whitman needed no further encouragement to speak at length about the breeding lines of his stock. Both Christopher and Mr. Robinson listened attentively and asked several clarifying questions. Sarah had been right again; Mr. Whitman didn't seem to mind Christopher's lack of knowledge on the subject of bloodlines at all. The man was more than delighted to explain everything about them in great detail.

"This is such a lovely estate," Christopher said to Mr. Robinson when the opportunity arose. "I am sure you have many wonderful memories of home."

The vicar's smile fell for only a moment before a forced look of pleasantness pained his features. "Alas, no. I did not grow up at Hanford but in my aunt's home near Portsmouth, and then I was at school and university. I became the vicar only a few months ago, after my ordination to the priesthood. It is one of the livings in my father's gift."

Christopher had put a boot into his own mouth. He should have heeded Sarah's counsel to be careful about mentioning the Robinson family dynamics. "Then, we are both new to the area. We will have to depend on Mr. Whitman here to show us around."

"With pleasure. But please call me H-Harry."

"Christopher."

"Brian."

"Do either of you know the area near Westbrook Park?" Christopher asked.

The vicar shook his head.

Harry sighed. "Not w-well. I'm a bowing acquaintance with R-Ralph Randolph. He was a year or two below me at school."

Whether it was Eton or Oxford, Christopher knew nothing of public education, but maybe he could share with them some knowledge about his specialty. "Sir Oscar is interested in rerouting a river to make a manmade lake. I was thinking about riding out there on Monday morning to get a better idea of the scope of work. If either of you would like to join me, I should be glad of the company."

Brian gave him a genuine smile this time. "I should be happy to."

"As would I," Harry said. "And I shall bring my best stud horse for you both to see. He's a champion and a thoroughbred."

"Do," Christopher invited. "And I am looking for a new horse. Perhaps I could purchase one of his offspring."

Harry clapped him on the shoulder. "I have just the mare for you. She's a sweet stepper and is well up to your weight."

After more talk of horses, Christopher politely left his new friends to find his wife. She was standing near a patch of daffodils and looked as if she belonged in a painting. She was speaking to Miss Iphigenia Wentworth, who must have been a more pleasing conversationalist than her prejudiced mother, for Sarah gave her bell-like laugh. Christopher glanced around and saw Margaret sitting near the two elder Lake sisters. Deborah and Miss Lily were playing a boisterous game of lawn bowling. He watched his youngest sister throw the wooden ball across the grass, and the pins scattered. She laughed in triumph. Her face was bright, and she looked happier than Christopher could remember seeing her. His gaze moved back to his lovely wife, and without thinking, he began to walk toward her—as if she had been his destination his entire life. He just hadn't known it before.

Once he arrived at her side, Sarah moved closer to him. He wished to hold her hand but contented himself with offering his arm, which Sarah readily took. She smelled of flowers and sunshine.

"Christopher, may I introduce you to Miss Wentworth? She has the charming idea of starting a young ladies' sewing circle and would like to invite your sisters to join it."

He bowed his head to her. "A happy thought."

Sarah gave the young woman a gracious smile. "Perhaps you can invite them right now, Miss Wentworth. I am sure Miss Moulton and Miss Deborah would be delighted to be included."

"I shall, Lady Sarah. And perhaps I will try my hand at lawn bowling. It appears that Miss Deborah has not an equal amongst the other girls. I shall see if I can challenge her."

Sarah and Miss Wentworth curtsied to each other, and the younger lady left to speak to Christopher's sisters. He was glad to have a private conversation with his wife.

She leaned her head briefly against his shoulder. He held his breath, but it appeared to be a sign of affection. He exhaled slowly and was disappointed when she lifted her head.

"I see that you were able to speak with Mr. Whitman and Mr. Robinson."

"Ah yes, Harry and Brian are to accompany me to Westbrook Park on Monday."

Sarah beamed up at him. "On a first-name basis already. You are a fast worker, Christopher."

"Indeed. I married you after knowing you for only one week."

Her countenance sobered. "And do you have regrets at the speed of our relationship?"

Shaking his head, Christopher did not fight his smile. He picked up her free hand and gently kissed the top of her glove. "Not even one."

CHAPTER 14

SARAH COULD HARDLY BELIEVE THAT she'd been married to Christopher for longer than she'd known him. Nine days. She supposed, however, that if one's entire relationship was less than a month's acquaintance, it wasn't entirely surprising.

Except that it was.

She had never intended to care for her husband. She didn't wish to love obsessively like her father had. Not that she was in love with Christopher. Nor was she obsessed with him. She merely liked him more than anyone else of her acquaintance. Like her cousin Ralph, he treated her like an equal and not like a silly female who couldn't understand complicated things. But unlike Ralph, Christopher sought actively to please her. Her London suitors had brought her hothouse bouquets and chocolates. Christopher would bring her one solitary yellow flower that he'd plucked when he'd thought of her.

And when he'd returned from visiting Reverand Robinson in the village on Thursday, he'd brought her an entire box of ribbons, tassels, and lace. He said that he had stopped at the village shop, and since he did not know precisely what Sarah would like, he'd purchased the lot, along with a lovely set of threads. It was the most thoughtful gift she'd ever received.

He'd also brought home small gifts for his sisters. He'd given Margaret several sheets of music, and she'd thanked him quietly. Deborah had squealed when he'd handed her five silver bangles. She'd instantly put them on her wrist and danced about the room.

Sarah had discovered that her youngest sister-in-law had quite exuberant spirits. She never walked when she could skip and had great difficulty sitting still. After breakfast each morning, Sarah had begun to teach both young ladies how to play the harp. Margaret picked up the notes and fingerings quickly. Sarah felt confident that Margaret was quite capable of fulfilling her dream to learn more musical instruments. Deborah, however, did not have the patience to listen or to practice the harp, nor the pianoforte. Although, she did have a lovely singing voice and happily sang while her sister played the keys.

This morning Margaret had played a simple piece of harp music perfectly. Deborah was still working on her scales and humming. Sarah doubted the younger sister would become proficient at the instrument. After squirming for most of the lesson, she'd left early to prepare for the arrival of the sewing circle.

Margaret had stayed in the sitting room to practice the pianoforte. Sarah strummed the harp to match the tunes her sister-in-law played. Margaret was a very talented pianist, having learned at school. Sarah could not recall ever hearing a better performer amongst the young ladies of the *ton*. If ever asked to present, Margaret would shine. Deborah was another matter, but Sarah needn't worry about her presentation yet. Younger sisters were not presented into London Society until their elder sister was married.

Margaret played the final chord from Handel. "Will you come to our sewing circle?"

Sarah had not wished to overshadow her sisters-in-law, nor had she much interest in the gossip of young ladies, so she had not attended the first meeting on Tuesday that was hosted by Miss Wentworth. "With such an invitation, how could I refuse?"

The younger woman smiled as she stood up from the pianoforte. "Deborah asked Mr. Wigan to set up a circle of chairs in the blue parlor."

"The perfect room for this time of day. Allow me to collect my kit, and I shall join you both there." Sarah stood reluctantly from the harp. She'd found herself practicing it in earnest when Margaret and Deborah were not there and had hoped to spend more time playing it today. The tips of her fingers had been sensitive at first, but after several days of strumming the strings, they'd toughened up. When she played, she would close her eyes and pretend that her mother was there listening to her. Sarah wished she hadn't ignored the instrument for so many years, because playing the harp made her feel closer to her mother.

Sarah brought her new threads from Christopher to the young ladies' sewing circle's second meeting, only three days after their first. Sarah did not think the sewing circle needed to gather quite so often, but she was fairly certain that the young ladies were simply delighted to have an excuse to get together and gossip. She took a seat but allowed Deborah and Margaret to greet and welcome their friends as the hostesses. She happily set about to alter her wedding dress for Nelly. Not even her lady's maid was better than Sarah with a needle.

"Miss Everett is visiting her grandmother. Should we invite her to join our group during her stay?" Miss Wentworth asked.

Margaret looked up from her sewing. "Who is Miss Everett?"

Miss Lily smirked. "She is only the daughter of a sailor. Her grandfather Mr. Stephens was the vicar before he retired and Mr. Robinson took his place."

The other young ladies paused for a little sigh at the mention of the handsome new vicar.

Deborah stuck out her chin. "If she's the daughter of a sailor, I bet she smells of fish."

The younger Whitman girls, as well as Miss Lily, laughed loudly at Deborah's wit. One of them even made fish lips.

"Besides, there are not enough seats," Miss Whitman said with another chuckle.

Sarah, however, was not amused. The daughter and sister of canal men should not turn up her nose at the daughter of a lieutenant in the navy. She opened her mouth to correct her sister-in-law but then closed it again. Most of these young ladies were nearly ten years her junior. Their ideas and impressions were still forming. It was often easier to laugh with the other girls than be laughed at.

Clipping the end of her thread, Sarah said, "Some women create their positions in Society by tearing other women down. My mother made her mark by building other ladies up, and in my opinion, if there aren't enough seats at the table, then we can always fetch another chair."

The girls did not laugh or smile at Sarah's statement, but Deborah's face turned a dark red. Sarah had not meant to embarrass any of them—only to help them realize that individually they were much nicer than they were as a group.

"There are plenty of chairs at Manderfield Hall," Deborah said at last. "I, for one, would like to invite Miss Everett to join us. I daresay Wigan wouldn't mind carrying in another seat."

"And if there aren't enough chairs, we could always sit on the blankets outside," Margaret added. "The weather is so lovely this time of year."

Sarah smiled approvingly at both her sisters-in-law. They were good girls. They just needed an older woman's experience and guidance. Sarah had said and done many foolish things in her youth, and her mother's gentle reprimands had helped her become a kinder, wiser woman.

Miss Lily clapped her hands. “I should love a sewing picnic. Perhaps at my house next Wednesday?”

Miss Wentworth set down the little dress she was sewing for the poor. “I shall stop at Mrs. Stephens’s rooms today and invite Miss Everett on my way home, if that is agreeable with you all.”

There was not one naysayer in the group.

Sarah left the room to call for tea. Mr. Wigan assured her that he would bring tea and a generous spread of cakes and biscuits for their guests. Walking back from the servants’ quarters, she saw Christopher coming in from the front door. He was wearing his riding coat. The handsome garment had only two capes—many fashionable gentlemen wore as many as twelve—but her husband didn’t need extra padding in his shoulders. He was a strong and handsome man. And every time that she saw him, Sarah’s breath caught a little, and it felt like there were butterflies in her chest.

Smiling, Christopher strode up to her. The fluttering in Sarah’s chest expanded to her belly. She felt a subtle warmth all over by just being near him. “Did you enjoy your ride with Mr. Whitman and Mr. Robinson?”

“Very much. We marked where to divert the river and the path it would take to create Sir Oscar’s lake,” he said, pulling a letter out of his coat pocket. “And I stopped at the postmaster and picked up the mail.” He opened the letter to reveal a poster with her mother’s picture in the middle, including details of where to give information of her whereabouts for a modest fee. He handed it to her. The wood printing was not quite as accurate as Christopher’s sketch, but it was still a remarkable likeness to her mother. “I authorized my man of business to put posters at every port and send copies to our foreign contacts. I am hopeful that someone will send word of having seen Lady Manders.”

Instinctively, Sarah rolled onto her tiptoes and brushed a kiss against his cheek. “Thank you, Christopher. You have made me more hopeful than I have been in years.”

His skin tasted both sweet and salty, and he smelled like the forest. Sarah felt her cheeks flush with pleasure. Her husband’s face turned the same shade of dark red that Deborah’s had only a few minutes before. Sarah wondered how it would feel to brush her lips against his mouth. Their first and only kiss had happened so quickly. Would his beard still feel scratchy on her skin? Or soft like the curls on the top of his head? Would he taste salty or sweet? She realized that she was staring at his lips and forced her eyes away from his handsome face.

"I was wondering if you would like to go with me to meet some of the tenants today," he said in a low voice. "Or another time, if that would be better."

Her husband was as nervous with her as she was with him. A surge of warmth grew in her chest. She could be friends with such a kind and thoughtful man. She might even grow to love him.

Sarah smiled at him and tried not to stare at his lips again. "Your sisters are hosting their first sewing circle, and I don't think they need me. Am I correct to assume that you prefer to ride rather than take a carriage?"

Christopher gave her a curt nod. "Aye. I don't like being closed in."

Sarah nodded. "As it happens, I have sewed myself the most beautiful new riding habit, and I have been itching to show it off. I used some of the blonde lace you gave me for the embroidery work on the bodice. It turned out very pretty, if I do say so myself. If you'll give me a quarter hour, I'll get changed."

His lips quirked upward, but he held in his smile. As she walked back to her dressing room and pulled the cord for Nelly, she wondered why he was so reluctant to show his emotions. Perhaps it was because Christopher was a man. The male sex was supposed to be reserved with their feelings and not wear their hearts on their sleeves. Not that either Uncle Oscar or Ralph had ever attempted to mask their emotions. Everyone knew when Ralph was joyous and when he was miserable. He had always been a terrible cardplayer; he could not keep a straight face. And Uncle Oscar smiled often, usually when something vacuous or nonsensical was said. He delighted in the ridiculous and was affectionate with his wife and children. And with Sarah.

She couldn't remember ever hugging her own father, nor having him pat her head or shoulder, like Uncle Oscar did. Come to think of it, Papa had openly showed his emotions. Mostly his anger. He'd yelled, stomped, punched the wall, and thrown things. When Sarah had been little, she'd been grateful he wasn't interested in being in the same room as her. Sometimes she'd curtsied to him before he and Mama went to dinner, but she never ate her meals with either of them. The only time she'd been allowed to play with her mother before she'd been sent away to school was in the early afternoons.

"Already tired of the younglings?" Nelly asked.

Throwing back her head, Sarah laughed. "Were we ever that small and silly?"

Her maid answered with a straight face. "Sillier."

Sarah nudged her friend with her elbow. "Particularly over a very handsome footman by the name of Guy."

She could see her friend's dimple peeping out as she pretended to be serious. "You rang for me, my lady?"

"Yes, Miss Mills. I need you to try on your wedding gown. I think I've made all the needed alterations. And then I would love assistance in putting on my new riding habit."

Sarah played the maid first and helped unbutton Nelly's day frock and set it on the bed. She carefully pulled the wedding gown over her friend's head. The dress was truly a work of art, and Sarah enjoyed seeing another person wear it. Nelly beamed and looked more stunning than ever. The soft white accented her gorgeous dark hair. She turned around in a full circle, admiring her reflection in the mirror.

"I think I shall bring it in a little here and here," Sarah said pinching the two areas on the side of the bodice that needed darts to better contour to Nelly's frame. "Then it shall be perfect for you to wear in a fortnight. I can't wait until Guy sees you in it."

Nelly twirled around one last time. "He'll lose his mind, he will."

Sarah helped Nelly take off the gown, and she pinned the two places she wished to take in. Then her maid helped her put on her purple riding habit with blonde braided lace in rows on the bodice. It was both fashionable and original. She hoped Christopher would lose his mind when he saw her in it.

CHAPTER 15

Christopher's breath caught when he saw Sarah descending the stairs in her purple riding habit. She looked like a royal princess. Like someone impossibly above him. But with each step down, she was coming closer to his level, and the smile on her lips was for him. He also thought that a bit of her smile was for her own handiwork. His wife was like sunshine and smiled a good deal. He'd come to learn that different smiles meant certain things. Happiness, mirth, ridiculousness, and pleasure. This smile was because Sarah was pleased with both her skills and with his admiration of her work. He doubted even the most expensive modiste in London could achieve such a perfect cut and elegant lines.

He took her hand and bowed over it, before succumbing to the impulse of kissing her gloved hand. Christopher could still feel her kiss on his cheek from earlier. The softness of her lips. The sweetness of her words. She smelled of honey and honeysuckle. He was reluctant to drop her hand. To move even an inch from her.

Sarah twisted her hand in his, and he let go, only she did not. She intertwined her fingers with his. Being handfast felt more intimate than offering her his arm. "Thank you so much for inviting me, Christopher. It was very thoughtful of you. I can hardly wait to introduce you to all our tenants. They are the best people in all of Britain."

"I am sure they are."

Leading her out to the front of the house, Christopher helped Sarah into her sidesaddle before accepting the reins of his own horse from the groom. He thanked the man and swung up into the seat. Squeezing his ankles against the mare's flank, he urged the animal forward.

They walked their horses together side by side. Sarah was obviously in no hurry to reach their first destination, and neither was Christopher. He enjoyed spending time with her. She brightened every room that she entered and made conversation sparkle and bubble like a bottle of champagne. And when she wasn't with him, Christopher found himself wondering where she was and what she was doing. Not that he would dream of interfering with her schedule; he merely wished to bask in her sunlight as often as he could.

"If I may, I shall introduce you to Mr. and Mrs. Watkins first. Mr. Watkins's brother, Guy, as you heard on Sunday last, is to marry my lady's maid, Nelly."

"I shall congratulate Guy the next time I see him."

Sarah giggled, and his heart lightened at the sound. "The person who deserves your congratulations is Nelly. She's been trying to catch Guy for nearly ten years. The poor man finally surrendered and let her have him."

Christopher felt one side of his mouth quirk up. There was something about this part of England that made women bold. Sarah had also proposed to him. He'd been shocked at the time, but he was now glad of it. And why shouldn't a lady be able to propose if she wished to?

"A wise man knows when to let himself be caught by a beautiful woman," Christopher said, winking at her.

This caused Sarah to let out another set of giggles. She was a needle wit and understood his meaning. "I know it has been scarcely nine days since our marriage, but I hope you don't feel like I am being presumptuous when I say that I feel as if I have been a member of your family for much longer."

"I am nothing but pleased," he said, puffing his chest out a little with pride. "You are wonderful with my sisters. I have never seen Margaret so animated, nor Deborah so well-behaved."

Sarah raised her eyebrows. "And how am I with you? Are you pleased with me?"

"You are a lady. How could I be anything but pleased with you?" As soon as the polite words left his mouth, Christopher knew he'd disappointed his bride. Sarah had wanted to know how he felt about *her*, not her title.

Exhaling slowly, she sat taller on her horse. "You please me greatly, and it has nothing to do with this house or with the money in your bank. You listen when I speak. You play silly games with your sisters and me. You are a master at spillikins. You are trying to help me find my mother. And you are very handsome—which should not matter to me, but somehow it does."

Her words made him puff out his chest even more. A lady—no, Sarah, his bride—found him attractive. Even with his rough features, big work-hardened hands, and hidden scars. Perhaps looks should not matter, but they did. "Every time I see you, I think you are even more beautiful."

A smile grew slowly on her face. It was one of happiness. "It's just my fashionable clothes."

"No. It is the person inside them who is beautiful."

"My mother always said that a woman is only as beautiful as she believes herself to be."

His own lips upturned. "Then, believe your husband and know that you are the most beautiful bride and wife in the entire world."

A rosy blush formed in her cheeks, and she grinned for the entire ride to the Watkins' cottage. Christopher dismounted and then put his hands on Sarah's narrow waist to assist her off her horse. He set her feet on the ground and found that her face was very near to his own. He could feel her sweet and warm breath on his lips. Christopher wondered if her heart was beating as wildly as his own and if the sound was loud enough that she could hear it.

"Is that you, Lady Sarah?" a woman's voice called out.

Reluctantly, Christopher stepped away from his wife and turned to meet the person. Sarah placed her hand on his arm.

"Mrs. Watkins, what a delight it is to see you, and you are looking so well."

He guessed the woman to be around his age or perhaps a little nearer to thirty. She had a round, pleasant face with green eyes and a nose with a bump on it. But what stood out the most was that the woman was great with child. Both of her hands rested on her round stomach.

Mrs. Watkins rubbed her tummy. "Any day now, the midwife says."

"Then, I will have to finish your baby's baptism dress this very night. I shall have Guy bring it over in the morning, if that is agreeable to you."

The woman nodded. "'Tis kind of you, Lady Sarah. Most third babes do not receive a pretty new gown for their christening."

Christopher had known that Sarah sewed for herself, and he'd seen the alterations she'd made to his sisters' wardrobes, but he had not known that she used her great skill with the needle for their tenants and neighbors. Even for the third baby of a farmer.

"Perhaps your darling baby could wear the dress again for your brother-in-law's marriage," Sarah said with a wink. "And I was wondering if you would allow me the great pleasure of throwing the wedding breakfast for the happy couple. I know you and your husband would provide a most wonderful party, but I fear that it would be difficult for you so near to the birth of your child."

Few farmers or their wives could compete with a party thrown at a great estate and the food prepared by a professional cook, but Christopher liked how Sarah had couched the request in both a compliment and the idea that the Watkins family was doing *her* a favor by allowing her to help. His wife seemed aware of how the woman of a lower class would feel, and she was careful not to offend her feelings.

Mrs. Watkins rubbed her belly again. "That would be a relief, but I'd like to bring my apple tarts. They're the best in the village."

"And the county, at the very least," Sarah assured her. "But where have my manners gone a'begging? Mrs. Watkins, please allow me to introduce my husband, Mr. Moulton."

The pregnant woman gave him an awkward curtsy, no doubt because of her condition. "Nice to meet you, Mr. Moulton. My man would be pleased to make your acquaintance too. Our new roof is as tight as a pewter bowl. Not even a drop comes through the thatch."

Christopher bowed his head to her. "I will pass your compliments on to my steward, Mr. Pryce."

Sarah bid Mrs. Watkins a merry farewell, and Christopher helped her once again into her sidesaddle. He enjoyed the feel of his hands on her waist and being near her. It was quite his favorite part of the rest of the afternoon.

He met Widow Sears and her son, Mr. Sears, Mr. and Mrs. Fisher, Widower Lewis, and Mr. and Mrs. Dibble. At each stop, Christopher was received graciously, but it was clear that his tenants adored his wife. Not that he blamed them. He was beginning to adore Sarah himself. She was so much more than her title. She was a giver, and her kindness touched everyone around them.

***

Christopher was not particularly excited about the Wentworths' dinner party that Sunday evening, mostly because he'd never been invited to such an event before. He'd done business with merchants and lords, but he'd never before attempted to socialize with either class. The only exception was that he'd looked in at one or two of the tradesmen's balls.

When he'd met Mrs. Wentworth, he had not liked the woman. She'd uttered deprecating comments about his friend. He could only hope the woman would be civil to the vicar when he was her guest. However, Christopher couldn't be certain. He'd seen more than one person give Brian an insolent stare. He rubbed his mustache, grateful that it hid his physical deformity from people like Mrs. Wentworth. Only a small white scar on his upper lip could be seen, and it was less noticeable if he kept his lips together.

Not that his father had ever been able to forget it was there, right underneath his nose and down to his mouth. When Christopher was born, there was a separation underneath his nose all the way to his upper lip. A physician named James Cooke had sutured the skin together when he was only three months old. Christopher remembered the scar but nothing of the surgery. Mama had said that the physician had told her to keep Christopher awake for twelve hours before the procedure. That way he would sleep after the surgery. His mother had also given him some cordial in a bottle to ease the pain.

But he did remember his father's embarrassment over his son's "imperfection." His repaired palate was the reason Papa did not have social pretensions for Christopher. That he'd never expected his eldest son to marry well. Nor did his father originally plan to leave his canal company to Christopher. At eleven, before any whisps of hairs on his chin or lip had grown, Papa had sent him to learn canal work starting as a digger. His parents had purchased a new home in London, and his father did not want Christopher's face to be the reason the family wasn't accepted by the fancier neighborhood. Not that his father had said those words aloud. He'd simply insisted that Christopher learn the trade.

Christopher had not been welcomed back into the family home, in an even more expensive part of London, until his mustache had grown in, covering the scar from his deformity. Only then was he allowed to see his little sisters and grieve for his dead mother and siblings. He rubbed his mustache again. What would his father say now that his imperfect son was married to the daughter of an earl? And the most perfect woman Christopher had ever met? Sarah excelled at everything and was beloved by all. She had kissed his cheek and proudly put her hand on his arm. Even though Christopher was from a lower class, his wife was not ashamed of him. If only his father hadn't been.

But perhaps that wasn't fair. Sarah didn't know the true reason he refused to shave his beard. If she did, maybe she, too, would find him underserving of her affection. Sighing, Christopher thought of his mother. *She* had never blamed him for this face, nor herself for bearing a child with a deformity. Mama had said that God had made Christopher that way and that God didn't make mistakes.

Christopher turned to the sound of footfalls on the stairs. Sarah was walking slowly down, like a queen. She wore a seafoam-green gown that shimmered like the fins of a mermaid. The dress had a high waist and short, puffed sleeves. She wore long gloves that had been dyed the same seafoam green. Her glorious mahogany hair was a perfectly ordered riot of curls with a pearl string weaved around her head. A necklace with three strands of pearls encircled the pale column of her throat. Her brown eyes were luminous when they met his, and she smiled at him. Marrying her had not been a mistake. It had been the best choice he'd ever made.

He held out his hand to his wife, and she placed hers inside his palm. Christopher had never been a dandy and didn't claim to be a swell, but he couldn't resist lifting her hand up to his lips and brushing a kiss on the top of her long green glove. "You look beautiful."

Sarah exhaled, and he saw that there were tears in her eyes. "If you keep telling me that, I might start to believe you."

It had never occurred to Christopher that Sarah might be unaware of her allure or insecure in her appearance. He had not thought her beautiful the first time that he'd seen her. Striking, yes. He'd been drawn to her fashionable clothing and the neatness that characterized her person. Her curly brown locks were her crowning glory, and her facial features had grown prettier with every moment he'd spent time with her. From the first he'd found her attractive, but he was not exaggerating now when he called her beautiful. She was. From inside her large heart to her enticing outside.

Still holding her hand, Christopher placed a second kiss on her glove. "Then, I shall tell you twice as often, dove—I, um, mean Sarah."

His wife blushed at his use of the endearment, and he wondered if "dove" was somehow vulgar.

Sarah stepped even closer to him, until the material of her gown brushed his knee breeches. When she rolled onto her toes, Christopher thought she was going to whisper a reprimand into his ear, but her lips did not reach that far. They brushed against the skin of his cheek, right above the line of his beard. His breath caught. His fingers tingled with the need to touch her. To pull her close to him.

His wife didn't move.

Neither did he.

Christopher wasn't altogether certain that he could move. Her sweet caress had left him immobilized. He felt her warm breath against his beard and then his ear.

"I should very much like to be your dove, Christopher."

His hands tentatively reached for the sides of her waist, and she did not flinch when he touched her. She smiled more warmly at him than she had before. His heartbeat galloped like his new mare in an open field. "May I kiss you?"

Her face turned a shade of pink, but she nodded, the smile never leaving her lips. Christopher took one hand from her waist and gently cupped her face. Her skin was softer than the petals of a rose, and she smelled sweeter too. He leaned forward, and she closed her eyes. His scarred lip hovered a breath away from her perfect mouth. Christopher pressed his lips gently to hers.

Their first kiss as a married couple.

It was more wonderful than anything he'd ever experienced before. He had never felt such pure joy and delicious pleasure. He felt warmth from the top of his head all the way down to his toes—which curled inside of his boots.

"My dress is much prettier than yours," Deb said loudly.

Christopher and Sarah abruptly broke apart.

His wife opened the painted ivory fan at her wrist and waved it at herself. There was a deep blush in her cheeks, and her lips looked swollen. Sarah appeared more enticing than ever, but he should have been intelligent enough to embrace her in a more private setting. One where they would not have been interrupted.

"It's very pretty," Margaret said. "Both of our gowns are."

Seeing his sisters, Christopher thought that Margaret's deceptively simple silver gown was fit for a princess. The new way Sarah had taught the maids to do Margaret's hair flattered the shape of her face. And he could see that her pale complexion had color skillfully applied to it. If he hadn't known her better, he would not have recognized the bit of blush in Margaret's cheeks, nor the black kohl on her eyelashes, nor the bit of carmine on her lips. Sarah or her maid had achieved a most natural look. He'd never seen his sister prettier.

Perhaps that was why Deb was making a point of showing off her own dress, and there was nothing simple about it. The dark-blue gown had several flounces on the skirt and even a flounce on both sleeves. She looked charming, but so young. And the pout on her lips made her appear younger. More vulnerable, like a child wearing her elder sister's gown.

Christopher grinned at his sisters. "You both look enchanting."

Sarah's expression evinced no surprise. She must have assisted his sisters in preparing for their first dinner party. He recognized her special touch in every aspect of their appearance, down to the diamond bracelet on Margaret's wrist. Christopher had not seen it before, and he assumed that the priceless jewels his sisters wore belonged to his wife. He felt a surge of gratitude in his chest for Sarah. She was more than holding up her side of the bargain. She wasn't simply chaperoning his sisters; she was making them feel like family.

"Those who compare themselves to others will always come up second best," Sarah said. "No matter what they say."

Deb's lower lip stuck out even farther as she toyed with the five silver bracelets on her right wrist. "You're only saying that because you like Margaret better than me. You lent your diamond bracelet to her and not to me."

Christopher opened his mouth but closed it again when Sarah waved her hand at him.

She came closer to Deborah, and he expected her to discipline his surly sister. Instead, she unclasped the pearl necklace with three strands from around her own throat and put it on Deborah. "Sometimes I do like Margaret better than you—typically, when you are being petulant or mean to her. However, I *love* you both the exact same amount and consider you to be my sisters. Next time, if you feel slighted in any way, you simply have to tell me, not be unkind or throw a fit. I am more than happy to share my jewelry with you. Remember, there is always room at our table for another person."

He watched his youngest sister touch the stunning pearl necklace. Christopher thought it must be an heirloom of Sarah's family. The necklace appeared to be old and priceless.

Deb's defiant chin angled downward. "I am sorry, Sarah."

His wife placed a gentle hand on Deb shoulder. "It isn't me you should apologize to."

Deb harumphed and did not look Margaret in the eyes as she mumbled, "Megs, I'm sorry that I said my dress was prettier than yours."

He watched Margaret hug herself and shake her head. "I don't mind."

But Christopher *wanted* her to care. He needed Margaret to stand up for herself.

Sighing, Sarah took Margaret's hand. "That school of yours seemed to drum into you the importance of good manners above all else. But in your own home you are allowed to have feelings. You should be able to be angry, frustrated, sad, and annoyed. You are wise to forgive quickly and not to hold grudges, but you don't need to always suppress your negative emotions."

Frowning, Margaret tugged up on her glove. "A proper lady is always pleasant."

Sarah gave a short laugh as she shook her head. "Then, I am afraid I am not proper at all."

Christopher was not the only one whose jaw fell open at this statement from his wife.

Margaret shook her head in disbelief, and Deb said, "Of course you are. You're a real lady, Sarah."

His wife took a deep breath. "Then, proper ladies are allowed to cry and be disappointed and scared. When my mother did not come home that night, I was devastated. You do not have to bottle every feeling inside so that the world cannot see it. If you do that, eventually all your feelings will spill out when you least expect it, like uncorking champagne."

Still fiddling with the top of her glove, Margaret said, "I'd never thought of it that way."

Sarah took Margaret's hand from her glove, letting it fall to her side. "There is a difference between expressing emotion and making a scene. I trust you are wise enough to know when it is appropriate to show your feelings in public and when it is best to wait until you are in private. Now, let us go dazzle the members of our dinner party. I see three gorgeous young women whose gowns are second to none."

Deb laughed and grabbed Margaret's hand. "You are divine in silver, Margaret."

"And you look beautiful in blue," her sister replied, and they strolled out the front door together.

Christopher offered his arm to Sarah. "Thank you. I know Deb can be a handful."

Placing her fingers in the crook of his arm, Sarah smiled up at him. "They are both starved for affection and attention. Deborah is naughty so that she is noticed, and Margaret is good, hoping for elusive praise."

His face felt hot. "I have done my best."

Sarah squeezed his arm. "I am not judging them or you. I know this because I was once the same way. My father never paid me any heed, no matter how badly behaved I was, nor how angelic I tried to be. My mother showered me with love and compliments, and I eventually outgrew the need for attention. I am sure it will be the same for your sisters. Until then, we will both give them extra love."

Christopher nodded, because words would not form in his throat. Like Sarah, his own father had not paid him much heed. He'd been embarrassed by Christopher's facial defect and tried to keep him separated from the other children. Christopher had barely seen Margaret or Deborah before his father's funeral, and then he'd followed through with Papa's request to send the girls to school. Where they would still probably be if Deb hadn't gotten into trouble and he'd swiftly removed them. Perhaps Christopher had been too aloof with his sisters since his father died. Sarah was right. His sisters needed more love. But never growing up with much affection himself, how was Christopher supposed to show it?

CHAPTER 16

Her husband didn't mutter even a syllable during the carriage ride to Wentworth Manor. Not that he had much opportunity to do so. Deborah asked a dozen questions about the dinner party—it was to be her first. She wished to know the order of the evening. How large the house was. Whether Miss Iphigenia Wentworth had any siblings. Who else would be attending the party. And she wanted to know which gentleman would be escorting her to dinner. Sarah knew that Brian Robinson and Harry Whitman were coming, but she was certain that Mrs. Wentworth would include another gentleman in the party to make the numbers between the ladies and gentlemen even.

Sarah thought that Mr. Whitman liked Miss Wentworth, and with a little encouragement, he might even propose. She did not know whether the young lady returned his regard, but she was very much aware that Mrs. Wentworth did not. She wished for her only daughter to marry higher than a gentleman horse breeder. She often talked of going to London for a Season, but the Wentworths had never left Eden, and being practically minded, Sarah doubted Miss Wentworth had either the personality or the looks to succeed in the *ton* marriage market. She was a pretty girl with soft brown hair and eyes, a light figure, and pleasing manners. But her dowry would not be enough to make the difference needed. As Sarah had told Christopher, grand matches required good connections and a great deal of money.

They arrived at the neat and stylish Elizabethan manor with a redbrick exterior and long narrow windows. It was impressive without being large.

The door to their carriage opened, but instead of a footman, it was her cousin Ralph.

"Flames!"

"Freckles," he said, pulling her out of the carriage and into a tight hug. "I've been a complete and utter mule. I shall mind my own business in the future. Forgive me?"

Sarah returned the embrace before stepping back from him. "Of course, Ralph. And you can begin to earn your amends now. I have two beautiful sisters-in-law who need escorting into their first dinner party."

Her cousin chuckled and turned back to the carriage to offer his hand to Margaret and Deborah. Sarah thought she saw a hint of color in his freckled cheeks. Despite calling them cits before meeting them, her cousin obviously appreciated their lovely appearances. He offered each sister an arm and jovially escorted them inside the house.

Christopher alighted from the carriage without assistance. There was a line between his eyes and a look of dissatisfaction underneath his well-trimmed beard. Perhaps even jealousy.

Linking her arm with his, Sarah whispered in an undertone, "It would appear that Mrs. Wentworth is trying to snare a baronet-to-be for Miss Iphigenia Wentworth. How furious that lady will be when she sees your sisters are on his arms."

His mouth curved into his almost smile, and she could see the small scar that marked his top lip. She had the unaccountable desire to run her finger over it. Silly. Sarah and her husband were still getting to know each other, and after only one kiss, she did not dare take such liberties. Christopher was a reserved man, and she wanted to break through his walls. She wished to whisper her own secrets to him, knowing that they would be safe in his keeping. He was a good man and a good brother. And a good husband.

Christopher led her into the house, and they were met by Mr. and Mrs. Wentworth. The master of the house greeted them with a large smile and shook her husband's hand warmly. Mrs. Wentworth curtsied coldly, and Sarah wondered if the woman had only invited them by way of extending the invitation to Ralph. Her cousin hadn't mixed in Eden society before, but he would have done anything for Sarah, and the social-climbing Mrs. Wentworth seemed to sense that.

Unsurprisingly, Ralph escorted Miss Wentworth into dinner and sat on her right. Mr. Robinson escorted Margaret, and they seemed to be enjoying a quiet and serious conversation together. Mr. Whitman led Deborah, and the two were laughing boisterously like old friends. During the meal, Sarah noticed Mr. Whitman's eyes glancing across the table at Miss Wentworth, and the young lady's cheeks turned a pretty pink. Sarah hoped that despite Mrs. Wentworth's machinations, the young couple would tie the knot.

After the dessert courses, the ladies retired to the sitting room for coffee while the gentlemen enjoyed their port and cigars. The coffee was as strong as Mrs. Wentworth's personality and burned down Sarah's throat. Margaret and Deborah sat on opposite sides of Miss Wentworth, and the three girls appeared to be having a lovely chat together, which left Sarah with Mrs. Wentworth.

"How kind of you to invite us to your party," Sarah said, forcing herself to smile. "Your home is lovely."

Mrs. Wentworth sneered. "The new glazing of the windows cost over five hundred pounds." The historical manor truly was lovely, but it was a cottage compared to Manderfield Hall. The older woman was needlessly putting on airs.

"The entire facade is delightful," Sarah said. "I particularly enjoyed the picturesque view of your estate. Do I detect the influence of Capability Brown?"

The older woman sniffed before she smiled. "Indeed. My husband hired a landscape architect from London to design it."

"How wonderful."

Their awkward conversation was cut short by the entrance of the gentlemen. Sarah had never been happier to see her cousin's face, nor the handsome visage of her husband. She left Mrs. Wentworth's side and took Christopher's hand eagerly. He glanced at her in surprise before gripping it tightly.

Her cousin did not miss the exchange. He raised an eyebrow—a family habit. "I take it marriage is going along swimmingly?"

Sighing, Sarah smiled. "It is. Although, we have yet to go swimming." She turned to her husband. "Ralph and I swam in the river that leads to Westbrook Park most days in the summer growing up."

"I recall us splashing together in it only last year. Particularly the deep section by the old oak tree. You should show it to Mr. Moulton, and perhaps he can take you to the spot he marked of where to divert it for the lake. Papa has not forgotten his latest project."

Christopher bowed his head. "I have advertised for workers. A crew should begin digging as early as next week."

"Everybody," Mrs. Wentworth said in a loud voice from the other side of the room. "My daughter, Iphigenia, has been prevailed upon to play the pianoforte for us."

Sarah smirked. Clearly the older woman did not like Ralph speaking to her and not paying court to her daughter. Christopher led Sarah to a settee, and Ralph took the chair next to them. It was the farthest from the instrument and caused Sarah to smile again. Poor Miss Wentworth's cheeks were a bright cherry red, as if she recognized her mama's awkward matchmaking attempts. She sat at the pianoforte and played two songs with nary a mistake. Despite the awkward beginning, she showed the poise of a duchess.

Everyone clapped at the end of the second song, and Miss Wentworth stood to leave the instrument, clearly making way for the other young ladies to perform. Sarah waited for Mrs. Wentworth to ask Margaret and Deborah to display their talents for the group, but the awful woman did not. Instead she said pointedly to Sarah, "Will you play the harp, Lady Sarah? There is no young woman in the neighborhood equal to your skill."

Swallowing, she saw Margaret's ever-ready blush and Deborah's obstinate chin. As a married lady, it was out of place for Sarah to display her talents, especially when there were two young ladies in the room who should have been asked first. Sarah was not about to allow her new sisters-in-law to be slighted by anyone, and certainly not by the likes of a Mrs. Wentworth. "But of course, Mrs. Wentworth. And, if I may, I shall perform with my new sisters. Miss Moulton plays the pianoforte beautifully, and Miss Deborah has the voice of an angel."

Sarah took Margaret's elbow. She whispered into her ear, "Play any song Deborah knows, and I will follow along on the harp."

Deborah met them at the pianoforte. "What are we going to do?"

"I'll play 'The Red, Red Rose,'" Margaret whispered.

Sarah squeezed both of their hands. "I know that song as well. It will be beautiful; I am certain."

Letting go, Sarah sat down at the harp and soundlessly ran her fingers over the strings. She was grateful that her new sisters-in-law had asked for lessons, for a fortnight ago, she'd been quite out of practice. But the fingerings and the notes had come back to her quickly. Margaret played the introduction to the song on the pianoforte, and Sarah plucked and strummed the harp. Deborah began to sing, and her voice was pure and true. Sarah had to remind herself to keep playing her own part; she could have happily listened to Margaret and Deborah perform for the rest of the evening.

She strummed the last note and then pressed her hands on the strings to quiet the harp. Christopher was the first person to clap, and Ralph got to his feet, also applauding.

"Brava, Sarah," Ralph said, his eyes filled with water.

He was the only person in the room who knew she had stopped playing the harp seven years before. He also knew the instrument reminded Sarah of her lost mother, and he seemed to realize the importance of her playing it again. It was healing. Sarah began to feel whole for the first time in seven years.

She glanced at Mrs. Wentworth, who looked as if she'd swallowed a prune. If she'd planned to get Ralph's attention for her daughter, she had failed miserably. His watery eyes were on his cousin and then on Christopher.

Mr. Wentworth politely asked them to perform another song. Margaret chose "The Briery Bush." The three of them were in perfect harmony. Miss Wentworth clapped loudly when they were done and made a point of complimenting them several times, perhaps to make up for her mother's lack of manners.

Mr. Whitman took the seat next to Miss Wentworth, and Mr. Robinson sat between Sarah's sisters-in-law. The only person who seemed unhappy with this arrangement was Mrs. Wentworth. Sarah returned to the settee to hear Ralph say in a low voice, "Mr. Moulton, I have wronged you. And Sarah. I thought she was marrying you only to stay at Manderfield Hall in case her mother returned. But I now see that your marriage is a good one. I have not seen my cousin so happy in years, nor have I heard her play the harp since my aunt's disappearance. If I had a goblet, I would toast you both."

"Perhaps instead you could have a piece of humble pie," Sarah suggested.

Ralph chuckled. "You know I will eat any type of pie, humble or not. Oh, how I've missed you, Sarah. May I visit Manderfield Hall, Mr. Moulton?"

She stiffened in her seat. She was not used to her husband being asked for permission instead of herself. It reminded her forcibly of her parents' marriage and her father's possessiveness. However, it was correct according to societal norms.

Christopher placed a gentle hand on her knee. "You will you have to ask Sarah that. She is the mistress of Manderfield Hall and of her own affairs."

"May I come, Sarah?"

Sarah's heart soared. She'd been right. Christopher was a good husband. "You're welcome at any time, Ralph."

"Then, I shall see you tomorrow morning at dawn."

She laughed, and her entire body felt lighter. Sarah had always been afraid that if she married, her husband would tether her down, control her actions and interactions with others. But Christopher made her feel free.

CHAPTER 17

Christopher knocked before entering Sarah's room the next morning. She sat on her bed with her beautiful hair down. She wore a lovely silk robe and was picking at her breakfast tray. She laughed when she saw him. "I am so glad that it is you, *Husband.* For a moment, I was afraid Ralph had kept his threat of visiting first thing in the morning."

Christopher felt his own lips twitching as he held up several letters. "I went riding with Brian and Harry this morning and stopped again at the postmaster's. He had quite a stack for you."

She patted the bed by her side, and Christopher gulped. He walked jerkily to the spot and perched awkwardly on the edge of her coverlet. Sarah took the letters from his hands and riffled through each one of them.

"Oh, they're all from members of my family. They are sending their best wishes for our marriage and hoping for a bit of gossip," she said and held up one. "This is from my aunt Beatrice. She is the Marchioness of Chapman, and she is hinting that she and her twelve children stay with us instead of Aunt Venetia for our wedding party. They've been rivals since they debuted thirty years ago. May I invite her?"

Christopher gulped again. Sarah had not been exaggerating when she'd said that she was related to many prominent members of London Society. "Like I said last evening, you are the mistress of Manderfield Hall, and you can do whatever you please."

"It would please me to invite my Aunt Beatrice and probably a few other families to stay with us as well, for Aunt Venetia has written that she has even included my second and third cousins in her party," Sarah said, holding up a lengthy page. Then she pointed to the remaining letter in his hand. "Is there any news about my mother?"

Exhaling slowly, Christopher broke the seal and opened the letter from his man of business. He scanned through the contents and saw that the bulk of the information was about canal stocks and shares. He also wrote to inform Christopher that his best foreman, Mr. Sinclair, was traveling to the area to begin work on the Randolph canal and lake with a gang of more than fifty canal men. There was only one line at the end that said no creditable information had been received about the whereabouts of the Countess of Manders. He knew that whenever a reward was offered, unscrupulous or desperate folks would try to give false information for coins, but he was fortunate that his man of business had a good head on his shoulders and could discern creditable information from false reports. He wished he had better news for his wife.

He shook his head. "Nothing yet. But it has only been a week. I am sure we will hear something soon."

"You are right. I am sure it will take some time." Sarah attempted a smile, but it looked sorrowful. Her sadness pulled at his heartstrings.

Christopher wished to cheer her up, not give her further reason to despair. "You'll be happy to know that my finest foreman is coming to supervise the creation of your uncle's lake."

"Uncle Oscar will be overjoyed," Sarah said, but then she hung her head, and Christopher knew he had not succeeded in cheering her. "Perhaps Ralph is right. Perhaps my mother is never coming back, and I am foolish to wait for her return."

Christopher placed a finger underneath her chin and lifted it up so that he was gazing into her eyes. "We will look until we discover the truth. I promise. I will not give up. If you'd like, you and I could travel to the different English ports and ask around in person."

She shivered underneath his touch. For a moment, he thought it might be in revulsion, that she was rejecting him, but then he saw a tear fall down her cheek. "I can't leave Manderfield Hall until she comes home."

"Not even to look for her?"

Sarah shook her head, and another tear slipped from her eye. "I've gone for two months of the London Season for the last five years because my grandfather insisted upon it. But every day, every minute, I wonder and I worry."

Moving his hand, Christopher gently cupped his wife's wet cheek. "Then, we will stay as long as you need to."

"I don't want you to be stuck here too."

Christopher did not fight his smile. He allowed the edges of his lips to curve upward. "There is no other person I would rather be stuck with."

Her eyes shined with tears. "Truly?"

"Well, perhaps your Aunt Beatrice," he said, teasing her. "Ten children, you said?"

"Twelve."

"Good heavens."

Sarah gave a watery chuckle, and his heart jumped inside his chest. "Three of them are grown and married now."

Christopher was reluctant to move his hand from her face. He loved the silken feel of her skin. The way his fingers tingled where he touched her. His eyes dropped to her pink lips, but he did not want to ruin this tender moment. He was here to comfort her, not kiss her. Compromising, he brushed a gentle kiss on her brow.

At last he let her go and got to his feet. "I shall leave you to finish your breakfast."

He walked two steps before she said, "What are your plans for today?"

Christopher spun on his heel to face his wife. "I had thought to ride over to Westbrook Park and stake out the location of the lake. Would you like to accompany me?"

She leaned forward. "Only if we can go swimming first. I have a blue-and-white-checked linen bathing gown with little weights sewn into the hem to keep it from coming up. I can wear it underneath my riding habit."

Christopher had seen other women swimming or, rather, wading into the water, but he hadn't thought ladies did. He was very eager to see her in her bathing gown. "Shall I have a groom bring our horses in an hour?"

Sarah grinned up at him. "That would be perfect, and don't forget your bathing suit."

It wasn't until that moment that Christopher realized he didn't *have* a bathing costume. Men usually swam in the nude. He'd never frolicked in the water in the company of a woman. Nay, a lady. And he had no wish to shock his wife, nor to give her a distaste of him by behaving improperly. He would ask his batman what to do.

Entering his own chamber, Christopher pulled on the cord for Mr. Harris. The young man arrived only minutes later, red-faced and breathing hard. Christopher felt his own color rise. Perhaps he'd yanked the cord a little too hard.

Mr. Harris bowed. "Sir."

Christopher's hand went to his mouth, and his finger touched the scar on his upper lip. "I am to go riding and swimming with my wife. What would be the proper clothing to wear?"

His batman bowed a second time. "I know just what you require, sir."

A quarter of an hour later, Christopher emerged from his rooms feeling like a gentleman, not merely a canal man who knew no better than to swim in the altogether.

He wandered down the stairs and followed the sound of music to Sarah's favorite sitting room. Except that she wasn't there. Only his sisters were. Margaret was playing the piano and singing the alto part, and Deborah's strong voice soared above hers in a sweeping soprano. The entire effect was lovely. Even lovelier that they were working together as opposed to competing with each other. He attributed the transformation between his sisters to his wife and recalled her words about showering them with love and attention. Christopher's mother had been loving, and he could be too.

When his sisters finished the song, he clapped loudly and said, "Brava! Brava! I have never heard a better performance. Not even in London."

A pretty pink stole into Margaret's cheeks.

Deborah didn't blush, but she beamed back at him. "We were rather good, weren't we? The next time we attend a dinner party, Margaret and I will be ready to present with all the other young ladies."

"You don't wish for Sarah to accompany you on the harp?"

Margaret stood up. "Sarah is always welcome. We just—Deb and I thought that she was surprised to be asked is all—as a married woman."

Exhaling, Christopher nodded. Now that he came to think of it, the haughty and horrible Mrs. Wentworth had not asked his sisters to perform—Sarah had insisted that they join her. His wife had ensured that his sisters were not snubbed or left out. It had been his lucky day when his solicitor had suggested that he purchase Manderfield Hall. He had not known then that Sarah would come with it, nor that she would be a constant source of warmth and joy in his life. But she was.

He walked over to Margaret and held out his arm to give her a half hug. He waited for her to acquiesce by moving toward him before he pulled her close to his side. His father had not been affectionate, and Christopher was probably going about it all wrong, but before he could let go of Margaret and hug Deborah, his littlest sister claimed his other side and squeezed him tightly.

Christopher spoke to the tops of their heads—it was easier that way. "I, um, don't always say how I feel. But I want you both to know how much I love you and how grateful I am to be the brother of the two most accomplished young women in the county."

Margaret tipped her head up to look him in the eye. She wrinkled her nose as she smiled. "Did Sarah tell you to say that to us?"

A smile danced on his lips. His sister was as sharp as his wife. "Not precisely. She, um, did mention that it was important to express how I feel to those I love."

Margaret rolled up onto her tiptoes and kissed Christopher's cheek.

Deb copied her and asked saucily, "Have you told Sarah yet that you love her?"

"She is my wife."

"You haven't realized yet that you love her?" Deb pressed. "She makes you happy, Chris, and no one else makes you smile."

Dropping his arms, he stepped back. Christopher admired his wife. He respected her. He was grateful to Sarah for how she treated his sisters and helped nudge them toward womanhood. His pulse quickened in her presence, and he loved how she smelled. Even more, he loved how his fingers tingled with sensation when he touched her silken skin. And when her perfect lips had touched his imperfect ones, the warmth he'd felt throughout his body. He had never known such pleasure, nor such joy.

But their marriage bargain had not been for love. It had been for Manderfield Hall and his sisters. Did Sarah want more from the connection? Christopher was reluctant to offer his heart only to find it rejected. And if his wife spurned his words of love, their perfectly happy existence would be ruined. There would be no more cards, spillikins, or hide-and-seek as a family. The easy and comfortable atmosphere of their home would be stifled and constrained. Christopher had never been so happy before. It seemed foolish to want or to ask for more than what he'd already received from Sarah.

"I believe Sarah is fond of you as well," Margaret said in a quiet voice. "She seems to light up when you enter a room."

He rubbed his mustache and the scar beneath it. "Her countenance is always bright."

"True," Deb said, poking his arm with her pointer finger. "But Margaret is right too. Sarah practically sparkles when you are near her, and I overheard her telling Miss Mills how handsome she finds you. Then Sarah and her maid both giggled like a pair of schoolgirls."

Did his wife truly find him handsome?

Christopher knew his sisters were trying to be helpful, but he could not think of a time when he'd felt more uncomfortable, nor more revealed, with or without a bathing suit. And he hated feeling vulnerable in front of anyone.

He preferred to hide his physical flaws behind his beard and his emotions behind a wall of reserve.

"I am going for a ride to stake out Sir Oscar's artificial lake. I shall be gone for most of the afternoon."

Deb plunked down on a sofa. "I daresay Sarah will keep us company."

Pulling at his collar, Christopher said, "She will be joining me."

Margaret sat next to Deborah and simply raised her eyebrows.

Feeling the heat rush to his face, Christopher turned his gaze away from his sisters and out the closest window. His sisters laughed together, and despite his great discomfort, he was glad they were getting along so well. He hoped Sarah and he would too.

He left the room abruptly, and when he closed the door, he heard more laughter. Christopher hadn't felt so embarrassed since before his first mustache had grown. He'd been teased mercilessly as a child for his scar. One neighbor boy had even called him a monster. He thought of his beautiful wife. How could a lady love a monster? Or an imperfect man like himself?

"What are the girls laughing about?"

Christopher jumped. He had not heard Sarah walking up to him, but there she was at his elbow, wearing her purple riding habit. He was grateful that his reaction had not been to flatten her to the floor with his elbow. He did not like being surprised.

"I am not certain."

Sarah smiled up at him. "Well, giggling is much better than quarreling, isn't it?"

Offering his arm, he agreed. "I believe so."

They walked out of the house, where two horses were waiting for them. Christopher lifted Sarah into the sidesaddle, and the groom handed her the reins. He swung up onto his own new mount and touched his hat to signal his thanks to the groom and for the man to let go. Sarah urged her horse into a canter, and they rode together for a couple of miles before she called to him to turn to the east. Christopher heard the sound of the river before he saw it. The forested area was quite dense with trees and debris. Sarah led them through a dirt path that looked well-traveled, to an area of the stream that appeared deeper and wider than the rest.

She slid off her horse and glanced over her shoulder to look at him. "Ralph and I used to say that this was where bears took their baths. Happily, we never met one here."

"At least they would be clean bears."

Sarah threw back her head and laughed merrily at his small joke.

He alighted from his horse and took both pairs of reins. He led the horses to the river to get a drink before he tied them to a tree. By the time he turned around, Sarah was already undressed—or, rather, ready in her bathing gown. It was a loose, smock-like gown that resembled a chemise. There was a tie at the throat, and the hemline barely covered her knees. Her calves were shapely underneath it. His pulse quickened, and he forced himself to stop staring at her legs. He didn't want her to find him vulgar or unseemly.

Christopher shucked off his coat, which was now a great deal tighter after Sarah's and the tailor's adjustments. He also removed his waistcoat, cravat, and bespoke shirt. He kept his breeches on. Mr. Harris had said that this particular pair would dry quickly after their swim.

Sitting down on a rock, he yanked off his boots and stockings. Christopher saw that Sarah had hung her dress and riding habit on the branch of a tree. Her boots and stockings were stowed tidily underneath them. He put his shoes near hers and picked up his discarded clothing and made a pile of them on the rock.

He heard a splash. Sarah had jumped into the water, and she was wading in farther. He watched until the river reached all the way to her shoulders.

She lifted a hand and beckoned him to come join her.

Christopher usually only swam after spending hours in the heat and sun. The cold rivers had always felt refreshing. Today it did not. One step in and the water was freezing. Gooseflesh formed on his arms, and the hairs on the back of his neck stood up. He wrapped his arms around himself for warmth. He had no wish to go any farther into this river.

"It's colder if you aren't fully submerged," Sarah called, beckoning him again with one hand. "Run in as quickly as you can, and then you won't feel so cold."

Rubbing the bumps on his arms, he was not entirely certain he believed her. But, on the other hand, he didn't wish to disappoint Sarah. Closing his eyes, Christopher ran and splashed until the water passed his hips and then rose all the way to his shoulders. He shivered underneath the water.

Sarah put her hand on his shoulder, and warmth emanated from her touch. "Isn't it refreshing?"

"That's not quite the word I would use."

She let out a gurgle of laughter that warmed his frozen heart, and then she grabbed his arm, tugging him deeper into the pool so that he had to tread water to keep his head above the river. Sarah floated next to him, a smile on her face, and then she splashed him. Christopher couldn't resist splashing her back. She dove beneath the water and pulled on his knees, bringing his face into the cold river.

Resurfacing with a sputter, Christopher dove for his wife. Sarah dodged his grasp and splashed him with a laugh. Never one to give up easily, he chased his wife as she swam away from him. After several circles and splashes, Christopher finally grasped Sarah by her shoulders.

"Now that you've caught me, are you going to dunk me?" she asked, grinning.

He shook his head. "No, I am going to kiss you."

Christopher released his hold on her arms, allowing her to leave or refuse his kiss if she wished to. He closed his eyes and leaned in, waiting for his wife to make the contact between them. He felt her cold arms around his neck, and he thought for a moment that she was going to dunk him again, but then her lips, cold and silky, brushed against his. Over and over. Each time his mouth grew a little warmer, and so did the rest of his body, despite being in a cold river. He wrapped his arms around her waist and pulled her closer to him. Sarah opened her lips slightly, and Christopher deepened the kiss. She tasted sweet and cold, but she warmed him to the very core.

Breaking the kiss, his lips moved to her cheek and made a trail to her chin, and then he nuzzled her underneath the delicate skin of her ear.

Sarah giggled breathlessly. "Your beard tickles."

He stilled. "Do you not like it?"

"Your kisses or your beard?" she asked with another laugh. "I confess that I like them both."

His wife demonstrated how much she liked them by fastening her lips upon his once more. Never before had Christopher felt such a tidal wave of feelings. Deb had been right: He loved his wife. And he even dared to hope that she cared for him too.

Sarah gave him one more heart-stopping kiss before splashing him and swimming away. They splashed, swam, and frolicked for nearly an hour before they made their way to the shore and found a sunny spot in the forest to stretch out and dry themselves and their bathing clothes. Sarah lay down on her back, one arm casually flung across her brow, blocking the sun. Christopher was on his side, perched on his elbow so that he could see her.

"We shall have to bring your sisters. You and I can teach them how to swim," she said.

He nodded slowly. Christopher was glad she wished to include them, but it was very nice to have Sarah all to himself today. Especially when she seemed so approachable. Her hair was wet and messy. Her bathing gown was modest but by no means fashionable. She looked as if she could have been a country girl. The sort of woman that a canal man would court and kiss and marry.

"I should like that," he said.

She gave another gurgle of laughter. "And perhaps we shall come without them sometimes too. We are married, after all."

His face warmed as he remembered their sweet embraces. He gazed down into Sarah's lovely face, to her pink lips tinged with a bit of blue from the cold. How he longed to warm them again for her. "Indeed we are."

Reaching up a hand, she caressed the side of his face, his beard, and then his chin. "I am glad you didn't listen to me and shave off your scruff. You look very handsome with it."

"Even if it tickles?"

Giggling, she nodded.

His heart leaped in his chest. His sister Margaret had not been telling a falsehood when she'd said that Sarah found him attractive. Christopher saw his wife's eyes drop to his lips. She traced his mouth with a solitary finger, and his entire body shuddered. Her soft finger lingered on the line of his scar.

"Was there an accident while you were working?" she asked.

Christopher felt a lie on the tip of his tongue. He could easily blame a shovel, a scythe, or any other tool for the scar. Sarah knew so little about laborers that she would never know the truth. He opened his mouth and then closed it. But he could not lie, even if it meant that she would no longer find him handsome. He wanted only truth between himself and Sarah.

Wrapping his hand around her finger, he lifted it to the top of his scar, underneath his nose, and ran it down to the end of the white line on his upper lip. "I was born with this—with a deformity. When I was a baby, a surgeon put in sutures to connect the two sides of my face together underneath my nose."

He let go of her hand, ready for her to shrink away from him in disgust. Instead Sarah traced the scar once more, her finger gently brushing the hair of his beard. "How painful that must have been. Does it hurt you at all now?"

Christopher shook his head, his scarred lips unable to make words.

Sarah leaned forward and brushed her mouth against the scar. His breath caught, and his heart pounded inside his chest.

"We all have scars, Christopher," she said softly, leaning closer to him. "Not all of them are on our skin for everyone to see. And your scar is nothing to be ashamed of."

He exhaled, then inhaled sharply and asked, "What are your scars?"

She turned her head away from him, and Christopher thought that perhaps he had been too direct. That she would not answer such a personal question. He watched her take a deep breath and then release it.

"The night my mother disappeared—it was my fault," she whispered.

"What do you mean?"

Sarah brought her hands to her face and covered her eyes, as if willing herself not to see this painful memory again. "My mother had learned that Papa had spent my dowry on his gaming debts and that I would have nothing to offer a suitor in the coming Season. She was angrier than I had ever seen her. I don't remember her ever arguing with my father. She never raised her voice before that night. She told him she hated him and that she would never forgive him for ruining my chances to make a good match."

She took another deep breath, and Christopher waited for her to finish her story, even though he already knew the tragic ending. She moved her hands from her eyes to her slender neck.

"My father was obsessed with Mama. He begged and pleaded for her to understand, but she said she never wished to look at him again. Not that I was eavesdropping. Their argument was in the entry hall, for every person in the house to hear. Foolishly, I came down the stairs to assure her that I didn't mind the loss of a dowry—which, of course, was not true. But I would have said anything to make her happy. She touched my face and said that she was going for a ride and that she would be back soon. My father tried to order two grooms to accompany her, like he always did, but my mother refused. She said she needed to be alone. I watched her ride off into the dusk and she never came back. All these years, I have known that it was my fault. If it hadn't been for my dowry, my mother never would have left."

Christopher brushed a wet curl from Sarah's face and gently caressed her forehead. "You didn't waste the dowry, Sarah. Your father did. If anyone is to blame for your mother's disappearance, it is him. You did nothing wrong."

"I-I didn't try to stop her. I didn't do anything."

He brushed a kiss on her brow. "I learned when my mother and my siblings died that sometimes there is nothing you can do."

Sarah shook her head jerkily. "No, my father rode out and looked for her from dawn until dusk for weeks. And I could not even take a step out of the house."

Christopher eased his arm underneath Sarah's neck and pulled her against him. "Dove, you are blameless. Your mother said she would be back, and what could be more natural than for you to wait for her? I am sorry you felt unable to leave the house, but that is no reason for shame."

His wife nuzzled her face into his shoulder. "I wish—I wish I would have done more. Sooner. I was so certain she would return. She never said goodbye to me."

He couldn't resist dropping another kiss into her hair. "I never got to say goodbye to my mother either. She died, and I had been sent away from home to work three years before that."

Sarah leaned back against his arm. "You must have been very young. Twelve? Thirteen?"

"Eleven."

"You were still a child."

Christopher brought his free hand to his scar. "But I was an imperfect child, and my father bought a new house in London and wished to join Society. He did not want me to ruin it for the rest of them."

Sarah grabbed his hand from his beard and squeezed it tightly. "Your father was an idiot."

A surprised laugh escaped Christopher's chest. It was the last thing he'd expected her to say, and yet somehow it was healing. Papa had been an idiot. Christopher had been an exemplary son, and it wasn't his fault that his father hadn't seen it. Besides, he didn't need Papa's approval anymore—he had Sarah's. And her opinion meant everything to him. "And so is yours."

She grinned, nodding her head in approval. "The greatest of idiots."

"We won't invite him to go swimming with us."

A tear slipped from one eye, but she was smiling. "Not that he would come. Papa has cut off all contact with me."

"Maybe it is a good thing."

She blinked. Her lashes were wet again.

"If he were to come to the celebration of our wedding, we might not have the space for him at Manderfield Hall," Christopher said in a straight voice. "Your Aunt Beatrice does have twelve children, after all. Three of whom are married."

Sarah gave a sudden chortle and rubbed her face into his sleeve. "I knew you were a good man, but I had no idea you were such a funny one!"

Christopher gently caressed the side of her face. "We are only beginning to get to know each other."

She took his wrist and kissed the palm of his hand. "Luckily, we have a lifetime to learn every detail."

CHAPTER 18

Sarah's hair had finally dried, but the heat in her cheeks remained. She did not think she'd contracted a cold from her swim. Rather, she'd been grinning and blushing since spending time with her husband. Christopher had listened to her like no one in her life had before. He was sweet. Kind. Funny. Handsome. And she may be ever so slightly in love with him. Having never been in love before, Sarah could not be certain. But if the heat in her cheeks and the inability to stop smiling were any indications, she was entirely smitten.

Tracing her lips, she remembered his warm kisses. The scratchy sensation of his beard and the softness of his mouth. His arms wrapped around her waist. For the first time in years, she'd felt whole. Since her mother's disappearance, Sarah had felt something was missing inside of her, as if she were a puzzle that was put together but lacked the final two pieces. Or, rather, three pieces: Christopher, Margaret, and Deborah. She'd needed a family of her own to love and to care for. And hopefully, in time, she and Christopher would add to their family. Being an only child, she'd always wished for siblings to play with. Ralph had made a wonderful substitute, but he lived a carriage ride away.

She huffed as she thought of Ralph. He'd come across Sarah and Christopher when her husband was staking out the lake and had joined their ride back to Manderfield Hall assuming that he would be welcome. And he was. For the most part. However, Sarah had been enjoying a private tête-à-tête with her husband. Christopher had been talking to her about his canals and the ports where he had businesses. They sounded nothing like London Society, which was the only other place she'd visited besides her school in Bath and the village of Eden. His words had made her wish to travel—to leave Manderfield Hall for just a little while.

Not forever. A couple weeks, perhaps. Certainly shorter than the two months of the London Season.

It would be nice to have a wedding trip without Ralph, Margaret, or Deborah interrupting their time alone. Indeed, her cousin had even invited himself to dinner that night. Ralph had always been welcome before and assumed Sarah would be delighted by his company. She hoped Margaret and Deborah would be the delighted ones this evening so that she could spend more time with her husband.

Alas, he would be at the opposite end of the table.

"No need to pinch them cheeks," Nelly said. "They're as pink as a piglet's and twice as rosy."

Touching her chest, Sarah explained, "While swimming, we bared ourselves."

Her friend winked. "I'm not sure what's so shocking about that. You are married to each other, after all."

Blushing hotly, Sarah pushed her maid's hand playfully. "Not that sort of bare—I meant that I shared the deepest feelings of my soul, and I believe he did too. I used to think love was like an obsession, like how my father treated my mother. He hovered, hindered, and hounded her. But it is not. Love does not trap; it sets one free."

"Free to leave Manderfield Hall?" Nelly asked with one hand on her hip.

"Free to let go of the past," Sarah said. "Christopher told me it wasn't my fault that my mother disappeared, and I needed to hear those words so badly."

Her maid shook her head. "None of us ever thought that it was your fault. Your father may have loved your mother obsessively, but the only person she loved was you. We all knew it as we all know now that if she could have come back, she would have, Sarah. Your mother loved you, and what she wanted for you more than anything else in the world was a husband and home of your own. She would be so happy for you now."

"Truly?"

One side of Nelly's mouth quirked up. "Almost as happy as she would have been for Guy and me."

Smiling, Sarah shuffled to her feet and patted down her lace overlay. "And how many days until your wedding, Nelly? Is it eleven? Have you started to count down the hours yet?"

A blush entered her maid's cheeks. "I've never been very good at mathematics."

"I've already had Cook begin to plan the menu for the wedding breakfast. Your sister-in-law intends to bring her famous apple tarts."

"That's mighty kind of her," Nelly said, biting her lower lip. "Will you be my attendant, Sarah? You're my oldest friend, even if you are my employer and a lady."

Sarah hugged her friend tightly. "I thought you would never ask. I have already planned which gown to wear—it's pretty but a muted blue, so as not to outshine the bride."

Nelly tugged on one of Sarah's curls. "You couldn't outshine me if you tried. I'll be wearing your wedding dress. Now, off with you, and don't forget to flirt with your husband. But try not to bare yourself in public. It's frowned upon in company."

Raising her eyebrows, Sarah said, "I shan't."

She felt as if she were floating instead of walking down the main staircase. Her green silk gown shimmered and moved like the waves of a river. She would need to sew bathing gowns for Margaret and Deborah. Or she could give them her mother's. For seven years, her mother's clothes had been in four trunks. One by one, Sarah had taken the dresses and remade them to expand her own wardrobe as her pocket money diminished to farthings. The last trunk held her mother's favorite gowns. Perhaps it was time to put them to use. Even if her mother returned, Sarah doubted she'd wish for outdated clothes. Bathing suits were a simple affair and didn't change much over time, but the fashion for evening gowns had completely changed. All she could do was make her mother's gowns over or reuse the material and lace. She would ask Nelly to have the last trunk brought to her bedchamber.

Following the sounds of music, she entered the sitting room. Margaret was playing the pianoforte while Ralph and Deborah sang loudly—and, in her cousin's case, a bit off-key. Ralph waved for her to join them, and Sarah, whose voice was nothing special, added her whispery soprano to the song. Christopher came in a few minutes later and joined in with a deep baritone.

Their singing set a jolly mood for dinner, and Sarah didn't think Ralph stopped talking once through all twelve courses. Everyone was laughing and enjoying themselves. Christopher, who had been so select in his smiles, was grinning freely. The only thing that could have made the dinner more enjoyable would have been to be at his side instead of at the opposite end of the table. Still, her chair was not without certain advantages. She got to watch his handsome face all throughout dinner.

After the dessert courses, Ralph suggested a game of jackstraws. "I should warn you all," he said in a conspiratorial whisper. "My cousin Sarah is impossible to beat. She has the steadiest hands I've ever seen."

Deborah stuck out her chin in defiance. "Well, she hasn't played me."

It was only a silly game, and Sarah should have let her sister-in-law win, except that she wished to impress Christopher. Ralph set up the game, and everyone took a turn. Christopher bumped another straw on his first turn and was out. Margaret managed to remove three pieces successfully before she bumped another. Ralph, Deborah, and Sarah had five straws each when Ralph got out. It was only Deborah and herself now. With a steady hand, Sarah removed a straw that was partially on top of another. Happily, it did not move at all. Deborah attempted to take a piece that was touching two others and managed to pull it off, but Sarah thought the bottom straw shifted a little.

Margaret pointed. "It moved. Deborah, you're out and Sarah wins."

Her little sister set down the straw. "It did not. You're just saying that because you want Sarah to beat me."

"Christopher," Margaret said, appealing to him. "You saw Deborah's straw move the one beneath it, didn't you?"

The look of contentment that had been on his face the entire evening was gone. In its place was the old mask of indifference. "It is only a game, girls. One that is rather stupid. Let us do something else."

"It's only stupid because you lost," Ralph teased.

Sarah smirked but wished that her cousin had let the conversation and the game die.

"It is not a stupid game, and I did not move a piece," Deborah said, standing up and stomping her foot as if throwing a childish tantrum. "Margaret was just lying for Sarah. She always has to be the favorite. The teacher's pet. The Goody-Goody-Two-shoes."

What little color was in Margaret's face drained from it. "That is not true."

Deborah stomped her foot again. "You're nothing but an ingratiating toadeater!"

"It is not my fault that you refuse to follow even the most basic of rules," Margaret said, anger spilling out of her voice like bubbling champagne. "At least I didn't kiss the dancing master, which disgraced us both."

Sarah had suspected there was a reason Deborah had left finishing school before she was at least seventeen years of age. She felt a surge of sympathy for Margaret, who had not made any mistakes but had been shamed and punished as well.

Ralph barked a laugh, which might have cleared the tension in the air if he had not added, "I daresay it was a handsome Frenchman with a mustache. Hard to resist that. Sarah had a tendre for her own dancing teacher, didn't you, Cousin?"

Nodding, Sarah tried to hold in her mirth at her own youthful ridiculousness. She needed to soothe the situation and not add sticks to the fire.

Deborah's hands clenched into fists. "Headmistress Mason would never have known if you hadn't told her!"

Red blotches formed on Margaret's face, and Sarah wondered if there was any truth in her sister's accusation. "Mr. Woodeford was preying upon innocent girls. He should not have been anywhere near the school."

"Yet we had to leave, and he did not."

"Because the lecher was the headmistress's nephew, and any fool could see that he was only after Christopher's money. He made up to all the young students with large dowries."

Deborah's eyes widened, and her jaw dropped. "How dare you say such a thing! Mr. Woodeford was not using me. How dare you!" She spun on her heel and ran from the room.

Christopher got to his feet, but Sarah grabbed his wrist. "Let her cool off before you try to speak with her."

"How glad I am that I invited myself to dinner," Ralph said urbanely. "I had no notion that amateur dramatics would be included. I should have brought my costume."

Sarah cast him a dirty look. "Flames, you're being insufferably rude and making everything worse."

Her cousin appeared entirely unrepentant as he got to his feet. "In that case, Freckles, I shall leave you. I confess I would love to see how the rest of this drama plays out, but it is getting dark and I have a long ride home."

"Good riddance."

Ralph blew her a kiss. "Good night."

He bowed theatrically to Christopher and Margaret before leaving the room and closing the door behind him.

Sarah exhaled slowly. "Oh dear."

Margaret grabbed the sides of her face. "It is all my fault, Sarah. Please forgive me. It was just as you said; it bubbled right out of me. For so long Deborah has blamed me for what happened, but I was only trying to protect her. And now I have created just the sort of scene you said not to and besmirched my sister's good name as well as my own."

Christopher moved and put a hand on Margaret's shoulder. "No. You did right looking after your little sister. I should have visited the school more. Written more letters. I should have watched over you better. I failed you both."

"No, Chris. I am to blame. The more I tried to help Deborah, the more she resented me. I was hoping Manderfield would be a fresh start for both of us, but we have fallen into the same silly squabbles."

"No one's name has been ruined," Sarah said reassuringly. "I am certain that Ralph will not breathe a word about your sister's indiscretion with the dancing master. My cousin loves to tease, but he isn't cruel. He would never hurt me or Deborah in that way. We need not speak of it again after tonight."

Margaret nodded, her eyes full of tears.

Sarah stood and pulled her sister-in-law into a tight hug. "I told you to stand up for yourself, and I cannot help but be a little proud that you finally did."

"Hear, hear!" Christopher echoed.

Margaret let out a watery chuckle.

"You protected your sister," Sarah said, "and someday Deborah will realize that. In the future, you must protect her with your silence regarding her mistake."

Her sister-in-law nodded again, and more tears fell from her eyes as she left the room. Sarah knew the argument had been so much larger than over a game of jackstraws. It was years of harsh words from Deborah and silent resentment from Margaret. She only wished it hadn't come to a culmination in front of Ralph.

She turned to meet Christopher's gaze. "I will send a letter to Ralph tomorrow and threaten him with bodily harm if he doesn't keep his mouth shut."

"I thought that my sisters were making progress."

Sarah swallowed. "Maybe they both needed to say how they felt before they can move on and move forward."

"Is there anything *you* need to say before *we* can move forward?" he asked, his tone gentle.

She blushed as she remembered baring herself to him earlier that day. "I think sharing our secret scars this afternoon was cathartic for me, and if you are still interested, I should like to go on a short wedding trip with you after my aunt's party. We can go and see all the canals you helped build. Because of you, I will no longer be tethered to my past."

"What are we to do with my sisters?" her husband asked. "Please say that they are not going to accompany us on our wedding trip."

A gurgle of laughter bubbled out of her. "They can stay with Aunt Venetia. She has a great deal of experience with girls. She had three daughters before Ralph was born."

Christopher leaned forward and kissed her cheek. "Just the two of us."

Sarah wrapped her arms around her husband's torso. "And hopefully we will add many more to that number."

He raised his eyebrows but grinned underneath his beard. "Do you wish for a dozen children like your aunt Beatrice?"

"At least a *half* dozen," she said, then lifted her face up to Christopher to be kissed.

CHAPTER 19

Sarah was snug in bed but was not yet asleep. She was reliving each of her husband's kisses and happily planning which gowns to bring on her wedding trip, which was in a little more than a fortnight. Nelly would be married in a week and a half and would return from her own time off before Aunt Venetia's party. Sarah would have to tell Christopher that they needed a footman to accompany them on their journey so that Guy could come too. It would be terrible for Nelly and Guy to be parted from each other so soon after their marriage.

Closing her eyes, Sarah sighed in blissful contentment until she heard a loud knock on her door. She bolted up in bed. "Come in."

Nelly peered through the crack of the door with a candle that illuminated her face. "Miss Deborah's taken a horse and run away! I was with Guy, and we saw her leaving the stable. This country isn't safe at night, and the miss doesn't know her way about."

Sarah flung off her coverlet and swung her feet onto the floor. "Wake every servant, from the butler to the batman. I want every candle and lantern lit for the search party."

"Right away," Nelly said, closing the door behind her.

Sarah didn't bother with a robe but pulled a loose day dress over her head and slipped on her stockings. Tugging on her boots, she quickly tied them before going through the dressing room to Christopher's bedchamber. He stirred at the light from her candle or the sound of her steps.

"Is everything all right?"

Her eyes burned with unshed tears, and her throat felt scratchy. She shook her head. "Deborah has taken a horse from the stables and run away, and it's my fault. I told you not to go after her. I thought I was giving her time to cool off her temper. I never dreamed—"

Christopher hopped out of bed, and his arms encircled Sarah before she could finish that sentence. He gave her a sweet kiss on her brow. "Nay, dove. 'Tis not your fault. If it's anyone's fault, it is mine. I have been the doting brother and not her guardian. I have not disciplined her or made her change her poor behavior."

Sarah swallowed heavily. "What if—what if she doesn't come back? Like my mother?"

Her husband cupped her face with one hand and caressed her hair with the other. "We will find Deborah and your mother. You are no longer alone. You will never be alone again."

Sniffling, Sarah let out a watery chuckle. "Not with a half dozen children."

With his thumb, Christopher wiped a tear from her cheek. "And a husband who esteems you higher than anyone else in the world."

Her breath caught. Christopher *esteemed* her. It was more than she had ever hoped for. Mama had told her to pick a wealthy and titled man who controlled his temper, drinking, and gambling. The best she had expected was a husband who treated her with respect. She had never considered that she could be esteemed. She hadn't wanted to be loved, if that meant a life like her mother's. One in which her husband hounded her every movement and demanded to know everything she said. But Christopher had taught her that Papa's love wasn't love at all.

Love meant putting a person's needs before one's own, like Christopher had done with his sisters.

Love meant time. Lots and lots of time. Playing hide-and-seek and quoits. Talking about everything and nothing. Swimming in cold rivers and riding on hot days. Attending inane picnics and snobby dinner parties.

"And I cherish you," Sarah whispered.

Christopher brushed his lips against her forehead. "Let's find Deborah."

He released her to pull on his breeches and took off his nightshirt to replace it with a shirt. His buttons were not in order, but this was hardly the time to fix such a thing. Tugging on his boots, he asked, "Who told you she ran away?"

"Nelly. I've had her wake every servant in the house and told her to light every candle and lantern."

Nodding, he got to his feet and took her gently by the elbow. "Deb can't have gone too far."

Christopher opened the door, and they walked down the stairs together. Sarah's heart was beating very fast, but this time she was not alone. She could feel the warmth of Christopher's touch.

Guy met them at the bottom of the stairs. He gave them a sharp bow. "Sir, my lady, all the grooms have mounted horses, and the rest of the servants and gardeners have lanterns. Mr. Wigan has directed them to form a circle around the house and walk straight forward so that every square inch of the grounds will be covered. And everyone has a whistle. If they find Miss Deborah, they are to blow it."

Christopher dropped his hold on her elbow. "Very well organized, sir. I shall saddle a horse and ride with the grooms."

Guy nodded and said quietly, "We have done this before."

"What do you want me to do?" Sarah asked.

Christopher turned back to her and kissed her cheek. "Stay here in case she circles back."

Sarah nodded and watched both Guy and the man she cared for most in the world walk out of the house and into the dark night. The only light in the entry hall were the two lanterns that Mr. Wigan put out every night for her mother. Sinking down until she sat on a step of the main staircase, Sarah couldn't believe that someone she cared about had gone missing again. Perhaps she had been too hard on Deborah. Young girls made many mistakes, particularly when they were trying to fit in with the popular crowd. She'd certainly done many silly things in school. She wanted desperately to teach both of her sisters-in-law that the best way to be accepted was not to be exclusive but inclusive. To dazzle the world with kindness. Mayhap she had expected too much too soon from the headstrong young girl.

Sighing, she thought of Margaret. She did not wish for her to be burdened by guilt for the part she'd played this evening. Deborah had thrown a tantrum, and Margaret, so often the target of her sister's frustrations, had finally stood up for herself. But if they were not able to find Deborah or if she were injured, Sarah knew that poor Margaret would blame herself, just as Sarah had blamed herself for her mother's disappearance. She would need to make sure that she gave Margaret extra love and attention. Christopher had helped Sarah work through her own guilt and made her realize that people were responsible for their own actions. Papa had spent Sarah's dowry. Mama had lost her temper and ridden off without her groom at sunset. The same could be said of Deborah. She was still a child, but she was the only person to blame for running away at night on a borrowed horse in a countryside that she did not know well.

Picking up her candle, Sarah got to her feet and went back up the stairs. She knocked quietly on Margaret's door.

A few moments later, she heard a groggy voice say, "Come in."

Opening the door, Sarah entered the room and saw that Margaret had sat up in her bed.

Sarah went to sit on the side of the bed. "I don't want to alarm you, Margaret, but Deborah has taken a horse and run away. All the servants and gardeners are out looking for her."

Margaret's face paled to the color of milk. "I am to blame."

Sarah took her hand. "It is *not* your fault. Deborah threw a tantrum and then made a poor choice. She is the only person at fault."

"But I—I shouldn't have lost my temper with her."

Squeezing Margaret's hand, Sarah said, "Then, you will apologize when she returns. I thought perhaps you might wish to wait with me downstairs until we have any news."

"Of course."

Margaret put on her robe, and the pair returned to the main hall. It was eerily shadowed in the night. The only sounds were the steady ticks of the wound-up clock. They sat on two chairs by the window and watched, waiting for news. Sarah could see little lights in the distance getting farther and farther from the house.

One hour passed.

Then two.

Despite the hour being well after midnight, Sarah was wide awake, her heartbeat quick and unsteady.

Another hour passed.

Sarah rocked back and forth in her chair, even though it was not a rocking chair. She could not seem to hold still.

Nearly another hour had passed when Mrs. Harmony and Nelly led the servant women back into the house. Sarah got to her feet and rushed to her side. "Did you find her?"

Her dear maid shook her head. "She's not on the grounds. We searched every cranny from the house to the outer fences. She may be in one of the fields, but the dogs caught her scent close to the road. Mr. Moulton and the grooms are searching the south area, near the forest and the main pike road and the river."

"And they sent you back to the house?"

"Yes, my lady," Nelly said, using the honorific. "We women are exhausted, and there was nothing else we could do right now. Not in the dark."

Sarah touched her friend's arm. "Of course. You were right to come back. Go to bed and sleep in as long as you need."

Mrs. Harmony curtsied to her. "We'll be up with the dawn to keep searching. Don't you worry, Lady Sarah; we will find her this time."

In her mind, Sarah added, *Not like last time.* Mechanically, she thanked them all and watched as they shuffled to the back of the house to take the stairs in the servants' quarters to the attic. The poor women looked exhausted and still needed to climb two flights of stairs.

Where could Deborah have gone? What had she hoped to prove by tonight's escapade? How were they going to find her?

Margaret got to her feet and walked toward Sarah. "Should we go to bed as well and search for Deborah in the morning? Tomorrow I wish to be useful and not simply sit and wait."

"Of course."

Her sister-in-law went to the stairs and took them slowly, step by step. Sarah watched until Margaret was out of sight. She was right. Sarah needed to be useful. She had sat for seven years waiting, and it hadn't done herself nor anyone she loved a lick of good. She put on her coat and Deborah's scarf, and picking up her candle, she left the house.

The night was full of the sounds of insects and creatures. Her candle cast eerie shadows on her path to the stables. She saw that most of the farm animals were still in their stalls, except for the horses. The only mare left was her own mount. Sarah did not have a great deal of experience putting on a saddle or getting on the back of a horse by herself. Ladies did not learn such useful skills. However, she'd been particularly horse-mad as a young girl and had watched the grooms perform those tasks hundreds of times.

Setting her candle in a safe place away from the hay, she turned to pick up the saddle. It was a great deal heavier than she'd expected, but she managed to lug it to her mare's stall and over the gate that held her in. Opening the stall, Sarah put a blanket and then the saddle on the back of the horse, only to realize that she'd done it backward. Huffing, she maneuvered the saddle around and fastened it underneath her horse's belly. She checked the strap twice. The last thing Christopher and their staff needed was for two women to have mishaps in the same evening.

Once certain that the saddle was secure, Sarah led her horse out of its stall and blew out the candle. Luckily, it was a full moon tonight and there wasn't an inch of Manderfield that she hadn't visited. It had been her beloved home and her beautiful prison. Sarah used a wooden box to climb onto the back of her horse. She was not quite securely on top when she realized that the saddle was not a female one but a male one. She'd only ever ridden side-saddle, but she didn't have the time or energy to start again with a different saddle. Lifting one leg over the other side of the horse, Sarah held on tightly to the reins and the pommel. If men could ride astride, she certainly could.

Squeezing her ankles, she urged her mare out of the stables and into the darkness of the night. She did not need a lantern to know which road went south. It was the way to her aunt Venetia's home, and she thought she could have ridden it blindfolded. Her horse galloped for over three miles before she saw the lights of the grooms. They were near the forest, a dangerous prospect in the dark.

She rode up to meet them and saw her husband. Christopher's eyes widened, and his mouth opened slightly.

Sarah spoke before he could. "I had to help. I *had* to this time. I couldn't wait any longer."

He bowed his head. "Be careful."

"I know this area better than anyone here."

Mr. Phipps grunted. "That's true enough. You and Master Ralph ran in and out of the forest like a couple of heathens when you were younger."

Holding the reins, Sarah asked, "Why have the dogs stopped?"

Guy doffed his hat. "They've lost her scent, milady."

Sarah pulled off Deborah's scarf. She only hoped her own scent hadn't covered her sister-in-law's. She handed it to the man. "This is Miss Deborah's."

Guy accepted the article of clothing and stooped down so the dogs could smell it. The hounds howled and began to move. Sarah was the first to follow them on her horse, and she had to duck to miss the branch of a tree as they entered the forest. It was a dangerous time to be in unknown terrain. The dogs were leading their party deeper and deeper into the forest, until Sarah could barely see the moon or the stars.

The dogs barked loudly in a clearing, and Sarah saw a shadow. She recognized a horse from the stables. She cantered to meet it only to find it riderless. Deborah was nowhere to be seen. Sliding out of the saddle without assistance was difficult even whilst riding astride. Sarah landed unevenly on the ground and would have lost her balance if she had not been holding tightly to the pommel. She walked over to the other horse and touched its nose before taking its reins and checking the saddle. It was not in the center of the gray's back but was tilted to the side. Perhaps Deborah hadn't secured it tightly enough. Maybe she'd fallen off. The dogs continued to howl at the horse.

"Any sign of her?" Christopher asked, his own chestnut snorting and huffing from exertion.

"I believe she was on this horse."

"You would be right, milady," Mr. Phipps said.

Christopher cupped his hands together and yelled, "Deborah! Deborah! Deborah!"

Her name echoed in the wind, but they waited for several minutes without hearing a sound. Deborah was either too far away or too injured to answer them.

"What do we do?" Sarah asked.

Christopher slid off his horse and took her hand. "We keep looking."

She nodded and was grateful for his assistance as he helped her mount her mare. She would not have been able to do so without him.

"The river is not far from here," Sarah said, gripping the reins. "Let's water the horses. The sun will be up in another hour, and we can keep looking."

Guy tipped his hat to her. "A good plan."

"Aye, milady," Mr. Phipps said.

Sarah saw that her husband was the last man to mount his horse. Swallowing despair down her throat, she led the thirsty men and animals to the river.

CHAPTER 20

Christopher splashed cold water on his face. He had never been so exhausted and yet so awake. Fear crept down his spine. He had believed they would have found Deborah by now. He didn't think she'd left the estate, but he'd been wrong.

Wrong about so many things.

His sisters didn't need a brother; they needed a guardian. A father figure. And since their own father had passed, it was his responsibility to protect and guide them. He had married Sarah hoping that she could curb Deb's temper and improve her manners, but the responsibility had always been his. Christopher had been hesitant to criticize his sister or to take her to task for her mistakes. His father had seen only Christopher's foibles and physical deformity, never his heart or hopes. But love required both caring and correction. He would do better.

Christopher watched Sarah pet her horse's mane. Her dress was rumpled and her hair a mess. Besides swimming, he'd never seen her appear anything but pristine and perfect. She looked more approachable like this. Less like a lady and more like his wife. Her eyes looked puffy and tired, but she had not gone back to sleep. She had come to help find his sister. Christopher didn't blame her one whit for Deb's behavior. The two people who were culpable were himself and Deborah. He knew his wife cherished him and that this was one of the reasons she was here. She also cared for his headstrong and wayward sister. But the primary reason she'd come was because she hadn't been able to find her mother; if she helped find Christopher's sister, perhaps she could finally close that sad chapter of her life.

His stomach rumbled with hunger.

Sarah gave him a tired smile and then a little laugh. "I suppose we are both a little worse for wear this morning, Husband."

Christopher felt a surge of warmth and happiness at that one word: *husband.* "I have drunk straight from a river, something, as a canal man, I would never recommend doing. But needs must."

Letting go of the reins of her horse, Sarah came toward him and began unbuttoning his shirt, which was askew. She lined up the garment correctly and rebuttoned it for him. Her gloved hand patted his chest. "There."

He covered her hand with his own. "Sarah, I can't begin to tell you how much it means to me that you are here. Your presence fills me with strength."

She raised one eyebrow. "And hope?"

Christopher picked up her hand and brought it to his lips. "Enough hope to fill up the world."

"We'll find her. I feel it in my heart."

He continued to hold her smaller hand in his. "And I in mine."

Yawning, Sarah pointed to the first tendrils of light filtering through the leaves of the forest. The sun was beginning to rise. Their search would be much easier in the light. "I think we should form a line from the river to the pike road. There are enough of us that we should be able to space ourselves every fifteen to twenty feet. And I believe we should follow the river. The horse Deborah took did not bolt back to his stall, so he must have been confused about where he was. I assume, although I could be wrong, that he lost his rider closer in the forest to Manderfield Hall."

Squeezing her hand, Christopher nodded. "I cannot think of a better plan to find her. You are good at everything you do, Sarah. You would make an excellent canal foreman."

His wife raised both of her eyebrows. "Are canal foremen allowed to swim with their husbands?"

Rubbing his beard, Christopher shook his head.

"Then, I am not interested."

He felt his lips twitch upward. "Still, I am grateful for your organizational skills. Allow me to help you onto your mount, dove."

He cupped his hands for her, and Sarah placed her boot inside them. He lifted her up onto the back of her horse, and once she had the reins, he swung up onto his own steed. Christopher nodded to Sarah, and she explained her plan to the grooms and Mr. Phipps.

Mr. Phipps squashed his hat back onto his head. "'Tis a good plan, Lady Sarah."

Christopher and Sarah rode about fifteen feet apart in the middle section, the grooms flanking them. Christopher urged his horse into a steady walk. It was better to be thorough than it was to be fast. Having worked near harbors and in the canal business, he knew that if one did not find a missing person in the first day, the chances of ever locating them were small. The world was a dangerous place, and naval-press gangs were known to prey upon those who were alone. But Deborah was not a man, nor was she alone, and the sort of madams who preyed upon innocent young girls were, thankfully, not to be found in the middle of Warwickshire.

"Deborah!" he called, but there was no response besides the twittering of the birds.

He swallowed down his fear and made his mind focus on looking at every tree, rock, nook, and cranny. His sister might be hurt or incapable of speaking. Christopher's heartbeat quickened, but he forced himself to keep a steady pace. He could see Sarah on his right side and Mr. Phipps on his left. He needed to stay with the line.

It took nearly an hour to go a mile in the thick bush of the woods, yet they were still no closer to finding his sister. The trees were closer together in this section of the forest, and it had several steep drop-offs. Tugging on the reins of his horse, he led the animal around a large rock. He now understood why the locals kept to the trails, like the path that Sarah had taken over to the river.

He heard a mewling sound, and at first, he thought it was the trill of the river gliding over the rocks, but the closer he got to it, the more certain he was that it was human.

"Deborah," he called again.

Bringing his horse to a halt, he listened intently for over a minute before he heard her reply. "Chris! Chris, help me."

His sister sounded like she was still far away from him. He pulled the roughhewn wooden whistle that Mr. Phipps had given him and brought it to his lips. Breathing in deeply, he let out three loud blasts of air.

Sarah was the first person to come to his side. "Did you find something?"

"I heard her. I think she must be somewhere near."

A tear ran down her cheek as she smiled. "I am so relieved."

"As am I." Leaning over, he brushed away her tear.

Mr. Phipps, Guy, and the five grooms arrived shortly after, and Sarah suggested they get off their horses and walk—they would be less likely to miss Deborah that way. Taking the reins of his tired chestnut, Christopher continued forward slowly with Sarah at his side. After nearly five minutes of walking, he stopped and called again. "Deborah, where are you?"

"I'm in a pit, and I have turned my ankle, Chris. I cannot stand or get out." Her voice was louder and clearer now.

Guy pointed northeast. "Her voice came from that direction of the forest."

The group turned slightly and continued forward, the brush so thick that Christopher could barely walk through it, and his poor chestnut struggled to follow him. He watched as Sarah's skirts kept getting caught in the undergrowth, but she didn't stop, nor slow down; she merely kept forging ahead. The bottom of her dress now had more burrs than flounces.

Christopher cupped his hands together. "Deb, keep talking so we can find you."

"I tumbled over the neck of my horse onto some sharp rocks and then fell down this horrible hole," Deb said, her voice stronger. "My whole body is covered with dirt and bruises—but that isn't the worst part. I felt something strange at the bottom of the hole in the night, and now that it is light, I am in a filthy pit with a skeleton. Did you hear me? A skeleton! Nothing but rags and nasty old bones."

He was grateful for the loud voice of his sister, but when she said "bones," he felt a shiver crawl down his neck. He prayed the skeleton belonged to a peasant from hundreds of years before, but he feared that they may have finally found the Countess of Manders. His eyes darted to Sarah, but her face showed only relief. His wife had not jumped to the same conclusion; perhaps he was merely being fanciful. He hoped he was.

"Is there anything in the pit with you besides the bones?" he asked.

"Mud and muck. It smells like a barn. I haven't been able to get one lick of sleep all night long."

Neither had he or any of their servants. He did not have much compassion for Deb's sleepless state, nor did it seem that she had any thoughts about how her actions had affected those around her. And it was Christopher's duty to teach her.

Following her voice, they found his sister in the bottom of a sinkhole. He pulled back the green overgrowth that covered the pit from their view. It was nearly eight feet deep. Deb was right; it was smelly, and there was a skeleton on the side opposite his sister. Without her voice, he never would have seen the sinkhole, as it was surrounded by a cluster of granite boulders and three thick trees. He wasn't surprised that his little sister had said she was covered in bruises. It was a miracle that she had survived such a fall.

"Can you stand up, Deborah, and take a rope if we lower one to you?" Sarah asked. "Or does someone need to lift you out?"

His sister stuck out her chin defiantly. "I don't need your help, *Lady Sarah*. This is all your fault!"

Christopher glanced at his wife and saw red blotches on her neck—he doubted she had ever been insulted to her face. "Well, I suppose that if you don't want Sarah's help, we will just leave then," he said.

Sarah stepped back from the pit.

"Chris! You wouldn't!" Deb shrieked, a slight tinge of fear in her voice.

Leaning over the sinkhole, he looked his sister in the eyes. "Yes, I would. For once in your life, Deborah, take responsibility for your own actions. Your foolish temper tantrum nearly cost you your life, and you have not taken one moment to think what grief your behavior has caused those around you. No person here has slept. They have all worked through the night, desperate to find you, and I have yet to hear one word of thanks or acknowledgment for their sacrifices."

"They're servants. It's their job."

Grimacing, he shook his head. "Servants are people, Deborah. Hardworking employees who should have received a good night's rest and not spent it searching the woods for a spoiled young lady who thinks only of herself."

His sister started to cry. "Papa would not have spoken to me thus!"

"No, he spoiled you, and so have I, but no longer. If you wish for help, you must ask for it nicely. But first you must thank every person here for their efforts in finding you."

Wiping her eyes with her dirty hands, Deb spread the muck on her face. "All right! Sarah, thank you for looking for me—even though I never would have run away if it hadn't been for you turning Margaret's head."

"Deb," Christopher warned her.

She rubbed her running nose. "Thank you, Mr. Phipps, Guy, and the other grooms whose names I do not know. I can imagine if your night was half as awful as mine, it was wretched. And I am sorry for it."

"Now will you answer Sarah's question?" Christopher said. Her apologies left much to be desired, but they were a start. "Can we lower down a rope, or do you need someone to lift you?"

Deb pushed off her hands and tried to get to her feet, only to fall back into the muck at the bottom of the sinkhole. She whimpered. "I think someone will need to help me out."

"Phipps, if you would get out your rope and tie it to the pommel of your horse," Christopher said. "Deb, scoot back as far as you can to that side. I'm coming down."

Guy put a hand on his arm. "You're our employer, sir. One of us lads can go down the hole."

"Thank you, Guy. But I would never ask an employee to do something I was not willing to do myself."

Sitting down on the edge of the hole, Christopher turned and put his elbows down to bear his weight. He lowered his legs, keeping his hands and forearms on the ground, grasping the grass for some sort of hold. His feet still dangled, so he eased his arms over the side until he only held on with his fingers. Kicking the side of the hole with his boot, Christopher let his body drop. It was only a couple feet, but the impact jarred his exhausted form.

He felt two arms wrap tightly around him. Deb had managed to get onto her one good foot, and she was hugging him tightly. A surge of warmth filled his heart. He would love and protect Deb for the rest of his life. And as her guardian, he would help her become the very best version of herself. He turned around and hugged her back.

"I'm so sorry, Chris." She sobbed against his chest. "I didn't think. I was just so embarrassed, and I wanted to get away."

"And hurt us a little too."

Deb nodded with another wail.

"You are going to need to learn to control your temper and keep harsh words to yourself. Margaret is not your whipping post, and I have allowed her to be for too long. You're right; she isn't your mother. And I am not your father, Deb, but I am your guardian. Sometimes I will need to correct you. Not because I don't love you but because I do. We will all need to do better, and I know that we can, together."

Rubbing her face against his shirt with the perfectly straight row of buttons, Deb whimpered. "Sarah won't forgive me, and now I've gone and ruined my good name."

He tipped her chin up with one gentle finger. "Sarah has been out all night looking for you. That doesn't sound like the sort of person who won't forgive you. Will your escapade cause gossip and possibly a few snubs from local society? Yes, yes, it will. But this time, we will not run away from the consequences, like I did when I took you out of school. The headmistress wanted to discipline you, and instead I removed you from the situation. The fault was mine, and you didn't learn your lesson. But you will this time. We both will."

Deb's eyes and nose were running freely, as well as being very dirty. She appeared very young and very sorry. "Will I never find a good match now?"

"Deb, you are only sixteen years old. Still a child. By the time you debut, all of this will have been forgotten. In the meantime, I would love nothing more than for you to be a part of my and Sarah's family. And we are in no rush to lose you to a handsome young duke with more estates than names."

His sister let out a watery chuckle. "I should like to marry a duke."

"Sarah and I will do our best, but let us enjoy you for several more years first."

Deb squeezed him again, this time tighter than before. He put his arm beneath her shoulders and lifted her to where Mr. Phipps had lowered the rope. Wrapping the cord underneath her arms but high on her chest, he tied a sailor's knot. "Pull her up gently."

He lifted his sister as the horse pulled the rope tight. Guy and another groom met Deb at the top of the pit and carefully lifted her out. She immediately thanked them, and Christopher felt proud of her. After untying Deb, the grooms threw the rope back down. Christopher did not tie it around himself but rather around the skeleton. Countess or commoner, this woman deserved a proper burial. The bones were light and held together with the remnants of a tattered dress, its original color no longer recognizable from the elements. The men lifted the skeleton up in a trice. Christopher felt relieved when the rope was lowered a third time, and he carefully tied it around his upper chest. "And up."

Rather than being hog-tied and dragged up the side of the sinkhole, Christopher put his boots on the side of the boggy dirt and climbed his way out of the pit as the men pulled. The first person he saw was his wife, tears streaming freely down her face as she knelt not by Deb but by the skeleton. Smelly and dirty, Christopher untied himself to kneel and put an arm around her. There was something in her hand. She turned it over, and Christopher saw a grimy green necklace. In its current state, it was impossible to guess the trinket's value.

Sarah wiped off the green slime on the top to reveal an engraving. "My mother always wore it around her neck. It's a locket with the Denham family crest. My father gave it to her on their first anniversary. I remember her wearing it that dreadful night that she left."

Christopher gently removed the necklace from the skeleton. He was no physician, but he could see that the late countess's neck had been broken. "Your mother's death would have been instantaneous. She would not have felt any pain."

"What happened to her?"

Sighing, Christopher shook his head. "I doubt we will ever know the entire story, but we do know that your mother never left you and that she always meant to come back to you."

More tears fell down her cheeks as Sarah nodded. "She did. She loved me."

Christopher wrapped his arms around his wife and simply held her for several minutes. He could have cradled her close to him for hours, if Deb hadn't made a sound of pain. "Mr. Phipps," Christopher said, "would you see that my sister is brought back on my horse to Manderfield Hall and a doctor called? Guy, would you take one of the saddle blankets and carefully wrap up these remains and bring them to the vicar? The Countess of Manders deserves a proper burial and funeral. The rest of you, once you've taken care of your horses, feel free to go back to sleep, and tomorrow I will give you all an extra week's wages for tonight's work. Lady Sarah and I will follow in a little while."

Quietly everyone left to do as he asked. Even his strong-willed Deb.

Christopher, covered in muck, sat on the forest floor and held his wife until she had no more tears to cry. He caressed her hair and whispered soft words of assurance. He'd been devastated when he'd learned of his own mother's and brothers' passing and that they had been buried without his attendance. There was nothing he could do for his wife but be there for her through her grief. Unlike himself, she would not be alone. And, holding her closer to his chest, he knew that thanks to Sarah, he would never be alone again either.

CHAPTER 21

It did not surprise Sarah that her father came to her mother's funeral. He had loved Mama in his obsessive way. Papa had been surprised to learn that the memorial service was for both the Countess of Manders and the late Mrs. Moulton and her children. When Sarah had spoken with Mr. Robinson to prepare for the meeting, she'd felt a prompting to include her husband's late family members. The service, she knew, would help give her closure with her mother's death, and she thought that perhaps Christopher needed that too. Unlike his father, Christopher's mother and little brothers had loved and accepted him as he was.

Mr. Robinson was certainly a young man, but Sarah felt moved by his sermon. In his short life he must have experienced a great deal of sorrow, or he was naturally gifted with empathy. Either way, he was an exemplary vicar. Her heart lifted as he read Isaiah 25:8: "He will swallow up death in victory; and the Lord God will wipe away tears from off all faces."

Many tears had fallen down Sarah's face, but she didn't mind them. Christopher held her left hand throughout the service and Aunt Venetia her right. Smiling through her tears, Sarah wondered which person had cried more—herself or her aunt. Cousin Ralph continually supplied them with fresh handkerchiefs; clearly he had prepared for how they would both behave. Deborah and Margaret sat on the other side of Christopher. Margaret, per usual, was a pattern card of perfection. Deborah looked surly, but perhaps it was her best attempt at being somber.

Christopher had asked Mrs. Harmony to give him a list of every person who worked at Manderfield Hall and requested Deborah write them all a separate note of thanks for their part in her rescue. Sarah's own note had been short, but she'd felt it was sincere.

After the services, Aunt Venetia hugged Sarah at least a half dozen times. "I am so, so sorry my dearest niece. I know that you have hoped for so long, and I prayed that my sister was still alive for your sake."

Sarah squeezed her aunt back. "As did I. But I find comfort in discovering the truth. Knowing is better than hoping, even if the result was not what we wished for."

Aunt Venetia cupped Sarah's cheek with her hand. "You have always been wise beyond your years. If there is anything I can do for you, let me know. It will be done."

The corners of Sarah's lips curled up. "What if I asked you to chaperone two delightful young ladies for a couple months? Christopher and I wish to go on a wedding trip."

"But what about my wedding party?" Aunt Venetia asked. "I've already sent out all the invitations, and everyone is coming. Even your ornery great-aunt Eunice."

One person Sarah wouldn't have minded refusing. "We plan to leave directly after the wedding party, Aunt. Indeed, Christopher and I are looking forward to celebrating our marriage properly."

"With cake. All proper weddings must have cake."

Despite the circumstances, Sarah grinned. "Of course. And I do believe you mentioned a most interesting tradition regarding the crumbling of the cake."

Her aunt smiled back at her and dabbed once again at her wet, red eyes. "Is it a good marriage, Sarah?"

Glancing over her shoulder, Sarah looked at Christopher standing with one arm around each of his sister's shoulders. Her heart felt full. She had a family of her own. "The best marriage."

"Excellent. I always liked his broad shoulders and his wealth. Your uncle says your husband's fortune is over half a million pounds in total."

Suppressing a giggle, Sarah solemnly agreed that both were very fine features of her dear husband. Aunt Venetia gave her one last embrace.

Then Uncle Oscar hugged her and kissed the top of her head. "The workers began digging the canal yesterday. In a matter of weeks, I shall have my lake."

A memorial service was hardly the time to discuss the creation of a canal with the sole purpose of forming a manmade lake. But people were messy, imperfect creatures, and Sarah loved her eccentric uncle just as he was. "I am delighted for you."

She turned to say goodbye to Ralph and was swept up into his arms and spun around the church. Her lips were smiling when he set her feet on the ground. "Christopher told me all about your trip. If it weren't a wedding journey, I would invite myself to join you."

Sarah loved hearing her husband's name on her cousin's lips. Ralph finally saw Christopher's worth. "That might be a tad awkward."

"Only a tad," Ralph said with a wink. "You and I were once an adventurous pair, but life happened, and you have been a kind and dutiful cousin. But I have missed the old you, and I see glimpses of her when you are with Christopher. Go and see the world like we always planned. Manderfield Hall and I will be here when you get back."

"You think you mean more to me than Manderfield?" she teased.

Not rising to her bait, Ralph shook his head. "I know I do. And that pair of sisters-in-law. Do not fear that I will say anything to hurt their chances in Society. Family squabbles should be kept in the family."

Sarah touched his arm. "Thank you, Ralph."

"Aunt Louisa loved you more than anyone else in the world, Freckles, to the very end."

Touching her mother's locket, which Nelly had polished back to perfection, tears filled Sarah's eyes as she nodded. "I know, Flames. I know."

Still holding the necklace, she thanked everyone in the neighborhood who had come to support her and Christopher. None of them had known her mother well, for Mama hadn't socialized with the gentry, but that didn't matter. Funerals were more for the living than for the dead. Sarah was grateful to have so many friends.

One by one they left. Her mother's bones were properly interred in the cemetery. It would be several months before her monument would be completed. Next to her mother's grave, Sarah had commissioned a second stonemason to create a statue in honor of Mrs. Moulton, John, Fred, and Francis. She wished Christopher knew where they were buried, but at least there would always be a place close to their home to remember them.

Her father was the last person to speak to Mr. Robinson and then to her. Up close he looked older and grayer. Wrinkles surrounded his eyes and mouth, and there was a sallow color to his skin, as if he'd been drinking too much.

He offered his arm, and Sarah couldn't remember ever taking it before. She had always been an afterthought to him. An unwelcome intrusion to his all-consuming relationship with his wife. Her mother had once said that children look like their father so that he will care for them. Despite having the same hair and eye color as Papa, however, he had never taken care of her. But perhaps that was best left in the past.

"Thank you for coming, Papa."

Her father patted her hand on his arm. "Dreadful business. But I knew your mother must have been dead. Nothing else could have kept her from me—from us. Your stepmother is also relieved, as you might guess. We were married by special license three days ago."

Sarah tried to smile. At least her father's relationship was legal now. Perhaps the new Countess of Manders would be a grandmother to Sarah's children. Sarah would try harder now; Mrs. Yardley was no longer the usurper. She was her father's wife.

"I only wish that my new stepmother might have accompanied you."

His response was a forced chuckle. "Ursula isn't overfond of the country."

"Maybe she can come the next time you visit," Sarah said as they left the church together. "I should like to get to know her better."

She saw that Mr. Robinson, Christopher, and the sisters were standing near a statue of the Virgin Mary just outside of the chapel. It reminded Sarah of both of their mothers.

Papa tugged at his collar with his free hand. "The thing is . . . Ursula isn't interested in visiting your mother's old home. She's still a bit jealous of Louisa's memory, and she should be. I will never love anyone like I loved your mother. And I will never forgive myself for that last night—the night she d-died."

"Everyone in the house knew what the fight was about," Sarah said quietly. "Neither you nor mother were particularly discreet that night."

"Then, you know it was all my fault."

Sarah took a deep, calming breath. "I know that you lost a great deal of money gambling and Mama was concerned that you were going to dice away my inheritance . . . a concern that proved to be most correct."

"I just had a run of bad luck is all."

Dropping her hand from his arm, she turned to face her father, eye-to-eye. "It has been more than a run of bad luck, Papa. You lost my dowry and then you lost my home. You left me with nothing, and you didn't even have the decency to tell me yourself. Your steward, Mr. Pryce, informed me that I had to leave Manderfield Hall and throw myself on the charity of my relatives."

"The Duke of Aylsham settled a little money on you."

Frustration bubbled up her throat. "Because you left me penniless from your gambling. I was not Grandfather's responsibility. I should have been yours."

"I was mourning your mother. I couldn't bear to be at Manderfield Hall when she was not there."

"My mother was missing, and you abandoned me for London and the gaming tables when I needed you the most."

Her father held up his gloved hands. "That is no way to speak to your sire and to an earl. Besides, it all worked out for the best. If I had taken you with me to London, you might not have landed Moulton. Rumor around Town is that he's worth over a half a million pounds at the very least."

Her heart sank deep inside of her chest. Papa hadn't changed at all. "You didn't come for me or for mother. You want money from my husband."

Papa shook his head. "Stop acting like a martyr, Sarah. When a lower-class businessman marries into an aristocratic family, he is supposed to pay the family for the privilege of joining their esteemed bloodline. I should have received tens of thousands of guineas from your wedding settlements. However, I am prepared to take only five thousand pounds by way of compensation."

Sarah could not believe what she was hearing. She leaned forward. "Why should Christopher pay you a farthing? You were not *here* to negotiate the wedding settlements. *I* was. And I received exactly what I wanted."

Her father's face grew red with an angry hauteur. "You would have your father ruined over a mere five thousand pounds?"

This was the man she remembered.

"I would not give you five pence, for it would be lost within a fortnight at the gaming tables. You must stop this madness. You have already squandered your inheritance and mine. Leave the dice and the cards alone."

Papa touched his chest dramatically. "Unnatural daughter. Do you not care for me at all?"

"Do *you* care for me at all, Father?" Sarah asked coldly. "I've often wondered. You've certainly never shown me any consideration before."

He shook his head dismissively. "I knew better than to talk to a woman about money. I shall speak directly to your husband. I am sure he will see the importance of meeting my needs. It would be bad for his business to have a father-in-law in debtors' prison."

Turning on his heel, her father walked away from her, as he had so many times before. She waited for the pang of disappointment and disillusionment, but it did not come. Thanks to Christopher, she knew what love was and what it wasn't. And she would no longer waste any time or energy trying for the affection of a person who was never going to love her back. She allowed herself a moment of sorrow for what might have been—a father who cared for her and a stepmother she might have been able to confide in. But she had waited for seven years, and she was finished waiting for what could never be.

Taking a deep breath, she followed her father to where he had confronted her husband, in front of her mother's grave. "Please do not give him as much as one guinea, Christopher. Lord Manders didn't come to see me or pay his respects to my mother. He came to bleed you for money."

"Now, now, daughter," Papa said in a falsely cheerful voice. "A woman knows almost nothing about finances. Allow me to speak privately with your husband. I am certain we can come to an arrangement that suits us both."

"You would be wrong, Lord Manders," Christopher said, moving to stand by Sarah. "Your daughter knows more about finances than any other person I have ever met, man or woman. She has taken care of Manderfield estate for many years and has a keen mind for how to make it the most profitable. I feel fortunate to have such an accomplished and intelligent wife. I would be a fool if I did not include her in all conversations about our finances."

Her father's smile turned into a sneer. "If I do not leave with a bank draft, I will disown you, Sarah, and never speak your name again."

At one time his words might have hurt her, but her heart was now an empty cavern as far as Papa was concerned. Sarah had waited five and twenty years for her father's love, and she had finally accepted that it was never coming. Sarah placed her hand on her husband's arm. She felt his strength and support. "Your choices are your own, Papa. Give my stepmother our best, and we wish you a fine journey back to London."

"Am I not to be welcome in the estate that was my birthright? In the halls of my ancestors?" her father said dramatically.

Deborah stuck out her chin defiantly. "Manderfield Hall belongs to Sarah and Chris now."

"And it doesn't matter if you disown Sarah," Margaret said, her cheeks turning a pretty pink. "She's a part of our family now, and we love her."

Both of her sisters-in-law moved to stand by her and Christopher in a physical sign of support. And Sarah's empty heart filled to the brim. She was a part of a family, and she felt loved.

Mr. Robinson stepped forward. "Lord Manders, shall I call for your carriage?"

"Insolent young man." Her father scoffed. "How dare you speak to an earl without being spoken to?"

"Yes, please, Mr. Robinson," Sarah said. "And thank you for your sermon today. I felt so much comfort from it."

Christopher pulled away from Sarah and took her father's arm. "Come, Lord Manders, you have outstayed your welcome."

Papa tried to shrug off Christopher's hold, but his arms were only used in dicing and cards, and Christopher dug canals. One awful earl was hardly a challenge. He half-carried, half-dragged her father to his carriage, and Mr. Robinson opened the door. Together they bundled the irate earl inside and told the driver to go.

Sarah sighed and felt two sets of arms wrap around her waist. Both Margaret and Deborah surrounded her in a hug. She held out her hand to Christopher, who joined their group embrace. They were a family.

CHAPTER 22

THE DAYS FOLLOWING THE MEMORIAL service were busy ones. It took Sarah and the entire sewing circle working several hours a day to finish making over her mother's dresses for Nelly's trousseau. Some of the girls were cool toward Deborah at first because of the whispers about her running away, but Miss Wentworth was so warm and welcoming that they soon all followed her lead. Deborah's chin still stuck out on occasion, but she no longer criticized or compared herself to Margaret. Christopher had told her to count to one hundred before she said anything in anger. Sarah often caught Deborah whispering, "Sixty-one, sixty-two, sixty-three . . ." Her young sister-in-law had not completely learned to hold her temper, but she was improving. What probably helped the most was that Christopher took her riding almost every morning.

Her husband understood that love meant time spent with someone.

He also gave time to Margaret. He taught her how to play a harmonica and let her teach him how to play the pianoforte. Margaret made great progress quickly, and Christopher did not, but they had a great deal of fun.

Sarah continued to tutor Margaret on the harp, and she thought that by the end of the year, her student would surpass her in talent. Dear Margaret had even expressed an interest in learning more instruments, including the violin. Christopher wrote at once to his man of business in London for the best instrument to be purchased and sent to Manderfield Hall. Playing the violin was not typically a female accomplishment, but the Moultons had taught Sarah that change could be a beautiful thing. And Margaret was certainly musically gifted.

Carefully, Sarah packed the last trunk that had once been her mother's. Sarah did not think that even a London debutante had a more beautiful trousseau. Closing the lid, she smiled. Her mother had loved beautiful clothing and would have enjoyed seeing these dresses have a second life.

Sarah pulled the cord, and a footman came to take Nelly's trunk. It was her maid's wedding day, after all. Nelly should not have to carry anything.

Sarah's own dress was nothing to sneeze at either. She had remade a gown from her debut and flattered herself that no one would guess that it was not new: dyed-blue silk with a matching overlay, tucks underneath the bodice, and flower-petal sleeves. She'd also dyed both her gloves and slippers to match. She had perhaps done it too thoroughly, for her hands were still the same color of muted blue. She would need to keep her gloves on.

She left her room and met Christopher. Her heart leaped in her chest as it always did at the sight of her husband. He took her hand, bent over it, and kissed it. Then he brushed a kiss to her brow. "You look enchanting, dove."

"You look very handsome yourself, my darling."

He held out his arm. "May I escort the bride's attendant down the stairs?"

Sarah loved placing her hand on his arm. "I should be most pleased, sir."

They walked slowly down the stairs to where they were met by his sisters, and then they left the house for the carriage, which was in a line with two others and two wagons. Every servant wore their finest and planned to attend Guy and Nelly's wedding. The ride to the chapel felt much shorter than it had on Sarah's wedding day. The route was lined with bunches of flowers, rushes, and herbs. When they arrived at the church, Christopher helped Sarah and his sisters out of the carriage, and they took their seats on the first bench. Sarah met with Mrs. Harmony. The housekeeper had awoken early to make the bouquets for the wedding. She picked up her own nosegay and Nelly's bouquet of white roses and camelias.

Nelly entered the church wearing Sarah's wedding dress. It looked even more gorgeous on her dear friend. Sarah handed her the flowers and hugged her friend. "If Mr. Robinson calls you the most beautiful bride he has ever officiated over, then you'd best believe him."

Her maid chuckled. "I am so glad that you are here. That you came back, Sarah. Manderfield Hall wasn't home without you."

Sarah straightened her friend's veil as she pulled it over Nelly's head to cover her face. "Nor without you, dearest Nelly. Enjoy your wedding week, but hurry back to us."

Winking, Nelly added saucily, "You'll need your lady's maid when you travel the world."

"We are only touring England."

"It's a start, my lady who is no longer in waiting."

"A wonderful start, my maid who never waited for anything."

They both laughed, and Sarah moved to let Mr. Wigan escort Nelly down the aisle. She took her role dutifully at her friend's side. Guy's brother stood as his attendant, but she could see Christopher sitting on the first row. It was the same church where her own wedding was held a little over a month before. How much had changed in her life, and so quickly. She had thought staying at Manderfield Hall would bring back Mama, and maybe it had. Sarah was able to move past her mother's death and remember only the good things. She'd given Mama's gowns a second chance to be enjoyed. She'd moved into Mama's rooms and made them her own.

She had married her husband for all the wrong reasons. She had married Christopher for her mother and Manderfield. How foolish she had been! He was worth so much more than an estate or a house. Manderfield Hall was only brick and mortar. It was the people who mattered. People like Nelly and Guy. Mr. Wigan and Mrs. Harmony. And all the wonderful people who made it home.

Christopher had married her to take care of his sisters. To give them an opportunity in Society and help them make good matches. She was glad that neither he nor herself were in any hurry to see Margaret and Deborah leave. Sarah had meant to be a good sister-in-law, but they no longer felt like a responsibility. She loved them, and they loved her.

Sarah's eyes moved back to Mr. Robinson. A light shone in his countenance as he performed the marriage service. He opened his scriptures to read from the Bible. "In 1 Peter 4:8 we learn, 'And above all things have fervent charity among yourselves: for charity shall cover the multitude of sins.' Charity is the purest love of God. If we replace the word *charity* with *love* in this verse, it gives us additional insight to the meaning: 'And above all things have fervent love among yourselves: for love shall cover the multitude of sins.'"

Love covers a multitude of sins.

Sarah believed that with all her heart and knew that she needed to tell Christopher she loved him. Her husband did everything in love. He was humble, gentle, and patient. She believed he loved her deeply but guessed that he felt too shy to confess his feelings first.

Mr. Robinson finished the ceremony and declared Guy and Nelly to be man and wife. The new bride and groom were the last to leave the chapel as the bells rang merrily. Their fellow servants, family members, and friends stood on each side of the pathway, ready to throw flowers and rice at the happy couple. Sarah was also hit with her fair share of projectiles and couldn't stop smiling. She felt only love, pure and holy.

The guests piled into the carriages and wagons to return to Manderfield Hall for the wedding luncheon. Farriers and carriers sat in the same dining room seats that had held dukes and kings, and they conducted themselves with great decorum. It was lovely seeing all the tenants sitting with them as equals, breaking bread with them and eating Mrs. Watkins's delicious apple tarts. Sarah devoured her own piece.

The wedding guests continued to eat and make merry, but Sarah could wait no longer. She took Christopher's hand and led him out of the dining room and the grand hall and from the house. She did not stop until she'd pulled her husband under the rose garden arch. It was quite private from the house and from prying eyes.

Christopher eyed her with surprise. "Is everything all right, dove?"

Leaning onto her tiptoes, she brushed a kiss against his cheek. "Everything is wonderful, my dearest husband. I couldn't have been happier if today were our own wedding day. I want you to know that I love you—utterly. And I can think of no greater honor or title than to be your wife."

"Y-you love me?" he asked, as if still unsure.

"I. Love. You. Christopher. Ambrosius. Moulton," she said, emphasizing every single word. "And. I. Will. Always. Love. You. Forever."

She watched as the smile slowly grew on his handsome face. She'd come to love his well-trimmed beard and the way his lips twitched before his mouth broke into a full grin. "I love you too, Lady Sarah Denham Moulton. Accepting your marriage proposal was the best decision I ever made."

Christopher placed his hands on her waist and pulled her against him. Sarah's arms naturally wrapped around his neck. "You're never going to let me forget that I proposed to you, are you?"

"Nay, dove. How could I forget the best day of my life?"

"I think today might be the best day of mine," Sarah whispered. She was close enough to her husband to feel his warm breath on her face.

"Maybe we should respeak our vows; you look beautiful enough to be a bride," Christopher said, then pressed a kiss to her cheek. "Sarah, you are beautiful, intelligent, kind, diligent, caring, and very fashionable."

She couldn't keep in a little chuckle.

Her husband placed a gentle finger on her smiling lips. "I could dig every day for the rest of my life, and I would still not uncover all that is wonderful about you. I will esteem, respect, protect, honor, and cherish you every day for the rest of my life. You are the woman I love. You are my wife . . . and I believe this is the moment for the ring."

A plain golden circlet was already on her fourth finger. Christopher gently took her hand and added an engagement ring with a large diamond surrounded by sapphires. She smiled so widely that her cheeks hurt. *This.* This was what love was supposed to be like. The poets spoke of passion, but a grand love was made up of small, precious moments like this one.

"Christopher, you have shown me by your words and your deeds what love is. I know you do not think you are perfect, and perhaps no one is. But you are perfect *for me*. Every perceived flaw makes you into the man you are. A man who is humble, hardworking, and unbearably handsome. I want to kiss you every hour of the day. Every minute, even."

"Nothing is stopping you, dove."

Giggling, Sarah pressed her smiling lips to his. Their previous kisses had tasted delicious, but this kiss was devastating. She felt their connection from their lips down to the depths of her very soul. It was as if their hearts beat together in steady harmony. She felt warm and wonderful wherever their bodies met. His hands pressed her closely against him. She tightened her hold around his neck and deepened the kiss.

How wonderful it was to be in love with her own husband!

One kiss became two. And after two, Sarah simply lost count. It didn't matter. The roses. The garden. Even the world faded away. The only things that remained were a man and a woman who loved. And were loved.

CHAPTER 23

Christopher could hardly wait to begin their wedding trip. Sarah's aunt Beatrice and her twelve children were enough to put a man into Bedlam. He felt a little sorry for the Manderfield staff, who would have to put up with them for an extra day after he and Sarah left on their journey. There was an itch to the soles of his feet and a tingling in his hands. He could hardly wait to be alone with his wife after the wedding party.

His wife.

He loved calling Sarah that. He loved her enough to be paraded in front of her numerous wealthy and titled relatives whose names he had difficulty remembering. Lady Venetia had invited the second and third cousins. His and Sarah's wedding party would be an event to be remembered for many years to come. Even her grandfather the Duke of Aylsham had arrived the night before. The old man was short and gouty, but he still had Christopher quaking in his boots. Christopher did not look forward to another conversation with the duke today. If he were careful, perhaps he could avoid one.

Knocking on the door that led to Sarah's room, he waited for her to speak before entering. Christopher had thought she was a vision of loveliness at their wedding, but her appearance today eclipsed even then. Every brown lock was curled and placed to perfection. She wore the pair of diamond earrings that he had given her and three strands of pearls, as well as her matching wedding ring. Without jewelry, she still would have sparkled. Her gown was bottle green and brought out the color of her eyes. The cut and style were unlike any he had seen before. Sarah did not follow fashion—she created it.

"You have left me speechless, dove."

She got to her feet with a queenly grace. "And you have made me wish to kiss you again, Husband."

Gently cupping her cheek, his hand nearly the size of her face, he brushed his lips back and forth over hers several times. "I am always happy to oblige, my wife."

Pink crept into her cheeks, and Sarah appeared even more beautiful and bridelike. "You always oblige me."

"Then, perhaps we can skip the party and head straight to our wedding trip?" Christopher suggested as innocently as possible.

Quirking up one eyebrow, his wife shook her beautiful head. "You know we cannot. Aunt Venetia has spent weeks planning this party, and you know how important wedding cake is to her. If we do not finally eat it, she will bring it up for the rest of our lives."

"It's not your aunt I am worried about."

Sarah's brow creased for a moment, and then she laughed. "You cannot be afraid of Uncle Oscar. Besides, you hired that gang of workers that started digging the canal over a fortnight ago. He will not plague you about his artificial lake at the party."

Christopher tried his best to raise only one eyebrow. He was pretty certain Sir Oscar would speak of nothing else.

He felt his wife's satin-like hands (which were blessedly no longer dyed blue) touch his cheeks and then move to his eyebrows. She lifted one of them. "Are you trying to give me a quizzical glance?"

"Is it working, dove?"

Shaking her head, she giggled, a sound that never failed to fill him with warmth and happiness. "I will protect you from Uncle Oscar."

"And your aunt Beatrice, the Marchioness of Chapman?"

Her nose wrinkled as she grinned.

"And your grumpy grandfather?"

"You can hide behind my skirts—no one will see you."

Christopher couldn't help but chuckle. He was a great deal taller and broader in the shoulders than his wife. There was no way he could ever hide behind her. "I'd rather play hide-and-seek with you."

"Who is doing the hiding and who is doing the finding?"

Attempting innocence, Christopher said, "I thought we could hide together."

"Did you now? And who is going to find us?"

"Hopefully, none of your relatives."

She swatted his shoulder playfully. "For shame. Come. I want to show you off to all of my family."

"Like a prized bull."

Sarah raised one eyebrow again in her satirical way. "Your words, not mine, dear husband."

Leaning onto her tiptoes, his wife gave him a long and lingering kiss. Truthfully, he would follow her anywhere.

***

Aunt Venetia had certainly outdone herself on the party. The three sets of ballroom doors were all flung open, and the wedding party flowed easily out into the gardens.

The wedding cake that Aunt Venetia had worried so much about was large enough to feed a village. Possibly two. The frosting was the same color as a Malmaison rose, a perfectly delicate pink. Decorative white sugar-icing figures garnished each of the three layers. Her cook must have spent weeks creating the figures that looked remarkably like real people. It was the most ornate and intricate cake Sarah had ever seen.

No one would forget her wedding cake now. She would ask her aunt to send a slice to all the members of the sewing society and her neighbors. Her parents had not socialized with the local community, and Sarah had discovered firsthand that being above one's company was a very lonely place to be. Neither she nor Christopher, whose hand she was holding tightly, would be lonesome today.

Aunt Venetia met them both with hugs and kisses. Christopher's face flushed a bright shade of red after her aunt kissed his cheek. Sarah couldn't keep her mirth inside.

Her aunt patted him on his bearded cheek. "You're even handsomer when you smile, Mr. Moulton. And you've kept our Sarah close to us, for which I will forever be indebted to you. Now, don't forget the cake, for you did last time!"

Still chortling, Sarah nodded and assured her aunt that neither she nor her husband would forget the wedding cake this time. She tugged her husband to Uncle Oscar, who hugged and kissed her. Happily, for her husband's sake, he only shook Christopher's free hand.

"The canal is coming along well," Uncle Oscar said, back to his favorite topic. "How many workers do you have out there?"

"Over two hundred," Christopher said.

"And it'll only cost me seven hundred pounds."

"Correct, sir."

Uncle Oscar patted Christopher on the shoulder. "You married a clever fellow, Sarah."

She blithely agreed, and they moved on to Cousin Ralph, who hugged them both. "When you get back from your trip, do tell me which London clubs you'd like me to put your name up for, Christopher. Someone needs to rescue you from a houseful of women."

Her husband thanked him and said he would think on it.

Sarah swatted her cousin's arm. "Any man should be delighted to live with three gorgeous women, Flames."

"Not if two of them are sisters," Ralph assured her and dodged her second swipe.

Aunt Venetia's daughters and their husbands were next in the receiving line. They were pleasant enough.

"We are so relieved that you finally found *someone* to marry," Cousin Eugenia said. She was married to the third son of an earl who had more hair than wit and only a respectable fortune.

Sarah was able to respond quite civilly, "Yes. I asked the handsomest and most intelligent man I have ever met to marry me, and it worked out perfectly. Did it not, dearest?"

Christopher's eyes twinkled, but he responded gravely, "Aye, dove."

Eugenia's face was a picture of surprise. "You asked *him*?"

Squeezing her husband's hand tighter, Sarah said, "Indeed I did. It was the best decision I have ever made. Come, darling. Grandfather is beckoning us."

Poor Grandfather was sitting in a chair with his gouty foot elevated. He looked like a spoiled despot king observing his court. He still wore the curly white wig that had been all the fashion a decade before. He claimed he didn't care for fashions, but Sarah privately believed it was because her grandsire was quite bald on top. Before he could berate her, she leaned down and kissed his cheek. "I am so glad you have come, Grandfather."

Her grandfather took out his quizzing glass and peered through it at Christopher, whose cheeks were a telltale red again. "Your husband has the build of a laborer."

Sarah kissed her grandfather's other cheek. "Yes, he is very muscular and strong, but my husband is also highly intelligent. Something the blood in our family definitely needed."

Cousin Eugenia's husband, the Honorable Mr. Felix Fotheringham, took that particular moment to use a tiny shovel to partake of his snuff. He snorted it out of his hand elegantly but coughed loudly and then sneezed onto his wife's blue gown.

Christopher flushed an even darker red, and the old duke guffawed loudly.

Taking Sarah's arm, her grandfather pulled her down to kiss her cheek. "Saucy minx! You are quite the cleverest of my grandchildren, and should you ever need anything, know that I will come. I should have done more for you these last seven years. And I would have if I weren't confined to this blasted chair."

Kneeling, Sarah held on to the side of his armchair. The old Duke of Aylsham could barely walk, but he was still a force to be reckoned with. "You have done everything, Grandpapa. You made sure I was provided for when my father gamed away my dowry, and I have always known you love me."

Her grandfather lifted one eyebrow, a little habit Sarah had learned from him. "It appears you have done pretty well for yourself without any help from me. Rumor has it that you are one of the richest women in England."

She glanced up at Christopher and had to agree with Grandfather, but not about the money. Christopher himself was worth a fortune. Giving her grandfather one last kiss on his brow, she led her husband to meet all her aunts and uncles, cousins and second cousins, and a few third cousins. He appeared a little daunted by the sheer number and size of her family, but he was kind and polite as always, even when she said she would quiz him on their names and titles afterward.

Uncle Oscar's butler announced that it was time for dinner. Sarah and Christopher were placed in the middle of the long banquet table. Looking around, Sarah sighed in contentment. Her father was not there, but he'd never been present for her. But her grandfather had been, as well as Aunt Venetia and Uncle Oscar. In fact, the dining room was full of her family. Sarah had been wrong; she had never been alone. There were so many people who loved her, including the man who held both her heart and her hand. She followed his gaze to where his two sisters were laughing with her younger cousins.

Her heart and stomach were full after an exquisite twelve courses. Aunt Venetia announced that there would be dancing after dinner, and on cue, a quartet began to play a lively country jig. Sarah realized she had never danced with her husband before, and that was something she meant to remedy immediately. Tugging him along behind her, they joined the set. Sarah curtsied to him, and he bowed to her. She saw Margaret dancing with second cousin Phineas, and Deborah with Sarah's first cousin once removed, Septimius. But once the dance started, Sarah had eyes for only her husband. She loved each touch of his hand and when they twirled together.

Christopher asked her for a second dance, and Sarah knew in her heart that she had never been happier in her entire life. She flew through the steps with both grace and joy. Then she danced the next with Ralph and then Uncle Oscar, who talked about his artificial lake throughout the entire set. Her next two dances were with her cousins, who were all agog to learn more about Christopher.

Was Moulton really worth a cool half a million pounds?

Had he truly dug canals with his own hands?

And was it true that she'd proposed marriage to him? They had heard such from Cousin Eugenia.

How might one purchase stock in his company?

Sarah danced until there were holes in her slippers, but her heart was finally whole.

Aunt Venetia beckoned her and Christopher to the table that held their enormous wedding cake.

"Now, take off your rings," her aunt said.

Christopher slipped off his plain gold band, and Sarah took off both her wedding circlet and the beautiful diamond-and-sapphire ring that her husband had given her to wear with it.

Her aunt instructed the butler to cut two pieces of cake from the top tier. "Now, Sarah and Mr. Moulton, you must put the cake through your rings."

Smiling at the absurdity of such a tradition, Sarah pinched a bit of sponge and dutifully pushed it through the hole of her rings. Christopher did likewise.

"Ralph, I shall need your help for the next bit," Aunt Venetia said. "We must follow the local traditions and break cake over their heads, and Mr. Moulton is a great deal too tall for me to reach."

Her cousin, with an enthusiasm that did not speak highly of his character, grabbed the largest piece of cake and lifted it over Christopher's head. Her aunt took the smaller piece and held it above her niece's. Sarah started to laugh, and her husband smiled when crumbs and frosting fell into their hair and onto their fine wedding garments. Christopher picked up a large piece from off his shoulder and put it into his mouth. Everyone laughed and cheered. Then he cupped Sarah's frosting-covered cheek and covered her mouth with a kiss that tasted of sweet cake. Their embrace was met with the loudest cheers of all.

Stepping back, Sarah shook her hair and spread crumbs into the crowd. Christopher hugged both of his sisters and covered them with pink frosting before taking Sarah's hand and walking through the crowd. Her aunts, uncles, and cousins threw flower petals at them, and Sarah had never felt like such a glorious mess! The party followed them to their open landau that had old pans tied to the back (courtesy of Cousin Ralph) and a great deal of ribbons (Margaret and Deborah). Christopher helped her inside, and together they waved until they could no longer see the wedding party guests.

Sarah picked a rose petal out of his hair and kissed his nose before placing her lips on his. This time her husband didn't taste of cake but of Christopher. The most wonderful flavor in all the world.

AUTHOR'S NOTE

Aunt Venetia was not the only person concerned about the wedding cake. Jane Austen wrote to her sister Cassandra in 1808:

> *Do you recollect whether the Manydown family send about their wedding cake? Mrs. Dundas has set her heart upon having a piece from her friend Catherine, and Martha, who knows what importance she attaches to this sort of thing, is anxious for the sake of both, that there should not be a disappointment.* (Roy and Lesley Adkins, *Jane Austen's England* [New York: Penguin Books, 2014], 11.)

The wedding cake was an important part of the marriage celebration and was shared with family and friends. Different areas in England had specific traditions; some included breaking the cake over the bride's and groom's heads or scattering it into the crowd. Others put the cake through the rings. Some even believed that if they took their piece of cake and slept with it underneath their pillow, they would dream of the person they would marry. In other locales, the tossing of the stockings was a tradition. Both the bride and the groom would sit on their bed; the bridesmaids would turn away from the couple and throw their stockings over their shoulders. Whoever's stocking hit the bride would be the next to be married.

Canon law decreed that weddings must take place between eight o'clock in the morning and noon. This law did not change until 1886. Persons under the age of twenty-one required parental consent before marriage. However, with parental consent, girls could marry as young as twelve years old and boys fourteen. Flowers, rushes, and herbs were placed along the route to the church. Commoners simply wore their finest clothing. The wealthy were able to choose white for the bride and often the attendants too. The ring was an important part of the ceremony because it was believed that the fourth finger had a small artery that ran to the heart. After the wedding, the church bells rang merrily.

Marriages were usually followed by a wedding breakfast. However, more elaborate weddings could last all day long and include other meals, dancing, and even games. Commoners and servants returned to work the day after their wedding. It would have been rare for their employers to give them time off like Sarah does for her dear friend Nelly. Nor did the concept of a honeymoon exist. However, some wealthy newlyweds would go on a trip, often in Britain because of the Napoleonic Wars on the Continent. But it wasn't a private affair. The couple often invited friends and relatives to come with them. And, of course, their servants! (See Roy and Lesley Adkins, *Jane Austen's England*, 10–11.)

The vicar, Mr. Brian Robinson, is based on a real person. This account comes from the journal of William Holland in 1805:

> *I met young [Brian] Mackey, who is come to see his father . . . This young man is his son by a negro woman, and has had from the father an excellent education, and is in [holy] orders and has two livings, and is in good circumstances.*
> (Roy and Lesley Adkins, *Jane Austen's England*, 41.)

Mr. Mackey studied at Oxford and was the parish priest of Coates in Gloucestershire. Unfortunately, William Holland continues on to complain in the same journal passage that Mackey is receiving too much money from his father and worries for the financial state of his stepmother. Despite his advantages, it appears that Mr. Mackey still experienced racism and prejudice, not unlike what Mr. Robinson receives from the most unpleasant Mrs. Wentworth.

Mr. Christopher Moulton made his fortune in canals. *Jane Austen's England* notes that in the 1790s there was "canal mania" (185). The creation of canals required hundreds of workers digging with hand tools and moving dirt with wheelbarrows. Canals were especially popular before railroads because they could be used to transport heavy goods and coal. Gangs of laborers traveled from canal site to canal site. A newspaper advertisement from 1810 announced positions for "two or three hundred good workmen on the Worchester and Birmingham canal, where liberal prices will be given to Agg Masters [subcontractors]; and good wages to workmen that are ready and deserving encouragement" (Roy and Lesley Adkins, *Jane Austen's England*, 186; capitalization modernized).

Fake ruins and false lakes? Lancelot Brown (1716–1783) was nicknamed Capability Brown because he saw the capabilities for improvement in English estates. He designed more than 170 parks and estates in Great Britain and created artificial serpentine lakes by damming small rivers.

DISCUSSION QUESTIONS

1. Where do you consider home to be? Do you agree with the phrase "There's no place like home"?
2. Are there any circumstances in which you would consider marrying a stranger like Lady Sarah and Christopher do? Do you agree with the Countess of Manders that "marriage is the greatest gamble of all"?
3. Lady Sarah is guided by many of her mother's maxims, such as *A lady is only as beautiful as she believes herself to be*, *Kindness is always in fashion*, and *Bad behavior should be ignored or isolated.* Do you agree with her maxims? What are some things that your mother taught you?
4. Aunt Venetia is very concerned about the lack of a wedding cake. How have marriage customs changed over the last two hundred years? How have they stayed the same?
5. Lady Sarah says, "Those who compare themselves to others will always come up second best." Why does Deb compare herself to Margaret and the other young ladies?
6. Lady Sarah tells Christopher, "We all have scars. Not all of them are on our skin for everyone to see." What scars is she hiding? What are Christopher's unseen ones?
7. Lady Sarah tells Christopher, "The better listener you are, the better conversationalist people will believe you to be. Everyone loves to speak. Only a few people understand the value of listening." Do you agree?
8. Lady Sarah says, "Some women create their positions in Society by tearing other women down. My mother made her mark by building other ladies up, and in my opinion, if there aren't enough seats at the table, then we can always fetch another chair." How do you make room for new people in your social circles?

9. Lady Sarah defines love as "putting a person's needs before one's own" and as time. "Lots and lots of time." How would you define love?
10. Do you agree with Lady Sarah that "knowing is better than hoping"? Did the ending surprise you?

ABOUT THE AUTHOR

Samantha Hastings met her husband in a turkey sandwich line. They live in Salt Lake City, Utah, where she spends most of her time reading, having tea parties, and chauffeuring her four kids. She teaches World Literature at Brigham Young University. Her young adult fiction books are Junior Library Guild Gold Standard selections, and her historical romances are published around the world. She also writes murder mysteries under Samantha Larsen that *Publishers Weekly* called "wildly enjoyable."

Learn more at SamanthaHastings.com.